# I LOVE YOU DON'T DIE

*also by Jade Song*

*Chlorine*

First published in the UK in 2026
by Footnote Press

An imprint of Bonnier Books UK
5th Floor, HYLO, 105 Bunhill Row,
London, EC1Y 8LZ

First published in the US in 2026
by HarperCollins Publishers

Copyright © Jade Song, 2026

From "The Future Is Between Us" from *The Sunflower Cast a
Spell to Save Us from the Void* by Jacqueline Wang. Copyright ©
2021 by Jacqueline Wang. Used by permission of the author.

From *The Politics of Friendship* by Jacques Derrida. Copyright ©
1997 by Jacques Derrida. Used by permission of the publisher.

All rights reserved.
No part of this publication may be reproduced, stored or transmitted in
any form or by any means, electronic, mechanical, photocopying or otherwise,
without the prior written permission of the publisher.

The right of Jade Song to be identified as Author of this work
has been asserted by them in accordance with the Copyright, Designs and
Patents Act, 1988.

This is a work of fiction. Names, places, events and incidents are either the products of the
author's imagination or used fictitiously. Any resemblance to actual persons, living or dead,
or actual events is purely coincidental.

A CIP catalogue record for this book is available from the British Library.

Hardback ISBN: 978-1-80444-353-8
Trade Paperback ISBN: 978-1-80444-357-6

*Also available as an ebook and an audiobook*

1 3 5 7 9 10 8 6 4 2

Design and Typeset by IDSUK (Data Connection) Ltd
Printed and bound by CPI (UK) Ltd, Croydon CR0 4YY

Every reasonable effort has been made to trace copyright holders of
material reproduced in this book, but if any have been inadvertently
overlooked the publishers would be glad to hear from them.

The authorised representative in the EEA is
Bonnier Books UK (Ireland) Limited.
Registered office address: Block B, The Crescent Building
Northwood, Santry Dublin 9, D09 C6X8 Ireland
compliance@bonnierbooks.ie
www.bonnierbooks.co.uk

*For my friends,*
*who taught me love*
*and saved my life*

*Because the catastrophe doesn't exist so long as I delay perceiving it. Can a book parry catastrophe? Let another temporality be my home! But death is everywhere in the book.*
—Jackie Wang, "The Future Is Between Us"

*For to love friendship, it is not enough to know how to bear the other in mourning; one must love the future.*
—Jacques Derrida, *The Politics of Friendship*

## author's note

The poet Gu Cheng wrote that though the shadows gave him dark eyes, he would use them to search for light.

This novel carries darkness such as depression, anxiety, self-harm, disordered eating, suicide, and suicidal ideation—please be aware of this content, and, if needed, refer to the resources at the back of the book for support.

But in the darkness, there is light too: friends, lovers, and selves—the moments together and the moments in between.

This story orients toward the light.

Thank you for being here.

Shall we step into the shadows?

# *work*

She doesn't care how or where she will settle down, because to settle down implies a belief in free will and she knows she has none. Nobody does. Nobody is free. Every choice is dependent on cash flow or community or citizenship—the combination of such or the lack thereof. Yet because the question of *settling down* occupies the minds of many people her age, she tries to care. To be like everyone else. Since she's already deviated far from societal normalcy and expectations. She is deranged enough. She wonders, when she does magically happen to *settle down*, if her body will do what everyone else's does, which is to place a golden band of commitment around the fourth finger of her left hand and enter a self-induced suffocation by mortgage and white picket fence. Or if her body will perform the action that *settle down* implies: an act of flesh sagging into a warm and cozy place, never to emerge again—like a grave, or her bed.

Oh, her bed. How she loves her queen-size bed where she can splay her tired limbs. To be alone in her bed, with only her bed and no one else. Gifts are her love language, so she gifts her bed with fancy: two silk pillowcases she had stalked the direct-to-consumer lifestyle bedroom brand for its Labor Day sales so she could buy them half off; the washable 100 percent cotton hypoallergenic weighted blanket she had "borrowed" from Jen when she had slept over for two weeks while searching for a new apartment; the eye mask and foam noise-blocking earplugs, to ensure total peace, which she keeps packed and easy to reach on her nightstand in a zhizha box printed with illustrations of diamond rings and pearl necklaces.

She has never understood why life advice proclaims it better to jump out from under the blankets as soon as the alarm blares. Why can't she *settle down* in her unmade bed for the remainder of her pointless, silly life? What goals are even worth achieving if they cannot be achieved from the pleasantries of the bed? Why voluntarily embrace the doom of consciousness in this sad, sad waking world of the alive when an offer of blessed, dreamed-of death is right there in the bed?

*Alive, alive, alive,* rings her alarm.

Time to act alive—five minutes before work begins, variations on a wakeup: 8:55 a.m., 9:25 a.m., 10:55 a.m., 1:25 p.m. Every night she changes her alarm, setting it for five minutes before her first meeting of the day.

*Alive, alive, alive,* rings her alarm. *Time to act alive.*

She lifts off her eye mask and takes out her earplugs and reaches an arm down. Drags up her laptop from its spot on the floor, where she stations it every night next to her bed like a loyal pet. She opens the screen, eyes half lidded. Clicks the video meeting link. Keeps her camera resolutely off.

Her boss, Dan, smiling, camera resolutely on. She stares at the pixels composing his face, identical to the two other creative directors at the company. Together, Dan, Dean, and Derek are triplets—shaggy-haired white men in their mid-thirties claiming disruption while adjusting their black-rimmed eyeglasses, wearing black hoodies with expensive logos and sleeves over skinny forearms painted in bold, saturated American traditional tattoos: swallows stretching their wings, anchors atop ribbons, skulls with daggers stabbed through the eye.

"Vicky. My favorite copywriter!"

"Hi, Dan."

"How are you today?"

"Good morning. I'm great. Happy Monday," she croaks while rotating her head on the pillow, looking for a glass of water. Finds none within reach. Her hydration levels are always low; her pee, a radioactive yellow.

"No camera today? I'd love to see your face."

"I'm eating breakfast. I'll turn it on when I finish my oatmeal," she lies.

"Okay."

"How was your weekend?"

"Fun. DJ friend had a rooftop party. Played his new set. Yours?" He does not wait for her response. "Anyway, jumping to business—new brief!"

Her finger jabs the volume down, offended by Dan's excitement over the pile-on of tasks. She has never been able to discern whether his disposition is real because he believes in the nobility of work or faked because he is paid to do so.

He shares his screen. A presentation slide reading "The Ernie Opportunity" designed in Onwards's black-and-gray branding zooms forward.

"As you know, we've been focusing on subsets of our target audience in recent campaigns. They've been going well, and we want to maintain our diversity and inclusivity outreach, but we also can't lose sight of our original Onwards heart: Ernie! We wouldn't have Onwards without him. He is, after all, the main draw for our urns. So. This brief highlights Ernie. We'd love to spotlight him in a disruptive, earned media–worthy campaign that . . ."

Vicky's throat tickles as Dan drones on. She mutes herself to cough. She feels feverish. Clears her morning mucus. Grimaces at the sweat sheeting under her armpits. Her apartment is like every other New York City apartment rented by those in her socioeconomic class: falling apart. Her faulty window air conditioner unit splutters—empathetic, apologizing for its inadequacy. The noise severs her already drifting attention despite Dan's enthusiasm. She wonders if it would be worth the extra time and effort to scroll through the Buy Nothing Chinatown and Lower East Side online group to scavenge a working unit. She opens a new tab in her browser, begins to type—then stops when she thinks about the scrolling, the messages, the venturing out to the pickup location she will have to do. The lugging back to her apartment. The desperate texting to the super begging for installation help. No—the amount of effort required is insurmountable. She decides she would rather die of heat exhaustion. Vicky slumps deeper into her pillow, gaze catching on the zhizha air conditioner unit she had cut from her zhizha two-story house, both of which she had placed on the sill next to her real air conditioner as a reminder of what she is working toward: riches like working air conditioners and a home of her own so she can *settle down*—perfect paper fantasy positioned next to defective reality. With proximity, would the flawed absorb the refined? Or would the ideal degrade? Or would both enter stasis? She feels stuck and stagnant. In between. Unremarkable.

"Any questions?"

Startled, unprepared, she unmutes herself. "No."

Her air conditioner sputters again.

"You good?"

"Yes. Sorry, that was my air conditioner. It's a window unit. I bought it used from a neighbor. It's been breaking down. I should probably get a new one."

"Oh, no problem. I used to rely on window units too. I know how loud they can be," Dan says.

Dan, who earns triple her salary. Dan, whose apartment she's seen through the video calls and whose address she'd searched online for: a three-bedroom with his long-term partner in a newly constructed central-air luxury building with an in-unit washer and dryer, a gym, and a pool on the top floor in Brooklyn Heights, steps away from the waterfront. She cannot fathom his limber privilege condensing itself to fit an apartment like hers: a six-floor walk-up, one room, the kitchen in the living room in the bedroom with its paint-thickened-yet-chipped corners and malfunctioning appliances and thin walls. Plodding to laundromats with hauls of dirty clothing over her shoulder and quarters jangling in her pocket. She tells herself at least she lives alone in New York City. At least she has a job that lets her work from home most days. At least she can live in Chinatown, where the faces are familiar. It could be worse. She had lived worse before.

"So. The new brief."

"Yes."

"To highlight Ernie and his leadership in urn innovation and end-of-life industry disruption. Focus on Ernie's natural celebrity. What he brings to the table."

"Right."

"You got it?"

She had not fully "got it"—she had not been paying attention. But it wouldn't be hard for her to highlight someone like Ernie. Or, rather, Ernest Hayworth the Third, named after his father, who had been named after his father—three handsome white male actors over six feet tall capturing the hearts of American generations, Ernie's one variation from his father and grandfather making him perfect for contemporary stardom: Ernie, gay! This fact of his sexuality enough to erase from public consciousness his status as nepo baby, as did his immense talent, both inherited and cultivated by the industry's most famous and expensive acting coaches, along with his habit of donating dividends of his generational and personal fortune to charities ranging from supporting queer youth to protesting puppy mills. Everybody loved Ernie. Even Vicky would admit she admired him. His career from child star to teenage idol to mature adult artist to successful start-up founder had never deviated from its upward trajectory.

"Got it!"

"Good, good."

"Already have some ideas mulling around. I'll get to jamming." She grimaces at her use of creative corporate jargon even as the words mask her distaste. She can pretend enough to get by. As long as her camera stays off. She lacks the strength to pretend in both facial and vocal expression.

"Cool. Let me know if you have any questions. We'll plan to check in tomorrow afternoon on your ideas. I'll throw something on the calendar."

"Great! Can't wait."

Dan waves.

The call ends.

She does not move. Stays in bed, the laptop purring, heating her lower stomach. She massages her wrist. Moans. Wonders if the carpal tunnel plaguing her is sparked from her habit of typing horizontal, though the wrist pain is worth the bed. Shifts on her mattress, wincing at the damp sweat underneath her back. She craves better sheets—five hundred thread count, OEKO-TEX certified, crisp light fabric with sweat-wicking and cooling material, the kind that would cost her too much yet would free her from the blistering cruel heat, a sticky late June preempting the oppressive July and August. She knows a New York City summer is better than a summer anywhere else, marking trips to the romantic Riis Beach with the topless queers, ferry rides across the East River pointing at the underside of history's bridges, bike rides up and down the West Side passing by art museums and pretty piers, orange sunsets glowing through Manhattan's metal ravines—experiences that would be hers if only she could muster up the energy and get out of bed.

The vitality eludes her.

She can't get out of bed and conduct her work meetings with her camera on, hair brushed, sitting in a chair with good posture. Can't get out of bed and respond to the messages—the endless messages!—from her new matches on the dating app she hates and from Jen, dear Jen, who sometimes comes over to get her out of bed, dear Jen who texted her this morning confirming their dinner tomorrow, dear Jen with the skincare routine and the color-coded calendar who is her one best and true friend. Can't get out of bed and do what Jen and their other mutuals sometimes do, which is to get informed, to go to a protest, to post an infographic on social media, to head to the food distribution meeting point, her apartment protecting her from the headlines pounding at the door:

**MASSIVE LAYOFFS SWEEPING ACROSS
INDUSTRIES INDICATE RECESSION RISK**

**SUPREME COURT RULING FURTHER
WEAKENS ORGANIZED LABOR**

**JUDGE'S RULING PINS BLAME ON SOCIAL
MEDIA FOR COLLEGE STUDENT'S SUICIDE**

**MASS SHOOTING RAMPAGE MOTIVE REMAINS MYSTERY;
NO KNOWN CONNECTION BETWEEN VICTIMS**

**U.S. HEALTH PANEL RECOMMENDS ANXIETY AND
DEPRESSION SCREENINGS FOR KIDS AGE 8 AND UP**

**FAMILIES DEVASTATED BY FENTANYL DEATHS
RALLY OUTSIDE WHITE HOUSE**

**INEFFECTIVE PANDEMIC RESPONSE LEADS
TO "CYCLES OF DESPAIR AND NEGLECT"**

**INSURANCE RATES UNDERESTIMATE GROWING
FLOOD RISK FOR COASTLINE HOMEOWNERS**

**MANY AGE 25–35 REPORT HAVING A DRINK
TO COPE WITH FINANCIAL STRESS**

Everybody is unhappy and everybody is dying. It isn't that Vicky doesn't care. More that she cares so much that the inordinate amount paralyzes her. Easier to ignore the truth of imminent monotonous disaster. Easier to stay in bed. Easier to pretend everything is fine. Everything is fine! Everything is fine. Everything is fine—

*friendship*

Vicky shoves a clump of leaves into her mouth. A stem of spinach leaks from her lower lip; she slurps it up, imagining herself a cow. Slaps her upper arm with her free hand like a cow's tail swing when a mosquito buzzes toward her skin. Drops her fork and sprawls in her chair, lolling her head around, gaze settling on an interesting target three tables away: A gender-rejector rocking a septum piercing and feathered hair shorn at the chin, attempting to wrangle an asparagus stalk onto their fork, accompanied by a much older man slicked in a tailored suit and gelled hair.

"Don't bother."

Vicky glares at Jen, who has followed her interest across the outdoor dining area.

"They're clearly busy with him," continues Jen as she turns back to her meal, spooning a clump of coconut peanut butter curry with her brown rice. "Why don't you hook up with someone not on a date with a finance bro or sugar daddy?"

Vicky grimaces. She's the cow *and* the mosquito too, buzzing with incessant lust. Craving to bite, craving to be bitten. An annoying pest sucking on others' insides, offering fast departures and irritating marks, hunting on summer city nights for bare skin to feast upon. Only Jen tolerates her pursuits.

Vicky stretches her arms above her head, hoping the conspicuous movement will catch her target's attention. She could show them a far better time. The finance bro might pick up their check, but she could pick up their pleasure in bed. She hasn't had sex in months because she has not had the energy to meet anyone—staying in bed, too alluring. She wanted to use her rare costumery that evening to her advantage: She is dressed in a floor-length fishnet dress over a bra and biker shorts rather than her typical plain T-shirt and black pants. Her outfit had not been libido motivated, but rather because she managed to exit the bed minutes before noon. Had conducted her presentation to Dan with her camera on, the success of her three Ernie-centered creative ideas and her meeting-free calendar afterward motivating her enough to open her closet and pick something presentable for dinner with her best friend.

"Can't you go for someone who's actually available? Like him." Jen uses her fork to point at the hot waiter they both admire.

"There's no way he's available when he looks the way he does."

"Maybe he's also into queering relationship structures."

Vicky grins. She adores when Jen quotes her manifestos. Her best friend offers more than simple acceptance—Jen gives affinity. Affection. For Jen, there is nothing about Vicky to accept because acceptance implies the existence of rejection, which has never been in the realm of possibility anyway.

"Don't you think that if he was actually interested, he would have, at the very least, asked our names?"

"He could be nervous like you are."

"I'm not nervous! I just don't want to ruin this restaurant for us."

They are regulars at the organic, plant-based, bowl-style restaurant on the border of Chinatown and the Lower East Side. La Botanical would not be Vicky's first choice—or her second or third, nor even on the list, because she prefers holes-in-the-wall that serve plates of plump dumplings for four dollars, with dirty mirrors and boxes of Chinese drinks stacked behind the counter as decor—but she goes here because Jen is her best friend, and Jen is a person who likes colorful vegetables in her healthy, calorie-conscious dinners featuring a good balance of carbs and protein and fat.

The hot waiter catches them watching him. He walks over with a smile. "Everything okay over here?"

Jen wags her eyebrows at Vicky, who ignores her.

"Sorry, we're good," Vicky says.

He departs.

Vicky stabs a roasted carrot stick with her fork as Jen giggles.

"How's work been?" Vicky asks.

"It's fine. Gonna ramp up soon, since the fall athletic wear release is coming out soon. They want me to lead the campaign."

"Of course they do."

Jen runs a hand over her slicked-back hair, tugging the end of her ponytail. Vicky notices her unpainted nails, her faded microbladed eyebrows, her dark circles—at odds with the Jen who enjoys beauty upkeep.

"You seem stressed," Vicky says.

"I am. I mean, I'm excited to lead the release—it'll be fun. We're already planning things like outdoor workout classes with influencers. Lifestyle shit. I just gotta make it pretty." Jen lets out a breath. "Still, it's a lot of work, and I care less about the promotion than I do the raise. Eric and I want to save more money—everyone says not to worry about the recession rumors, since it won't hit our industries yet, but I can't help it. We're still trying to pay off our loans, and then we wanna help his mom pay off her house."

Jen had been dating Eric, a mutual friend from college, since the night of their graduation four years ago. He had confessed his unwavering crush over blaring music at an acquaintance's house party. Jen had hugged him in reciprocal delight. Vicky thought Eric too simple—he was always happy. Too boring—he was an accountant. Too inadequate—he was in debt. Typical student debt combined with healthcare debt after a surprise collapse on the sidewalk a year out from college while in between jobs, in between insurances, his mother unemployed and unable to bestow him dependent child benefits. He had been rushed to the hospital thanks to a kind bystander who may not have been so kind after all, for Eric had been pummeled with exorbitant bills for everything from the ambulance fee to the triage fee to the facility fee to the physician fee to the medical supplies fee—fees, fees, never-ending fees. Though the financial assistance program for state residents reduced some of the bill, the credit card charge was astronomical enough to still be accruing interest, adding on another type of debt. Jen, enamored with her blossoming serious relationship, had promised to help him pay them off, against Vicky's advice.

*You are drowning in student debt yourself, and you like to spend money on fancy things,* Vicky had pointed out.

*But we're a team,* Jen had insisted.

*I thought we were a team,* Vicky had bit back. Left the words unsaid. Jealousy was ugly.

Nevertheless, Vicky had to admit Eric was good for Jen—he might be in debt, but so was Jen, along with everyone else in America, and if everyone was miserable, then misery became the norm. Even better, Eric was emotionally stable, and Jen needed a semblance of control to steady her. Vicky had seen Jen at her worst: head in the toilet vomiting up her last meal, hair torn out from anxiety before exams, lines of cocaine snorted off a visiting creative director's bare chest. Eric was good for Jen because, like wellness, he was constant.

"You deserve both a raise and a promotion. Aren't you supposed to be senior level by now? You've been loyal to Roller for years."

"Yeah, well, it depends on the results of the campaign." Jen drops her silverware in defeat, slumps in her chair. "Meanwhile, I'm working on social images for the smoothie delivery collab— we're featuring produce like dragon fruit and jackfruit, not just the typical berries and bananas." She grimaces. "At least the pictures will be pretty. I assigned a photographer I love. She really knows how to play with shapes, colors, and textures. The lay-flats will be interesting, but also manage to look yummy."

Vicky nods along as she chews her leaves. She likes to listen to Jen talk about her job. Not because she likes advertising or wellness, but because Jen is good at art direction, and it is nice to listen to someone she loves talk about a skill they are good at. It hadn't always been this way—they had both been clueless when they first met in their undergraduate creative advertising program, two pimply Asian freshman girls in a sea of people uglier and stupider than them, or so they told themselves in delusional self-encouragement as they holed up in that stuffy study room in the library stacks five sleepless nights in a row to think of ideas, any idea, on how to sell a dog care and accessories product line to millennials (the brief!). They had run through three dry erase markers and two packs of Post-its before realizing that millennials were delaying marriage, parenthood, and homeownership in favor of dog adoption (the strategy!), and that these same people craved identity through aesthetic consumption (the insight!). So, they would create a kitschy jewelry line for dog owners to match their dogs' collars (the idea!). Millennials would be able to customize the chokers, and they'd offer limited edition themes for each month's holiday. Pictures of matching dogs and owners would blow up on social media and highlight the entire dog care line with it. Their idea was the perfect campaign, the customization even inclusive of people of color and queers, something their industry hadn't managed to figure out yet—of course their professor awarded them the mock business after their class presentation.

They could have been the best creative team to come out of that school, Jen the art director and Vicky the copywriter, predicted by their professors to win every award in their industry (and there were many awards—too many; creatives have outsize egos).

A good creative team needed to project both business-appropriate tidiness and creative disorder, and they complemented each other well, not just in art and copy, but in mannerism and dress too—Jen, the extrovert preppy presenter who could woo any client through banter and jokes; Vicky, the moody goth-lite who hated public speaking, hated the spotlight, had a mini panic attack whenever she was forced to present, yet her careless bursts of creative talent turned people favorably toward her despite her jagged edges. But they valued their friendship too much—the work-wife bond would forever be constrained by its corporate sanctions. When the university held its job fair for incoming upperclassmen, they arrived together, looked at each other, nodded, and split up. Went down separate aisles, collected different brochures. They both renounced the ad agencies, which were a dying business, to go in-house with better benefits and perks and salaries. But the houses they wanted were not neighboring—their career goals diverged. Jen wanted to go into wellness because she believed in wellness: fancy workouts, fancy gear to wear to the fancy workouts, fancy salads to fuel the fancy workouts. Jen still believed in the feeling wellness could give: the feeling of being alive, of prolonging that alive, of making that alive look prettier and, therefore, giving that alive a purpose. Jen loved her job at Roller, founded by a white woman in her thirties who was not skinny but *fit*, who had, according to Roller lore, visited more than thirty-five male venture capitalists before finally finding one who trusted a woman founder enough to drop some bucks into her brand. Roller was named after the many rollers found in wellness—the jade rollers in skincare, the foam rollers for sore muscles, the dough rollers for cauliflower pizza crust, all kinds of rollers sold at Roller designed to make life roll smooth—which

Jen got for free and passed on to Vicky, who stored them unused and dusty in the back of her closet, because Vicky did not believe in wellness. She believed in death. Wellness optional; death inevitable. Death, the safest industry. Everyone would die. Everyone was already dying.

Neither girl regretted her choice of career, though Vicky would admit her job in death, though a reliable necessity, deadened her inside the way Jen's in wellness seemed to reinvigorate. In college, Vicky had dreamed of the future, but now, at the present, she could barely even think of tomorrow. Confrontation of a tomorrow involving headlines and urns and bosses required an inner stamping against her natural personhood, which had once enjoyed dancing sweaty on ecstasy until 6:00 a.m., gorging herself on five pints of ice cream, and dragging to the bathroom whichever person looked her way first in the bar to fuck with her leg propped up on the pee-drenched toilet seat. Only during self-destruction could she remember she had a self. But now, because she had a job that paid for her apartment, her healthcare, her sustenance—she no longer let herself chance healing through damage. Safer to pursue a career with salary raises and campaign productions as benchmarks of a life: her Valentine's Day campaign where single people could send their exes Onwards urns with engraved copy like WISH YOU WERE DEAD, her April Fools' Day idea where people could use an Onwards AI bot to generate and send out their fictional personal eulogies, and the Onwards zine series she wrote featuring death traditions from around the world, from endocannibalism, the mortuary ritual of consuming the dead, to Famadihana, a ceremony of the Malagasy people, who brought forth corpses from their family crypts to be rewrapped and danced with. Never mind that her creativity was used toward a profit margin end; never mind that Jen, who knew her best, occasionally asked her, in a worried tone masked as nonchalance, if she was okay, because she hadn't seemed like herself lately—*No, like, are you really doing okay?*

Bowls empty, table cleared. The hot waiter comes over: "Dessert tonight?"

"No, thank you, check please," Vicky says. As he leaves, she rolls her eyes at Jen's eager expression. "Stop. He's never gone past pleasantries."

"So? He probably just doesn't want you to think he's creepy."

"Well, I don't want him to think I'm creepy by hitting on him at his place of work."

"How are you going to get fucked if you don't at least try?"

"I am trying. It's summer, so I'm on the apps again, okay? You know winter always forces me into abstinence."

Jen flips her palm, wiggles her fingers.

Vicky shakes her head.

Jen does not retract.

Vicky sighs, gives up. Slaps her phone into her best friend's hand. Picks up the check. "Why do you care so much about my sex life anyway?" she grumbles.

Jen raises the phone toward Vicky's face, unlocking it. She begins tapping through the dating app. "You're getting pathetic, and we've been talking about work too much. You need to give me some exciting sex or dating stories—I have to live vicariously through you, remember? Ooh! Who's this hot couple? They sent you a like!" Jen flashes the screen, and Vicky sees a photo with a film-grain filter of a man and a woman holding hands as they stand on what looks like a street in Lower Manhattan. Neither smiling. Both good-looking in that artistic New York City way, weird looking if transported anywhere else. Both are slicked in all black, the boyfriend's fingers jazzed in silver rings brushing his bangs, the girlfriend short and tan, rocking a bob streaked with blue.

"'Kevin, he/him, artist and gallery assistant. Angela, she/her, organizer. Looking for someone interested in dating us as a couple, open to dating on our own for the right person. No pressure on first meetup!'" Jen raises her eyebrows.

"Classic," Vicky says while totaling the tip and signing the receipt. "There's always no pressure. Pressure to do what, exactly? Why are they on the app in the first place? They should just add the unicorn emoji. Makes the search specific."

"Yeah, but I thought you liked dating couples? Less commitment, more pleasure, and they mostly leave you alone 'cause they've already got each other." Jen returns her phone.

"All true, but I still think they're annoying."

"You think everyone's annoying."

They stand, chair legs screeching against the pavement. Vicky sneaks a glance at the table where she had spied her interest, only to find the mismatched couple gone. No matter. She would have disappointed the gender-rejector eventually anyway, because she knows herself by now. She is a good friend but a terrible partner.

She waves to the hot waiter as they exit. He waves back, but she knows by the way his eyes slide past her that the reciprocation is mere politeness. He will not recognize her when they return next week.

"Come over for a bit?" Vicky asks as they stand on the street. She does not feel ready to be alone.

"Sure." Jen is typing on her phone. Vicky pulls her gently by the elbow to safety as a delivery biker zooms past on the sidewalk.

Jen doesn't glance up. "Thanks. Hold on. Let me just send this email."

They meander the fifteen blocks back to Vicky's apartment, weaving through the sidewalk bustle, Jen trailing behind as she taps. Vicky watches others without their noticing, a method she has perfected during her city walks. The quick judgment of those worth watching because of their strut, or their outfit, or the force of their loneliness, or their matter of difference—a good difference, always a good difference. She watches the construction workers on break crouched in shuttered doorways sharing tacos; she watches the old ladies draped on bus stop benches, so still they appear like street art sculptures; she watches the sweaty women striding past in matching colors of athletic wear, perhaps purchased from Roller—she'd never confess to Jen her inability to distinguish which leggings are Roller's and which are from any of the other hip wellness brands. The two head south into Chinatown proper, Jen still on her phone while Vicky watches the gaggles of backpack-laden teenagers sipping boba and sharing bites of pork buns; she watches the souvenir hawkers spin their key chain displays as they discuss prices with tourists; she watches the fishmongers dump their melted ice into the sidewalk gutter as they close up for the night—how she loves even that damp odor of raw fish emanating from the puddles, how she loves the reminder of rotten death streaking the street with water reflecting the sunset like veins of gold. Past 8:00 p.m. on this summer evening, twilight dancing with the building shadows, brief breezy minutes when the city resembles the fantasies, though Vicky had never experienced the destruction of New York City dreams that others experienced upon arrival, ground down by high rent and high stress. She had never harbored desires for city glamour and high power, never believed she'd even come close. She had simply moved in and felt at home in that younger, happier version of herself, freshly in New York. A sense of comfort walking seven miles a day—because why not, it was better to hurt in feet than in mind—wandering around Chelsea in and out of free galleries to stare at pretty paintings; buying leafy variations from Chinatown's street stands that she wishes she had the fortitude to cook before they wilted, feeling grateful to live in the neighborhood of affordable diverse produce; barricading her tender self in her shabby apartment above a Chinatown funeral parlor, the one she thinks is the prettiest, with the green and black and bronze exterior—likely why her rent is so low, because who, other than her, would want to live above death? She is, again, deranged, for she would have happily paid a normal rent for the apartment. She likes sleeping, eating, puttering about, being depressed, above Chinatown's mourners, Chinatown's dead bodies, Chinatown's funerals. Feeling like she's above grief—perhaps another reason she doesn't mind working at Onwards. Sometimes, when she mulls over a difficult brief, she wonders if she should lie on the floor in hopes of absorbing the funeral parlor wisdom six floors down. She's jealous of the poetic mottoes in black calligraphy running down each side of its entrance, characters she had painstakingly copied into an online Chinese-to-English translator: AFTER ONE HUNDRED YEARS RETURN TO EARTH BLESS OFFSPRING on the left and OUR BUSINESS ATTAINS VIRTUE BECAUSE WE HAVE PRECIOUS TREASURE on the right. She does not fully understand what the mottoes mean, sure that there is something lost in translation, but she appreciates the sentiments nonetheless, and how they accentuate the paper rectangles announcing the day's funerals hung in the parlor windows next to the entrance, inked names like MARY CHIU, SHING KWAK, SUE HONG, and WEN YI CHEUNG: names she'd hear drifting through her open window in weeping tonal variations by the deceased's family and friends—she believes it the most poetic soundtrack as she works in death from home. Living above the parlor has furthered her acclimation to the sound of grief, her acclimation to pain, making her the perfect candidate to reside in New York City, for yes, the city is dirty, miserable, and crowded, yet why would she choose to live anywhere else during her stupid, stupid life? A life that could end at any instant—illness, freak accident, gun violence. A hot dog vendor cart breaking free, speeding down the street, running her over. An air conditioner window unit from twenty stories above dropping onto her head. A collapsing sidewalk cellar door, her weight breaking the spongy hold, causing her to plummet and splatter. A horde of angry pigeons pecking out her eyes. A rabid rat biting her exposed big toe on a day she risks flip-flops on the subway. There were so many ways to die in the city. It was better than dying anywhere else.

She digs for her keys at the bottom of her tote, rustling through three sticks of gum, a ball of receipts, two face masks. Creaks open her building door, holds it for Jen to enter first.

"No funeral tonight?" Jen asks as they climb.

"Not in evenings. Usually day." She conserves her words while they ascend—the six-floor walk-up requires full capacity of lung power. Her body has never managed to adjust to the stairs.

Jen, wellness-loving Jen, is fine. "You haven't gone to one yet, right?"

She shakes her head.

Jen pauses mid-stride to peer over the railing, where Vicky is half a flight behind. "You should."

"Why?" Vicky huffs, catching up to Jen.

"Could be interesting. You've lived above the parlor for so long, why not check it out?"

Vicky, speechless out of fatigue, gestures for Jen to keep advancing.

Jen shakes her head and ditches Vicky. "You need to exercise more."

They meet on the landing, Jen's sneakers already lined neatly on the welcome mat.

They enter the apartment. Vicky kicks off her boots and rushes to open the window leading to the fire escape, hoping the evening air might ease the stuffy atmosphere.

Jen surveys the room from the doorway. "Damn. Did you get more zhizha?"

"Oh. Yeah. I did." Vicky, embarrassed, though she knows Jen will not judge her for the zhizha collection that had begun when she arrived in New York City. When Vicky showed up to view the apartment, she had been curious about the paper alcohol bottles, mansions, mahjong tiles, luxury cars, handbags, cell phones, cosmetics, woks, and white woman maids she passed on the street, sun-bleached of color while displayed in store windows with signs reading FUNERARY SUPPLIES. After the broker handed over her keys, she entered one supply store in curiosity and, on a whim, bought a paper bottle of Rémy Martin Cognac in celebration for her first night in the apartment, toasting herself and tipping it back, her saliva dampening the paper. It was only after Jen had come by a week later with an actual bottle of alcohol—a cheap champagne as a housewarming gift—that Vicky learned these paper constructions were called "zhizha," Jen patiently explaining that these were neither fun toys nor weird art but offerings, burned as sacrifice so the dead could own the depicted riches in the afterlife. Jen thought after educating Vicky that the zhizha would be thrown out, but to Vicky, the grim connotations made the papers all the more fascinating. Why did the dead need laptops, dim sum, pet cats? Drawn to the spiritual currency, she window-shopped every time she exited and entered her apartment, stopping into a supply store once a week to treat herself to a new zhiza, the merchants—like the hot waiter—never remembering her face. Another proof point of her mediocrity. She placed her treasures wherever she could find an open space in her apartment: on the windowsill, the bookshelf, the side tables, even hanging flat-bottomed zhizha, like mansions and perfume bottles, on the wall, where they jutted out sideways like coat hooks. She had once made a vow that every time she received a raise, a promotion, or some sort of financial windfall, she would pluck a zhizha from its resting place, throw it out, and buy its counterpart in real life—but the vow had quickly fallen away once she realized just how much she loved the zhizha. And how expensive life really was.

"I haven't bought any this week yet," she said. "You just haven't been over in a few weeks."

Vicky pushes a red Lexus zhizha back and forth on her table like a child would with their toy car.

Jen pokes the top of a beach umbrella zhizha stuck in the nose bridge of a pair of luxury sunglasses zhizha—Gucci branded, though the logo is askew, crooked, like a real Chinese knock-off. "Why's there a beach umbrella? Is the afterlife sunny?"

"Life's a bitch, afterlife's a beach."

"Shut up," she said, then stage muttered, "Stupid punny copywriter."

"A copywriter who hasn't taken a vacation in years. Why don't we travel somewhere beachy this summer?" Vicky nudges Jen. "Sardinia? Ibiza? Goa? Bali?" She rattles off premium destinations she's never believed she'd actually be able to afford visiting—and still couldn't now.

"You know I wanna pay off more of our loans before a fancy trip, and I have all those weddings for Eric's hometown friends this summer." Jen pouts, then brightens with a new thought: "Besides, let's dream bigger. More than just a vacation. Shall we move to, hmm, the coast of Portugal? Quit our jobs, buy a place by the beach, open up a surf school?"

"We don't know how to surf. And we'd miss Asian food after three days."

"Good thing you have a zhizha for that." Jen points to the hot pot zhizha, packed to the brim with graphics of vegetables, tofu, meat, and seafood, tucked on the top of her fridge. "Just bring it along."

"As if you'd ever quit your job."

"You never know. Maybe if you burn an 'I quit' letter zhizha for me, it'll happen."

"Zhizha is only for the dead, and you aren't dead yet."

"Yet," Jen echoes. She frowns, then switches the conversation by turning her attention to her bag, rummaging around until she finds her box of cigarettes. Flourishes it forward. "Ta-da!"

Vicky grins. "What would your health-obsessed coworkers say if they knew you smoked tobacco?"

"I only have so few pleasures."

"I'll make sure to burn packs after you die so you can have cigs in the afterlife."

"I only want them if you smoke them yourself, all at once."

They duck below the open window, clambering onto the fire escape, where night has descended, though it is a darkness not total but gentle, softened by streetlights and glowing apartment windows and neon bar signs. The two sit facing each other, cross-legged on the metal platform. Jen sticks a cigarette in her mouth, then briefly illuminates her face orange with the Hello Kitty lighter she always keeps with her—a gift from Vicky, purchased from their collegetown's Sanrio store in celebration after they had won the dog collar brief. Jen takes a drag, blows clouds.

"Gimme," says Vicky.

Jen hands her the box, then the lighter. Vicky palms out a cigarette, pops it between her lips, lights it with Hello Kitty. She loves how Jen refills and reuses the cheap lighter year after year, dropping it off at a Chinatown repair stand rather than disposing of it after the fluid ran out—one of the many inconsequential objects cherished over a long friendship, like postcards or books or hair clips, exchanged over the years to mark moments and their love.

*I wanted to give you this.*
*It made me think of you.*
*Thank you for being my friend.*

The nicotine prickles through Vicky. She loves the buzz, the smell, the exhalation, the flirting with death; most of all, she loves the excuse to evacuate ceilings for stars, with a friend, a lover, a soon-to-be friend who might just turn into a lover. She supposes it would be better for her health if there were tobacco-free excuses to step out, but she finds cigarettes themselves romantic, she can't help it—she loves the thin tube resting on lips and the graceful movement of a traveling hand, drawing attention to strong fingers and warm mouths; the ephemeral drifting smoke; the excuse to step away and step out; the temporary tenderness counting down minutes by the length of its paper.

They do not talk. They smoke in quiet. They had discussed so much in the past. Drunk and sober shared secrets and jokes and fights and gossip. Trauma's various genres. They would again in the future. Enough now to sit in silence, sharing a smoke. Company as conversation, the soundtrack of the city accompanying: pedestrians laughing, buses wheezing, lights humming.

Jen takes her final drag, stubs the cigarette, discards the butt in the ashtray Vicky stores on the bottom step of the fire escape.

"Gonna head out," she says.

The two uncrinkle their limbs, stand, and scramble back through the window, into the apartment.

Jen hugs her. A familiar comfort of touch upon every meeting, every parting.

"Tell Eric I say hi."

Jen nods, waves, steps out.

Vicky locks the door behind her. Plops onto the love seat, putting her feet on the scratched table she had filched from the sidewalk last year on trash day. Eric had helped her carry it up while Jen cheered from the sidelines.

She takes out her phone and opens the dating app. The couple Jen fawned over stares at her. Kevin and Angela. She thinks of Jen's succinct summary at dinner of Vicky's winding explanations of why she prefers couples. Less commitment, more pleasure.

If there is a zhizha in any of the funerary supply stores representing commitment, she is sure it would be a wedding ring, though she cannot fathom in the hedonist possibility of the afterlife why a soul would still want to entangle themselves in a marriage, a state-sanctioned concept devoid of pleasure. She is less sure what a zhizha representing pleasure would be—a lover? A partner? Neither, both? Pleasure is subjective. Nevertheless, the choice is inconsequential, because: one, she would be dead, unable to ask for her own zhizha; two, she's sure it's considered bad luck to burn a paper rendition of someone alive. Zhizha were meant to be things promising joy, happiness, prosperity—not people, though she has seen cleaner, maid, butler, and nanny zhizha sold in stores. Perhaps servants were not humans but objects to those who hired them.

She looks around her apartment at her zhizha and wonders if people like Kevin and Angela, clearly open-minded in romantic structures, would be further open-minded to her strange zhizha quirks if they came over—rarely has she tested anyone other than Jen before, opting to go to her lovers' places instead to avoid the awkward questions—and because it is easier to leave than it is to kick someone out. She has a bad habit of leaving. Of disappearing when she is too sad. Too stressed. Too tired.

She looks at their picture again and decides she likes Kevin's slim hands drenched in silver rings—she could imagine sliding the jewelry off, sucking a finger, licking a trail of vein. She likes Angela's nonchalant pout, how her lips curl upward without smiling. She likes how they are posed holding hands, indicating their connection, while leaving enough space between their bodies for whomever they might stumble into when swiping. Despite what she had told Jen, she likes their up-front, truthful bio too—she has met up with many women from dating apps only to discover their boyfriends waiting in the shadows of the bar like bats, planning to swoop in from the sidelines.

Why not. She's bored.

She presses the heart to match with Kevin and Angela. Swallows her nonchalance, her contempt, her exhaustion. Sends a message.

hi

# work

She winces as Dan greets her too loudly and too early. Her wrists ache. Head pounds. Throat bristles from dehydration and last night's cigarettes.

"Ernie loves your Urnie stunt. He thinks it's buzzworthy, funny, and on strategy. He wants to launch in the upcoming weeks, so I've already set up a meeting later with a team of producers. They'll start looking into cemetery venues, budget, and name-change petitions. If the formal court procedure takes too long, Ernie says we can frame the ceremony as an announcement of intent."

"Great!" Her voice, hoarse. "If he'd like, I can draft a speech for him to read."

Dan wrinkles his eyebrows. "It's fine. You know Ernie will have something prepared."

Ernie, an actor, celebrity, and founder, always with a grand script for everything from company parties to press announcements. Vicky can't recall any Onwards event featuring Ernie where he did not step up to the podium.

"Right." At least she showed initiative. Dan believes in initiative.

"Let's work with Strategy to figure out the best way to get media intrigued—we're thinking a spin on how names are sacred, especially Ernie's because of his father, so the name change emphasizes his commitment to Onwards urns. In the meantime, can you add a slide in the planning deck with a short paragraph that summarizes the campaign and our thinking? I'll use it to brief Production."

"Will do."

"Thanks, Vicky. This'll be a good one. Ernie's excited."

"Me too."

"Talk to you soon." Dan waves, his hand a blurry mass on the computer screen.

She exits the meeting, slumps onto her pillows. Checks the time in the corner of her screen: 10:22 a.m.

She opens the presentation titled THE ERNIE OPPORTUNITY _Creative_June.

Adds a new slide. Hovers her fingers over the keyboard.
Attempts to think.

Nothing.

Needing a distraction, she picks up her phone, face down on the mattress. Checks her texts—nothing new from Jen, her last message a picture from her smoothie photoshoot of a pineapple wearing sunglasses. Vicky had sent back a laughing face emoji.

She checks the dating app.

Her last message glares: hows tmrw afternoon 4ish? i can leave work early

Sent Thursday afternoon, now Friday morning. No response in twenty-two hours. She is unsure whether it had been Kevin or Angela messaging her with full sentences and proper punctuation from their shared profile. Perhaps they composed each response together, judging Vicky as they cuddled. But nothing now.

She drops her phone. Stares at the blank presentation slide, the text box's blinking cursor mocking her. Mentally motivates herself: *The sooner you finish work, the sooner you can go back to sleep.*

She'd presented three ways to show her range of thinking. But when the Ernie-Urnie parallel had popped in her head, she'd known any other idea would be subpar. She can recognize a good idea. She can do the work. She shuts her eyes. Allows her fingers to take on their own life and type words without her mind pausing to judge. *Tap tap tap*—her body can perform when her brain goes blank, like when she wanders around the city without an intended destination, yet somehow arrives at her favorite city spots: the Chinatown ice cream shop with the pandan flavor, Jen's apartment building entrance, the used bookstore with neither sign, nor name, nor online presence but many overflowing one-dollar carts.

Opens her eyes and reads:

Ernie Hayworth (born Ernest Hayworth III), Onwards founder, humanitarian, philanthropist, and former actor, film producer, and model, petitions the NYC Civil Court to grant him a name change to Urnie Hayworth. Through this transformative campaign, Hayworth expresses his commitment to fighting for a better death industry through Onwards. The shift from his famous namesake to the embodiment of Onwards indicates Hayworth's acknowledgment—and therefore acceptance—of death's inevitability.

Good enough.

She rereads, looking for any spelling or punctuation errors. Dan is detail oriented. If her work is sloppy, she will be viewed as unreliable. Unnecessary to the company. Fired. And without her job she will be stressed, and with stress she will not be able to sleep, and when she doesn't get enough sleep her defenses against despair are lowered, which means that despite the coping mechanisms she's gathered over the past decade, she will descend back into her nightmares, the visions that had her screaming awake when she was fifteen years old after the death of her grandfather, which had brought the realization that no matter how hard and how deeply she loves someone, they will still die. A childhood lesson: Love did not save. Love meant grief.

She had dreamed of her mother collapsing from sudden cardiac arrest after one of her long Sunday morning runs. She had dreamed of her father, who did not like to carry around his EpiPen because it would make him seem weak, suffocating to death from the anaphylaxis caused by a wayward peanut. She had dreamed of her ex–best friend, Gabriel, a talented ice skater, his throat slashed by a skate blade after a flip gone wrong, bleeding out onto the frozen rink. She had told Gabriel she didn't want to be friends with him anymore, and then she had stopped dreaming of his death. Better to love less so she could sleep better.

Vicky's sleep is so valuable that she'll never forget the best night's sleep of her life. She had been a college student laboring with Jen over a mock campaign brief in the library lobby café when simultaneous screams around the building burst free, signs of life in the bleak wasteland of stressful final exams. Breaking news: paparazzi vultures, fans, and journalists descending onto the scene, broadcasting the carnage for citizens panicking over their beloved Hollywood royalty; Vicky and Jen and every other long-suffering student huddled breathlessly around their laptops, phones, and televisions, refreshing and scrolling and sharing, their study guides forgotten in the face of tragic spectacle. Ernie and his boyfriend, parents, and grandparents had been speeding to the Gay & Lesbian Association Against Derogation annual convention, where Ernie would be honored for his role in the hottest summer blockbuster as a political public relations consultant hired to spin a presidential candidate's homosexuality, a markedly different character from the one he'd played in the comedy that had launched his career, as a teenager fighting for the right to wear a dress to his high school prom. A fanboy, tracking Ernie's location through social media stalker accounts, had launched his vehicle in front of their limo, intending to force the chauffeur to brake so he could express his undying thanks. But the driver, startled and slow to react, had instead swiped the fan's car, then swerved into the side of the Pacific Coast Highway. The feeds recorded Ernie's mother's charred ankles curving into her iconic red heels and Ernie's father's wrist, ravaged but still rocking the precious metal and stone million-dollar timepiece handed down from Ernie's grandfather, who himself had nothing the cameras could capture because his body had been incinerated in the wreckage. The feeds recorded emergency medical technicians wiping the soot from their cheeks onto their ragged shirtsleeves, the blue and red glare of ambulance and police lights, and the fan's car, ditched on the side of the road, decorated with printouts of Ernie in the prom dress, Ernie in a tuxedo on a movie premiere red carpet, Ernie kissing the cheek of his boyfriend—photos hanging in the front, back, and side windows, so obstructing the driver's view that it was a wonder the fan had spotted the limo in the first place, moreover driven the car at all, though wasn't the hazard of death worth any glimpse of your idol's face? And the feeds caught Ernie, dear Ernie, emerging unscathed from the flames but for the scorched bundle in his handsome, muscled arms—a lover clearly dead, yet Ernie so alive in his grief, collapsing to his knees, wailing over the bloody flesh that had once animated the top half of his boyfriend, sliced clean in the collision from the legs Ernie had spent innumerable nights kissing. Parents dead, grandparents torched, lover bisected, all in a violent and unavoidable formula: a car crash, a natural occurrence of post–Industrial Revolution contemporary human life, a risk ignored whenever anyone contorts their frame into a metal wheeled cocoon, whenever anyone agrees to a monthly auto loan repayment, whenever anyone zooms twenty miles above the speed limit down a highway with the windows open, blasting some song whose lyrics sing of being alive until they stop being alive because the car crashes and the journey ends. They die. We die. The Hayworths died.

Vicky woke up the morning after the crash not feeling like herself—she woke up feeling refreshed, alert, and motivated. The power of a solid nine hours of sleep. Her witnessing of such horrific ends had chased away her dreams of death: facing her fear had compelled her fear to flee. No more nightmares of Jen's head cracked open after tripping down the stairs drunk at a party; Jen strangled by the creepy male shadow she imagined behind her every time she walked home late from the library; Jen crumpled from a heart attack after too many cocaine binges.

Vicky knew she loved Jen because she dreamed of her death. To love meant to fear death.

Vicky had begun watching clips of people dying every night. Her favorite macabre bedtime stories became people falling off building roofs, wasting to nothing in hospital beds, wandering astray on expeditions gone wrong. Her search engine delivered her a canceled television show called *Ten Thousand Ways to Die*, and she ran through every season twice, eventually emailing the network's listed support contact, begging them to revive the show. She slept well. The nightmares ceased.

A month later, Vicky and Jen skipped class to watch together on Jen's bed what the paparazzi were calling the event of the year: the televised funeral for Ernie's family and partner (the chauffeur and fan, forgotten), scheduled at 12:00 p.m. EST, 9:00 a.m. PST, though it could have been midnight, could have been 3:00 a.m.—every American would wake and watch and pray and cry. Anything for Ernie, darling Ernie, his first public appearance in weeks. He appeared impeccable in a black suit tailored to his body—only those with unceasing budgets for tailors, assistants, stylists, beauty experts, and lawyers could look so perfect in mourning, and Ernie needed to look *perfect* while standing at the cemetery podium—because he had an important announcement to share after his heartfelt eulogy. Viewers around the world sobbed into their tissues over his tribute, as Ernie wiped the tears from his face and explained how he could not bear the grief. The agony. The absence. He ran away to where rich people could go to feel better: India, for a meditation retreat led by bearded gurus who deemed him worthy, bestowing their ancient funerary wisdom unto him. Human body as temporary vessel. Cremation as purification. The releasing of the soul, which equaled the freeing of the soul.

Ernie declared his intent to launch a funeral innovation start-up inspired by his experiences. He never wanted his loyal and devoted fans to face the same ordeal he had. He would protect his people from predatory funeral directors, exorbitant funeral homes, and the inequities of burial. He would teach how to prepare for death and for grief. He would guide fans in death the way the gurus had guided him. And he'd keep it in the community, corralling his three best friends from childhood: Ned, Barrie, and Yves—two tall, beautiful, chiseled white men and one tall, beautiful, chiseled white person, all from American celebrity and artist lineages whose last names adorned museum wings and college buildings. Combined with Ernie, they composed a best friend group christened ENBY—the initials of their names, non-appropriative because Barrie, the designer, was nonbinary—by adoring fans who had watched them grow up. Ned was a sculptor and Yves was a model, though you could deem all four of them simply creatives, because their practice did not align under one discipline. They had the freedom—cash, privilege, safety net—to try many things and be good at them too. ENBY combined brainpower with brand power and launched the first line of Onwards urns, five prototype designs, each named after Ernie's deceased loved ones; ashes from their cremated bodies, and in the case of the incinerated grandfather, residue collected from the crash scene, were scattered into the urns' paint before being fired in the kiln. A double burning as its own form of spiritual rejuvenation. A double cleansing. Grief and rebirth, claimed Ernie. Well designed, low cost, and convenient too, the ideal vessel to march Onwards to the afterlife, Onwards to after-grief.

*Wow*, Jen had said, her head nestled on Vicky's shoulder as they gazed at the laptop screen together. *It's a bit perverse.*

*I think it's a good idea*, Vicky said. She understood Ernie's reasoning. She'd defend him until death for giving her the gift of a good night's sleep.

Vicky kept tabs on Onwards as the weeks passed, clicking through articles in the business section about Ernie's endeavors. Famous people were always launching brands, from skincare to alcohol, mobilizing their fanbase to purchase cheaply made products dressed up in celebrity chic. But none had attempted to shake up the funeral industry before, especially so personally, and the media was frothing to report on the innovations. How, despite Onwards's business model of cutting out the middleman, funeral homes and directors recognized the opportunity Onwards—rather, Ernie—offered, presenting plans for collaborative expansion into funerary features such as coffins, land plots, bouquets, even meal delivery—an idea capitalizing on how grief made simple tasks like cooking difficult. How investors too clamored to seize a piece of the death start-up, a soon-to-be unicorn nearing valuation of $1 billion, but Ernie, no longer nepo baby but nepo orphan, remained resolute in his initial foray: urns. He had no need for outside investment or product development. He had himself, he had ENBY, he had fans—who showed up for him. The elderly close to death, babies just born, those sick with terminality, those healthy running monthly marathons. Some people bought urns because of Ernie; others wanted options when death inevitably struck. Some bought because Onwards urns were pretty enough to decorate a home; others for status objects, to prove they had the courage to face death. A select group was even popular: deathfluencers, urnfluencers. Onwards consumers were an astounding business school case study. "Onwards is transforming funeral preparation into an aspirational lifestyle for all generations," wrote one *Fast Company* journalist. And to further encourage the Onwards community, Ernie prioritized connection for customer experience: Onwards grief support groups, Onwards-led death café discussions, an Onwards-branded team of grief counselors and funeral directors to consult with customers through urn selection. The growth and expansion of Onwards—all while the brand remained true to Ernie and its roots—made Vicky realize that Ernie led the sort of company her professors had presented as timeless examples of American innovation. *If you have a chance to work at a place like this, take it. Don't worry about money. The money will come,* they had said, pointing their hands that had never known begging to lecture slides of historic company logos representing fast-food revolutions and smartphone iterations. Didn't Onwards deserve to be up there? Only Ernie had been the catalyst for her to discover what would chase away her troubled sleep; only Ernie had been brave enough to take on the very gay, edgy Hollywood roles that agents advised against; and only Ernie was brave enough to disrupt the business of death, untouched unlike the business of glasses, sportswear, makeup, razors, vitamins—safe consumer goods, but Ernie had never been interested in playing it safe; he was interested in *slaying*, as ENBY and their devout gay following would say, because every successful brand needed a reason to believe, a strong backstory, a David slay Goliath. And there was

Ernie, the handsome David slaying the Goliath of Death. Ernie, *Urnie*, was better than any holding company, any CEO, any advertising mascot. A c-suite's wet dream, an advertising creative's fantasy. The reason Americans began to eagerly anticipate death in order to soften its punch.

Vicky had headed down the aisles of her senior year college fair straight for the black Onwards logo without looking elsewhere. Tunnel vision. Single-minded determination. She had plastered a grin on her face to ingratiate herself to the recruiter, submitting her résumé, portfolio, and professor recommendation after multiple rereads and frantic texts to Jen asking if she could look over it again, just in case we might've missed a typo. Her attention to detail then had helped her be hired, but now set up an expectation of perfection that if unmet, as Dan stressed on every project, she would be fired.

When the offer letter came through weeks later, she and Jen had gone out to their college bar and split an entire fishbowl to celebrate Vicky's first job. Tackling adulthood with death—the ideal starting point of a life.

*love?*

Kevin, or Angela, or Kevin and Angela both, confirmed their date precisely when Vicky, annoyed at the delay in response, was hovering her thumb over the X button.

Instead of unmatching, she typed a response: cool see u!

Hours later, she stands under the left arch of the Gothic Revival bronze gate, perched at the top of the cemetery's winding driveway, offering her a high vantage point of the neighborhood:

the auto repair garage roofs, the retail bakery outpost wafting fresh-baked delights at odds with the industrial surroundings, and the murky waters of the Gowanus feeding into New York Harbor where the Statue of Liberty perches. She can spy the figures she's been waiting for too. She can tell they are dating, though they are not holding hands—their strides match well despite their uneven heights, like they have been gait-adjusting side by side for years. One is shorter and stouter; the taller walking slightly hunched, shoulders curled in and forward like a turtle poking its head out of its shell. Both are dressed in black like herself despite the heat. Vicky has repeated her outfit from the dinner with Jen, rescuing the dress from her apartment floor, inspecting it for stains, spraying it with room freshener, and flapping it like a flag to rid it of wrinkles.

"Vicky?" The woman speaks first when they arrive. Her face is shiny, her blue-dyed bangs matted.

"Hi." Vicky matches the woman's gaze and is struck by the saddest pair of eyes she's ever seen—shape tilted downward, gaze unfocused, mascara smears further staining the already dark and tired under-eyes. Vicky has only ever seen a similar appearance once, months ago, on a young girl riding the C train clutching a bag of apple slices and a stroller, whose baby alternated between stroking the subway pole and shoving his fingers in his mouth, until the girl passed him an apple slice, which he then promptly dropped on the floor. Vicky watched as the girl seized another slice and deposited it onto her baby's waiting tongue, as if the train's safe passage depended solely on his swallowing of apple nutrients; the girl then ran her saliva-stained hand over her acne-riddled cheeks, and though the girl had cooed at her giggling baby, Vicky could not tear her eyes away from the exhaustion, the sadness, the despair, radiating from that C train girl. A void sucking in spectators; a sorrow that had no definable shape but many shadows—and Vicky looked at this blue-haired woman in front of her at the cemetery and wondered if this woman's shadows were uncountable too. "Angela?" Vicky asks.

"That's me."

"Kevin." Not to be forgotten, the man waves, his silver rings glinting in the sunlight. Vicky has a brief, delirious vision of him removing them one by one to place in a neat row on a side table before sex like a dog meticulously circling its bed before lying down. She smothers her desire to laugh—her natural inclination is to be brash. Rude. Uncaring. She's learned by now her natural attitude should be revealed only on the third or fourth date.

Kevin is different from his dating app photos, which gave the impression of confidence. In real life, his caved-in shoulders make him seem like he is attempting to protect his heart. He's grown his hair out—shaggier, matching Angela's length—and he sports a skinny mustache. Vicky asks herself if she can still maintain an attraction to him despite the facial hair—decides that she must, if only to find out if he keeps his rings on or off for sex.

She shakes his hand. The palm is dry, the silver cool against her sweaty fingers. In the second before she relinquishes her grip, she resolves that she will ditch the couple if he dares to wipe his hand on his thigh.

"Sorry, Kevin's overly formal sometimes. Come here." Angela opens her arms. Vicky hesitates, then steps in, her posture stiff.

Steps back before she can soften.

"Shall we go?" Vicky motions toward the entrance.

They walk through the gate. She appreciates how Angela chooses to keep pace next to her, Kevin a few strides behind.

"Have you been here before?" Vicky asks.

"Yeah. For this Halloween concert in the catacombs, featuring dancers who performed inside the crypt. One of those random events you attend when you first move to New York City because you signed up for a newsletter that drops a list of weird free happenings in your email every day, and you go because you don't know anyone else and you don't have anything better to do."

"Sounds fun, though."

"It was."

"When did you move to the city?"

"Six, maybe seven years ago at this point? It's been a good time. Feels like home. First Halloween at the catacombs, second Halloween at a mutual friend's party, where I met him." Angela jerks her head back toward Kevin. "Can you believe it? I had been so close to not going, since work had me stressed, but I rallied. I threw on a witch hat and some black lipstick—the most basic costume—while Kevin showed up in a sexy loose black suit with a red tie, as the guy from *Rush Hour*—"

"You know. Jackie Chan," Kevin interrupts.

"Anyway, my dad and I used to rewatch *Rush Hour* every year. We'd quote the stupidest lines together. So I went up to Kevin to tell him I loved his costume, and he asked if black lipstick tasted like licorice, and I offered to let him sample, which was so fucking corny, but it worked. We made out, he asked for my number, and now we're here." Angela giggles.

"Cute," Vicky offers.

"Halloween's a special holiday for us now. We throw a party at ours every year—you'd be welcome."

"Oh, uh, maybe. Can I let you know?" Vicky is surprised at

the invitation, arriving months in advance. Is she special, or does Angela offer such warmth to every first date?

"Sure, it's an open invite."

They arrive at a fork. Vicky gestures toward the left. "This way leads to a nice view. Wanna check it out?"

Angela nods.

"You're here often?" Kevin asks. "We liked your bio: 'Ask me about my favorite cemetery.'"

"Mm-hmm." Vicky visits Green-Wood often. Walks with Jen, walks with dates, and walks with herself, solo—she loves the wise trees, wide trails, quiet tombs.

"Why? You like being around dead people?"

"Better than being around alive people. The dead leave me alone."

Kevin laughs.

Angela frowns. "No, the dead haunt."

"Are you superstitious?" Vicky asks.

"A bit."

"Well, I'm not. My dead stay dead," Vicky says.

They saunter, Green-Wood's many magnificent trees granting shady respites from the sun. Vicky points out certain grave markers—she's traversed this direction enough to consider them familiar friends: the angel trio, carved so excellently that their stone dresses resemble real rippling fabric; Death, in a green oxidized cloak, stretching out his grubby hands as if to snatch spectators and pull them into his abyss; the goddess Minerva, concrete and wise, palm raised in the direction of Lady Liberty, her sister-in-wisdom atop the waters. Other gravestones whose dates and names have eroded, weathered by sun and rain and snow, denoting that the corpse below was loved enough by someone willing to pay for a marking of its final resting place even if the little arch jutting from the ground was unremarkable, no work of expensive art like angel trios or Minerva. There were inequities in cadaver interment too—never mind the privilege of having a physical body to bury, which catastrophes like natural disasters or war erased.

"Fucking beautiful," Kevin murmurs, stopping to examine a cast metal bear straddling a headstone, haunches saggy and eyes alert.

"Kevin's background is in sculpture, though he explores all mediums now," Angela whispers, not wanting to disrupt her partner's process. "His gallery assistant gig in Chelsea is just for inspiration. He spends a lot of time thinking."

Vicky resists the urge to say something scathing. It is still too early to be rude—to be herself.

"'Beard'?" Kevin reads the headstone's etching. "Oh, maybe that's why there's a bear here—isn't Beard that artist who painted animals doing human activities? Famous for painting bulls and bears on Wall Street?"

"I'm not sure," Vicky answers. "I don't know much about the actual people buried here. I mostly just pay attention to the monuments."

"For work? Your profile said you're at Onwards. That's the death start-up founded by Ernie Hayworth, right?" Angela asks.

"No, I have hobbies," Vicky says, though this makes her realize that perhaps they are the same. Disconcerted, she adds, "Green-Wood is peaceful. And it's fun to see how people commemorate their dead. Urns and cremation feel separate from cemeteries and burial. Besides, our urns have such a contemporary design that these old headstones can't teach me anything useful."

Kevin leaves the Beard bear and rejoins the group. Vicky spots the obelisk marking where to veer off the paved path. She leads them onto the steep, grassy hill.

As they hike upward, Angela asks, "Why'd you choose to work at Onwards?"

Vicky isn't ready to divulge her strangeness: the zhizha, the childhood-to-adult fascination with death, the daily acceptance upon waking up that the next twenty-four hours could be her last. "Pay is good," she grunts instead.

"Is it?"

"It's fine."

"Hmm."

"What?"

Angela shrugs. "It's nice to know which companies treat their workers well. Or don't."

"Not the best, not the worst. Same as any company."

"I'd disagree, but it's fine. We just met, after all." Angela giggles.

Vicky is silent.

"Aren't Onwards urns well-known for their designs? Which do you like the most?" Kevin asks.

"The Lucy urn." A classic design like its namesake, Lucy Hayworth, Ernie's dead mother, with red adornments in the same shade as her famous lipstick and a curvy shape borrowed from her notorious cleavage, which had catapulted her to fame back when women were not meant to be smart for plot but hot for audience. According to the Onwards consumer insight team, the Lucy was most popular among middle-aged husbands purchasing urns for their wives who had passed away from breast cancer.

"I'm surprised. Thought you would've chosen the sleek onyx one," Kevin says.

"Oh, so you know the designs well?" Vicky says.

"Not really. I just read an article about avant-garde death aesthetics. It featured Onwards and interviewed Barrie, the designer."

"Thoughts?"

"I guess Barrie and ENBY in general seem cool. Have you met Ernie yet?"

Vicky shakes her head. She had known this question would come—it always did whenever she met new people who learned where she worked. Why did people care most about Ernie, about celebrity? She wasn't famous, but she did work just as hard to make Onwards successful—where was her credit?

They arrive at the top. Their final destination. Vicky breathes in, fills her lungs to capacity, breathes out. The air feels good. She loves it up here, where she's never run into anyone else. Where she can relax undisturbed in the quiet shade of a marble sarcophagus surrounded by ghosts and graves to gaze at Manhattan's skyline, the silver buildings rising into the blue like headstones themselves. She loves looking at that far-off steely mass of fast walking and high rent where she's managed to make a life for herself—an inconsequential life, yet a life nonetheless. A life that is hers, or trying to be, and when she sits here, she can almost convince herself that the mere trying is the most meaningful act of all.

"Wow," Angela says.

"Nice," Kevin says.

Vicky decides she likes them. She pats the ground. They join cross-legged, her in the middle.

Together, they face the expanse.

"So." Kevin clears his throat.

This is where it begins: the endless personal questions about what Vicky is looking for and why—why a couple, and why them? Couples, sweeping aside decorum on the first date just because they could. Safety in numbers. Two versus one, safer than turning two into three. Couples who want to confirm that Vicky is delusional enough to date them, yet not delusional enough to believe that she could join them. Vicky braces herself. She's undergone this process so often that she knows her answers before the questions are asked, because the questions are always the same.

Yet, somehow, this time—

"Kevin, don't bother her with stupid questions. I like her."

Vicky looks at Angela in surprise and catches Angela watching her with a hungry yet careful expression, a calculation exposing both the predator's ravenous appetite and the predator's fear that her hunger is immoderate, extreme, terrifying—the predator should not scare off its prey before it can pounce—and this naked yet cautious gesture is what makes Vicky decide that she will love Angela. Not love in the romantic way, but love in the comfortable way, more a fondness in the way that Vicky likes to love, which is: *I will try to be there for you when you need me, and I will try to be there even when you don't, yet either way I will fail, because I always fail, but I am trying my best, I am. I promise.*

Vicky turns back to the skyline. "Thank you," she tells New York.

"Have you done this before?" Kevin asks.

Angela groans.

"Have you?" Vicky counters.

"Yes, but I can tell you why we've been looking again recently—"

"No need," Vicky interrupts. "Truly. No need to explain why you're looking for a third. To be honest, I don't really wanna know. Let's just have fun, okay? I like dating couples. It's not complicated. The intensity of monogamous coupling is too much for me in my current stage of life. I don't want the spotlight, I prefer the peripheral."

"Interesting," Kevin says.

"Is it?"

"Do you mind if I ask some questions?" he asks.

"You can ask me anything."

"How many couples have you dated before? What were they like?"

"You're maybe the fourth or fifth? I have a bad memory. But I do remember that they're similar to you. I have a type."

Kevin laughs. "And what type is that?"

"Creative. Honest. The couple should be in love, but not nauseatingly so. And to be honest, looks don't matter much to me. I like brains."

"So, you're a zombie?" Angela asks.

Kevin snorts.

Vicky grins.

Angela dips her chin, exposing the top of her head to Vicky. "Here. You can eat mine. Free me from reality."

Vicky pats the offered head. She likes the matching weirdness.

Angela raises her face.

Beckoned, Vicky leans in.

They kiss, tentative and soft. Angela moans gently, and, on cue, Vicky presses deeper. She dimly perceives a caress elsewhere on her body: Kevin, his fingers—no, his rings—stroking her arm, and she likes it, she does, this woman on her lips and this man on her body.

Vicky releases the kiss and opens her eyes and sees Kevin, sees Angela, sees the death around them and the city far off, and she is happy, suffused with the sensation of happy, for the first time that day.

Angela smiles. Brushes her fingers against Vicky's cheek. "Would you like to come over?"

Vicky wavers. The answer is yes. She would love to come over.

And yet.

She is tired. And her happy is fleeting—for her, happy arrives occasionally and departs often, and she does not want the inevitable comedown to happen when she is around someone she has just met, someone she thinks she could love.

"Maybe next time?" She adds, "There will definitely be a next time." She adds again, nervous, "If you would like a next time."

Angela kisses her in assent.

# *friendship*

"YES!" Jen pumps the air, her arm slicked in pumpkin spice, part of the new Roller fall athletic line releasing in a few months featuring colors of muted orange, rust red, soft brown—evoking marketing copy like "crunching leaves below your feet as you jog three miles," "picking apples with your besties," "cooking plant-based butternut squash stew (minus the cream!) for a cozy date night."

"So, she's hot? And the dude?" Jen probes.

"Both hot."

Jen pumps the air again. Vicky sips her coffee, smiling. She enjoys telling Jen her dating adventures because of the gracious reactions. She had once been afraid of Jen's judgment or boredom, but Jen had confirmed how she just wanted Vicky to be happy and how—because she and Eric rarely had sex—it was nice to know that one of them was having orgasms. Vicky had once pointed out that it was likely both Jen and Eric were ace, or at least gray ace, but Jen had shrugged, saying that the identity, the label, the definition, didn't matter much to her, since both of them were quite happy being a sexless couple in love. Vicky admired how Jen had spent her youth overthinking and overanalyzing until the anxiety became so unbearable that it bubbled over into nonchalant acceptance. Part coping mechanism, part realization that it is what it is. She is who she is; we are who we are. Jen had learned, as Ernie would say, to move onward.

Jen and Vicky sit in a diner, or the appropriation of a diner, on the border of Chinatown and what real estate agents were trying to market as Two Bridges. The diner resembles the several other businesses that have popped up in the past few years along the block, owned by Asian Americans who sought to fuse what they called the East and West. Jen and Vicky regularly used the spot for catching up quickly over a cup of coffee. There were other, more tolerable cafés and neighborhood bakeries nearby, but they had stumbled into this diner one day and never summoned the energy to find somewhere else. Besides, the music was quiet, the location convenient between their offices, the coffee bottomless, and it was rarely overcrowded. They knew what to expect. Vicky thought it ridiculous how tourists asked the internet for the best local spots—best coffee, best bagels, best parks—when she never went for the best, merely what was unexceptional, comfortable, close by. Long-term love, not infatuation.

"You'll meet up with them again?"

"Yes. Just gotta find time. Probably next week since they're going upstate this weekend. They asked to see me on Wednesday for a drink, but you know how it is with work—it's been hectic with the Ernie/Urnie renaming campaign. Can't swing a weekday."

"You're headed to the ceremony now?"

"Yeah. Producers landed the Marble Cemetery a few blocks away."

"I haven't been."

"It's a city landmark. We're staging the media event by the gate since its managers didn't want a crowd inside trampling the vegetation or tripping over headstones. But—still a win, since usually they won't even let people loiter in front. Just mention Ernie and people will do anything." Vicky rolls her eyes. "Good publicity. Also, I think the cemetery needs money. Apparently there's less profit in burial now that most people either can't afford it or just aren't religious anymore. They built an entire new columbarium recently. More accessible to the general public and doesn't take up too much space."

Jen wrinkles her nose. "You always talk about death and profit so nonchalantly."

Vicky laughs. "How have you not gotten used to it?"

Jen shivers. "I don't think I ever will." She checks her phone for the time. "I have to go. I have a meeting with the photographer for the apparel shoot." She shimmies, showing off her pumpkin spice. Stands and drops a bill onto the bar.

Vicky follows, stretching and yawning.

"What are you doing next Thursday?" Jen yells as they exit

into construction jackhammering, car honking, and subway grumbling within the concrete depths.

"Nothing. Probably a chill work week, since it's after production. Can do whatever. Give me an excuse to leave work early."

"The apparel shoot! It's a workout and dance thing in Fort Greene. We're working with a bunch of lifestyle and athletic influencers. You know the type. I'm leading creative—"

"Nice!"

"Yeah, but I'm anxious about it. I'll feel more confident if you're there. Come! There will be free shit."

"Yeah, I'll be there. Even though you know I hate working out."

The two hug, pedestrians parting around them like streams around boulders, reenacting familiar scenes of farewell in front of subway stations, stoops, cafés, office lobbies, food carts—the goodbyes, the *good to see yous*, the promises within *see you soon*s.

# work

"Dan! I'm over here!" Vicky yells. She watches her boss anxiously pace the breadth of the half-block-long Marble Cemetery gate, his head impaled with every step by its iron rods. Vicky lifts the collar of her T-shirt and wipes the sweat collecting on her forehead from her fast walk to the ceremony, then crosses the street with no regard for glancing left and right. A biker zooms by, swerving to avoid her.

"You're late," Dan hisses. "Didn't I tell you we needed all hands on deck to set up the stage?"

Vicky bites back her retort that he should be grateful she's there at all. She waves her phone at Dan. "I took some pictures from across the street if you wanna see how it might look on social. Everything looks great. The producers did a wonderful job."

Dan leans in. Together they stare at Vicky's screen showing the path outlined by white bouquets, starting from the corner's coffee shop—rented out for the day so Ernie could have a private space away from hungry spectators—leading up to the gate arch, where a podium had been placed. Used for burial eulogies, it had been lent out of storage by the cemetery managers. An Onwards logo sticker had been pasted onto its wood by one of the freelance producers they hired for experiential campaigns.

Vicky waits nervously for Dan's reaction. She can interpret from his pit stains, knuckle cracking, and mustache twitching that he's upset, her blatant tardiness adding to his general stress of being the lead creative director on a production—she feels the need to salvage whatever workplace reputation she's managed to establish by reminding Dan that even when she's lacking presence, this entire campaign was her idea. That none of this campaign and its peripherals, including—and especially—Ernie's approval, would be here today if not for her.

"We're starting soon. Walkway can't be messy. Can you head down the path to the café and make sure the flowers look good," Dan says, a command phrased as a question, and Vicky knows better than to reply that she thinks it looks fine.

"Of course." She turns away before Dan can request anything more. She dodges the mingling crowd of media and influencers as she stomps down the narrow path, angry. She's a copywriter, not an art director or set designer. If Onwards had partnered her with an art director as customary practice, then she wouldn't have to check on any visual aesthetics—she's doing the workload of two people, she fumes, as she tucks a wayward petal back into place. Wasn't it enough she had written the press release, the social media copy, and the media touchpoints flowchart? And she had arrived well before Ernie's speech, hadn't she? What else did Dan want from her? An orgasmic declaration of how much she loves working? A tattoo on her forehead of the Onwards logo to declare her ultimate loyalty? Her firstborn child, if there ever were to be a child birthed from her depressed womb? Maybe then he would be satisfied, convinced of her commitment to the company, finally offering a glowing review so she could get promoted, offered a raise—oh, the things she could do with a raise, an everyday fantasy, and in today's episode, she would buy Angela dinner, buy Jen brunch, buy herself a nice zhizha of a meal—Peking duck or dim sum, a paper illustration depicting baskets of crystal har gow . . .

"Vicky! Get out of the way," hollers Dan.

Startled, she rips the white petal she's been absent-mindedly stroking from its stem, crushing it between her fingertips. The background commotion ceases: media and influencers settle into their seats; cars and bikers change direction; pedestrians divert or else obediently wait at the ends of the block, incentivized by possible glimpses of Ernie, though a few charge through anyway, for this is a city and nobody has time to waste. Quiet, in deference as the man deserves, for Ernie has exited the café on schedule, a man respectful of his fans' time, unlike Vicky, who is frozen in the center of the pathway, the fondled petal lying crushed on the ground. She cannot move, not when this man—Ernie!—paces slowly toward her. Walking? No. Gliding, floating, like a god with blessed feet that do not deign to tread the ground of his disciples, a black cape attached to his suit rippling behind him, an outfit Death himself would crave. Vicky is sure that Death has never looked so good. That if Death came to everyone's doorstep with Ernie's style, face, and body, the world's population would cease, jumping into his embrace without haste to reach sweet forever sleep.

"Vicky!" Dan pulls her to flatten against the cemetery gate before Ernie can step on her.

Ernie progresses without a glance. She shivers—perhaps because of his height blocking the sun, casting her in shade, or the cold of the stone gate behind her back—but somehow Ernie emanates something—a force, a vacuum, a void. Not sweet and sympathetic like Angela or the C train girl, but a void threatening uncaring cruelty. Vicky bows her head. Looks down at the concrete. She's seen Ernie before during her years at Onwards—in body at company parties and productions, in pixels on company-wide Zoom calls and news articles and Onwards memos—yet every real-life meeting with the man who grants her a livelihood through death destabilizes her, as if she enters an unreality whenever faced with such an unnatural vision.

Dan pulls her to stand behind the seats. Vicky stares at her feet, wishing the ceremony would simply end so she could go home. Another jab to the side—Dan, again. A reminder to pay attention and do her job, even though she's already done it and then some. She lifts her head to watch, because she can, now. Gods are more bearable from a distance.

Ernie arrives at the podium, ascending the stairs.

He speaks. His voice thunderous. The microphone unnecessary. "My friends."

A camera click. A bird chirp. A passing New Yorker, harried, grumbling, shushed by the audience.

Ernie collects himself. Opens his mouth. Grows strength as he speaks, harnessing his dead and the dead behind him.

"You have heard of Death. You may know him well. He may have knocked on your door, invited himself in. Sat at your dinner table. Eaten your offered snacks. Then kidnapped your loved ones under the cover of night."

Ernie pauses. Dramatic effect. Vicky shivers.

"Or perhaps you have been lucky. You know of death as a phenomenon that happens to other people. Not you."

Ernie scans the crowd. Stares directly in each pair of eyes trained rapturous on him. Vicky tilts her face to the sky.

"Perhaps Death is lonely, and so he takes away the people we love in the hopes he will gain their love for himself. Perhaps Death thinks that is what love is—to take and never give. Perhaps Death believes our funerals are parties we throw in his name. He visits, hoping to dance. Hoping to be celebrated. Or to be remembered. Perhaps, in this way, Death is very human after all. But, my friends, let us be wary. Our funerals are for the living, because the dead are dead. The dead do not feel. The dead do not suffer Death—only the living do. The living! Us! Me! You!" Ernie points into the audience at everyone and no one.

"We must contend with a life with death. And so, out of necessity and out of love, we learn how to move"—Ernie pauses to impart the solemnity of the company name—"Onwards."

A truck could careen off the road and no one would budge. To be crushed by an erratic vehicle would be worth hearing Ernie's voice for one second longer.

"You know death like you know my father. My mother. My grandfather. My grandmother. My lover."

Ernie chokes. Swallows. The audience, with bated breath.

Ernie collects himself. His voice stronger:

"After the accident, I was afraid to sit in cars, too afraid to even talk about Death lest he come for me again. I was depressed. Waking every day in sunshine wondering why I perceived the sky as gray. I had believed stardom awarded immortality, so how could I, Ernie Hayworth, have suffered death? I had been jarringly made aware I could die at any time, and so I went to India, where I learned my fear could lead to awakening. Yes. I had been guided to the light, learning I must prepare for death or never truly live. Therefore, I called you here to announce my rebirth. My name change. I wanted you to hear it from me: I remain a Hayworth, but I am Ernie no longer."

Someone in the crowd whoops. Ernie nods, acknowledging his vocal fan, ever gracious.

"I am moving Onwards from Ernie to Urnie. *U-R-N-I-E.*" Each letter, enunciated clearly, without mistake.

"I may have lost my old family, but from these ashes I build anew. A family I could build because of you. Thank you."

The crowd leaps to its feet. Thundering applause. Vicky does not join in, but then Dan elbows her, glaring. She jolts, then slaps her palms together repeatedly in a mechanical motion. Reporters and fans rush to the stage for a comment, an autograph, a noticing glance—anything—from Urnie, while Vicky is shunted to the side, catching her balance before being nearly thrown onto the ground. Between camera flashes, Vicky spies Dan clapping while craning his neck—looking for her, she guesses—and before she can be called to do more by her boss, she turns and slinks away, thinking of her bed, the clamor of the production steadily replaced by car horns and pedestrian chatter.

## *work, again*

              Vicky chugs caffeine with a throbbing wrist as her body accordions in her kitchen chair. Another intolerable, indistinguishable weekday. She's wearing the same shirt she's worn every day and night the past week, its black color hiding coffee and drool stains.

"Where'd you go after the ceremony?" Dan asks. "I was looking for you. I wanted to introduce you to Urnie. Face time is important, you should be visible."

"Oh—I went to clean up, the producers asked me to transport some stuff," she lies.

"That's good. Creative should always help out where they can at productions. But I want you to be more present. Show some more initiative. It will go a long way in your career growth. Sometimes it feels like you've checked out of work even when you're at work."

"But I care a lot about what we do."

"Good, because you should be proud. The cemetery managers were thrilled with the partnership—they've emailed our producers a glowing note saying they'd love to work with us again. Urnie's pleased with the turnout and the media results," Dan says, the sound of his words lagging against the movement of his mouth. Her wi-fi has been faulty lately—work calls slow, TV streaming glitchy, porn videos taking so long to load that her libido dies before the actors even take off their clothes. Vicky makes a mental note to check the internet setup, already dreading the interaction with the landlord.

"Thank you." Dan's reprimand followed by a compliment twists her stomach. Even if her personality at work does not measure up to expectations, at least her creative output fits the standard. The campaign had been a resounding success: Onwards had gained more than four thousand followers to its social media accounts in the past week, with endless posts applauding Urnie's unflinching defiance against the doom of death, boosted by influencer videos of his speech and in-depth articles detailing the history of Urnie's family name. Im getting an urn right now and naming it urnie as a counterpiece and idc if its fucking weird, read a tweet linking to an essay recounting every milestone of Ernie and his dead lover's tragic relationship.

Of course, there was backlash too: people who wanted the old Ernie back, people who believed his name and his brand sacred, untouchable. But drama brought clicks, and to Urnie—and Onwards—all clicks were good clicks. Vicky finds the virality ridiculous; her life's work, minimal. Was it really so easy to manipulate public opinion? None of the buzz was organic—they had invited influencers and media partners under the lure of a scoop and an exclusive event. She wants to comment under every post: *You are talking about it because you were influenced to talk about it, not because you actually like it.* But she does not, because she is numb to her job's absurdity. Who would care about her comments, anyway? Why show initiative when nothing really mattered, why rail against her own victory? Her career growth hinges on the success of each campaign. She is neither an Ernie nor an Urnie. She is a nobody.

Vicky thinks about Angela. It had been over a week since their cemetery date, and though they had texted one-offs and quick greetings in a group chat, none of them had posed scheduling another meeting. Angela seemed busy, her last text saying she had to travel to an out-of-state picket line to support a fight for a fair contract, reducing the Ernie/Urnie endeavor to trivial in comparison. Embarrassed by the ultimate meaninglessness of her work, Vicky hopes Angela hasn't seen any of the Onwards publicity from the name-changing ceremony. She wonders if she should text and ask when Angela will return. Would it be overly enthusiastic, too cringey? Wouldn't trying to coordinate a date for sex seem silly to someone fighting for better labor conditions?

"You good with that?"

She jolts. "What?" Despite being off camera, she plasters on a smile in the hopes it will shine through her voice and hide her disinterest.

"Helming this next brief? Urnie wants you on it, and I agree."

"Really?"

"Of course. He was very happy with your work on the renaming campaign. And you're the perfect candidate for the next brief since you're gay. We want to make sure creative is ideated by someone in the community rather than an outsider."

Vicky wonders how Dan's reasonability manages to deteriorate within a few sentences. "Sorry?"

"It's July. Pride Month is over. We think now is the best time to lean into the cultural insight that Pride is actually all year long. The LGBTQ Opportunity. Urnie's been saying for a long time now: 'I'm gay all three hundred sixty-five days!' In general, we'd like to highlight our marginalized target audiences by spotlighting them for twelve months, rather than just one. You'll see—Pride is just the beginning. There's a Black History Month brief too—Anthony gets that one. And"—he winks, but the camera glitches, his eyelid staying shut like the swelling after a punch—"Asian month. Asian American month. Anyway, the LGBTQ brief will come sometime next week. Just wanted to give you a heads-up so you can get excited."

"But—I—" Vicky is still stuck on how Dan claimed she is gay, when she is technically bisexual, though like Jen and asexuality, she could not care less about the label any longer. Perhaps Dan is using "gay" as an umbrella term, a stand-in for "queer." She had, after all, filled out the diversity questionnaire when she first arrived, checking yes to the question "Are you of the LGBTQ+ community?" A week later, she had received an email inviting her to the monthly Onwards Pride meetings, two of which—both attended by fewer gays than straight allies who wanted an excuse to skip work for an hour and eat rainbow-dyed baked goods—were enough to teach her that corporations, even Onwards, were not community. She could not believe she had ever been seized by the passionate throes of company culture enough to take part in office affinity groups. Why were coworkers always searching for community in the workplace? It was the textbook definition of being paid to be friends—and true friends would never come from capital.

"What?"

"Nothing." Vicky shuts up.

"It's a good cause, good press: Urnie even wants to donate half of the profits from this Pride campaign to a queer youth suicide hotline," says Dan.

Vicky finds it ironic that helping to decrease risk of suicide would mean less death, which meant fewer urns and little Onwards profit. "Um, okay. So. We're targeting queer youth."

"Exactly! You're the perfect creative! It's a great opportunity. The brief will have more info." Dan lowers his voice. "Also, keep this between you and me: I'm not sure if you've seen or read any of the pieces that have come out recently, but there's been some negative, um, comments. From the LGBTQ community. It's all false, of course! But Urnie's aware and wants to remind the public how Onwards has always had the community's best interest at heart. Especially since he's part of the community too. Just—keep that in mind, okay? We wanna make sure the community is involved and feels seen in the idea."

Vicky smiles and nods into the camera in lieu of an answer.

Dan waves. "Thanks, Vicky!"

He ends the call.

Vicky does not move. Stares at the screen. She's sure the op-eds are the only reason Urnie wants to implement this new campaign—to sway public opinion, which is why she, as the only queer creative at the company, is being forced to work on a queer target brief. Yet Dan seemed to think she'd be excited—is her ability to appear enthusiastic a detriment rather than survival tactic? What if Dan assigns her more tasks than necessary because she seems eager for it? Yet overworked and underpaid is better than underperforming with a bad attitude. The latter carries a greater risk of getting fired, which she can't afford to happen, in both cost of living and will to live. Even employed she rots in bed—without her job, she's sure she'd disintegrate further into her sheets like a moldy body imprint at an abandoned crime scene. To work is to distract; to stay busy is to avoid. With more time she'd end up thinking more freely about her depression. Besides, her savings combined with unemployment would not cover her rent and groceries past two months. And—a mortifying admittance—if fired, she would miss the joy of creation. It is creation at the whim of client, strategy, and customer acquisition, yes, but creation is still thinking, and it is a joy to be paid to think. To be valued, even if minuscule, for her mind. How lucky she is. Young Vicky would be proud of the Vicky today. There is a certain pleasure in her relative corporate success that she cannot deny and does not want to admit, some burst of dopamine that keeps her mindlessly running for the next company win even as she yells at herself to stop, like how death stalks in the shadows while she fumbles and fails to turn on the light.

*friendship at work*

Vicky fidgets on the suffocating Canal Street platform. Tiptoes forward to the painted yellow line, craning her neck to check the tunnel, which remains a black hole. No beam of promise, though there is a wiggle of motion in the bottom area of her vision—three rats scampering through the rails. Even vermin move faster than she does.

She glares at the signboard, indicating the number of minutes until the next Q train appears, but like everything else in the city it is broken, a blank screen with a flickering vertical of pixels.

She steps back. Returns to her original position of leaning against a pole, which provides her with a sense of security against being pushed onto the tracks. Her T-shirt sticks to the skin between her shoulder blades—she hasn't arrived at the Roller workout and yet already is drenched in sweat.

She sighs. Takes out her phone to check the time, the subway an enabler to her bad habits like always running late.

A vibration—an instant smile on her face, which she hurriedly smacks back into indifference. How demeaning that the mere pop-up of Angela's contact name erases the swelter, the delay, the clamor of other irritated passengers. She has spent so long corralling her wild emotions into a cage that relinquishing control feels like killing a well-loved pet.

> Want to get dinner tonight? There's a good Italian place with nice outdoor seating close to our apt!

She types back: cant. sorry!! promised jen id come to this thing shes leading for work. gotta support. wish i could come tho

She frowns, annoyed at herself for her tinge of regret. She's never wanted to be the type of person who would ditch a friend for a date, lover, or partner. Yet the heavy insinuation of Angela's "close to our apt" makes Vicky yearn for a summer night sidewalk dinner, a sweet ten-minute stroll, an invitation up. It's been almost two weeks since they met at Green-Wood—the three of them are busy, though everyone is in New York City, even those without Vicky's introversion. She has begun to feel as if the cemetery date had been a fantasy conjured by her deranged brain.

Random texts from a bodiless entity named Angela and Kevin, a chatbot sending sterile, lifeless messages because it lacks flesh-and-blood fingers.

A vibration, a text:

> No worries! Have fun:) hope to see you soon

Vicky debates typing back *What are you doing this weekend?* But her other bad habits include not responding and not planning ahead, and she justifies them by arguing with herself that she could wake up tomorrow and want to stay in bed all day, a more common morning mood than not, and wouldn't it be less rude to feign temporary disinterest than to cancel completely at the last second? She wavers, her thumbs poised over the keyboard—but then the rattle of the tracks announces the overdue arrival, and she looks up and prepares to enter the car, shoving her phone into her bag.

"Where were you?" Jen hurries over, clutching a pile of clothes. In her haste, a sock falls from the bundle onto the pavement, ignored. Vicky chooses not to point it out—Jen seems too overwhelmed to deal with a wayward piece of fabric.

"Sorry, I didn't have wi-fi! Couldn't text you that the train stopped halfway in the tunnel." The train had screeched to a halt shortly after leaving the station, the conductor releasing an indecipherable garble of explanation for the standstill.

"You could've texted me when you exited—whatever. Forget it. Can you change into this? Hurry, we're starting soon." Jen shoves the heap of clothes at Vicky, who is unprepared for the abrupt exchange and nearly drops the chai-colored leggings, sports bra, tank top, and one sock, its twin lying dirty and forlorn on the ground feet away. Jen turns around and dashes toward the photographer, who is shuffling about the perimeter, fiddling with her lens.

"Hello to you too," Vicky grumbles. She looks around. Where is she supposed to change? She doesn't want to bother Jen to ask if she could change in the influencers' pop-up trailer, and Fort Greene Park is crowded on a sunny afternoon, filled with dog walkers and casual strollers and serious exercisers—she can't strip in the middle of the park unless she wants a nuisance charge, nor does she want to be naked in a public New York City bathroom.

She picks through the pile, noticing that the leggings are labeled XS. She uncrinkles them and holds them against her bottom half. Its legs are toothpicks, the waistband half the length of her belly—zero possibility that she can fit. She needs a size medium if she is mired in a low-energy depressive episode; she needs a size large if she is on her period.

Annoyed, she clenches the Lycra in her fist, then tells herself to relax. Drapes the leggings onto her forearm. She's here to support, she reminds herself. Jen knows her size and has never shamed her for it—Jen is just busy, Jen is stressed. It is an innocent mistake.

Vicky folds each article of clothing into a clean square. She deposits the neat stack onto the table of Roller-branded water bottles, then edges along the border of the pumpkin-spice and muddy-brown army stretching in formation to take her place at the back. The high-kicking feet and windmilling arms are attached to so many different kinds of bodies that Vicky thinks she's rushed into a farm patch littered with various gourds. The diverse demographic of influencers adorned in Roller's autumn colorways is astonishing for an advertising campaign—Vicky is proud of Jen for the inclusivity effort, even if representation is mere means to increase profits. With her black-and-gray outfit and average attractiveness, Vicky prays the cheerleader effect will allow the photoshoot to remain perfect despite her presence.

"Okay, everyone! Feeling limber?" The fitness instructor, head to toe in apple-red Roller spandex, grins a perfect set of straight white teeth. She claps her hands, ponytail bouncing, positivity so radiant Vicky wants to slap her. "We're gonna do four rounds of climbs! First round, every. Second, every other. Third, hop every. Fourth, hop every other. It's okay if you stumble or need a break! Remember, this is about loving yourself and what your body can do, not resenting it for what it can't!"

"Looking good!" Jen calls from the top of the stairs where she stands, flashing two thumbs-up silhouetted against the horizon, next to the photographer, whose head is misshapen, overtaken by the camera.

The instructor, incandescently well: "Three! Two! One—"

The front row blasts off, leaping up each step, hair textures fluttering and bouncing. They resemble a herd of elegant gazelles surging across fields, a school of fish darting through water, a flock of geese vaulting across skies. Vicky watches the second row run forward and jump, then the third, fourth, fifth, and she marvels at her best friend's art direction, how the collective yet disparate movements of autumn palettes make the bodies in flight morph into falling leaves, carried by air to their final resting place on dirt to be crushed by feet, scratched by rakes, shredded by clippers, rotted into nutrients, converted into methane, gone, disintegrated—then Vicky blinks, wills her legs to move, because her row has advanced and she has been left behind, inert, stagnant in her ruminations of death and decay.

After her second ascension, Vicky stops next to Jen, who hasn't left her perch. Jen stares at the distant downtown Brooklyn skyscrapers poking out from the treetops, calculating whether the skyline is worth featuring in a few lifestyle shots.

"Photoshoot's gonna look good," Vicky huffs, bending over to place her hands on her thighs, catching her breath. Her legs burn, her shirt neckline made white by a crust of sweat salt crystals.

"Hmm? Oh." Jen turns to Vicky, her face shifting from concentration to confusion. "Why aren't you wearing the clothes?"

"'Cause you—" Vicky catches herself, deciding not to make Jen feel guilty over the wrong sizes. "Don't worry, I put them on the table over there." Vicky points to the faraway chai-colored stack next to the bottles. "They won't get dirty."

"But—" Jen shakes her head, drops the thought. "What do you think of the location? I'm worried there isn't enough shade. The sun is too bright. Everyone's skin will be washed out."

Vicky pats Jen between her shoulders. "Relax. The photographer will take care of it. You're doing great. Fort Greene's the perfect location. Hilarious, honestly, considering its history."

Jen frowns. "Hilarious?"

"Of course."

"What are you talking about?"

"You know!"

"No, I don't."

"Fort Greene Park is a literal graveyard. Filled with bodies from the Revolutionary War. Prisoners of war who died while the British were holding them captive." Vicky points to a concrete slab below them jutting from the middle of the stairs, around which the cascade of mocha-, paprika-, and chestnut-adorned influencers part. "That's the crypt where they're buried." She gestures to the stone monument behind them. "You never wondered why this tower is here? It's the Prison Ship Martyrs' Monument. And that green thing on top of the column is an urn." Vicky giggles. "It always goes back to the urns."

Jen's eyebrows are contracting, her mouth bending into a frown. "Why are you always bringing this kind of shit up?"

"Don't you think it's ironic?"

Jen shakes her head.

Vicky presses on. "There are literal corpses under our feet right now. All these people you've gathered here today are attempting wellness to fend off death. To extend their lives. But death is at the top as an urn; death is below in the crypt." Vicky flaps her hands. "Death. Inevitable. Can't avoid it."

Jen's already flushed face grows redder. A drop of sweat trails from her hairline down her cheek. "I don't want to think about death right now. I'm leading a photoshoot; I'm at work. Why are you even saying these things?"

"Saying what? I'm here for you, remember?" Vicky's chest constricts. Panic, fear, the need to flee. How had the conversation changed into conflict? Did she do or say something wrong? The sun beats down, the influencers' footsteps a riling beat. Dizzy, she reaches out to Jen. To remind her that she is here. That they are here together.

But Jen rears back, avoids her touch, shakes her head. "You couldn't even wear the right clothes."

"I couldn't fit into the clothes!"

"Did you even try?"

"Did you even check the size?" Vicky, hysterical, the high temperature adding to the pressure inside her chest—her feral emotions are escaping their cage, climbing its walls, the jailer asleep.

"You could've grabbed a new pair, there's a ton over there!"

"You can photoshop me out, can't you? Just ask the retoucher!"

"Why should I? You're adding more work for me!" Jen waves her hands in frustration.

"Just do your job, maybe? The way I do *my* job?"

"Are you fucking kidding me? I'm doing more than just my job! Ten percent of my coworkers just got laid off!" Jen's voice jumps octaves higher with each sentence. "You're so busy being obsessed with yourself that you didn't even ask!"

"What? Layoffs?" The jarring news, coupled with the instructor announcing the next exercise, distracts her from the fight's original topic, and Vicky sees behind Jen the influencers, finished with their stair climbs, milling about the plaza below, glowing in their robustness, and Vicky's ferocity coalesces into loathing. She detests them for their airiness, their casual beauty, their *joy*, even if she is mature enough to realize she's projecting her own insecurities—perhaps these influencers too know the precarity that shadows her; perhaps they vomited up their breakfast before the shoot so they could fit into their Roller leggings; perhaps they have had their affection trampled on so often that they no longer attempt to revive it. Vicky attempts to collect her hatred, but it is easier to think these beautiful people as vain, vapid, and stupid, as stupid as this fight she is having, and her heart pounds frantically, violently, unrestrainedly, and she turns to Jen and tries to channel this frenzy into a frenzy of care: "It's fine, it's fine! You won't be laid off! Just lead the shoot like you've been doing, it'll be fine, don't worry—"

"Of course I'm fucking worrying!" Jen screeches, her volume so high that the influencers, instructor, and photographer turn their attention upward toward them, curious. What is this drama unfolding? Who are the actors, what is the plot, is it worth watching?

Vicky spies two influencers holding up their phones to film, and with this violation, the last of her desperate desire for empathy flees. No matter how high her level of stress, she has never lost her temper at an Onwards production. How had Jen become so unprofessional?

"You're messing your own shoot up," Vicky hisses.

"*You're* messing it up! You're just adding to the pressure! Look around! Why do you think there's barely any other Roller people here to help? Because they're all gone! Fired! I asked you to come support, but you show up late. You can't even change your clothes. And then you talk about death? Why can't you just be fucking normal?"

Vicky recoils as if Jen had slapped her.

Jen, ashamed. Her face settling, eyes widening. An expression Vicky recognizes because they are best friends—she had seen this face in college, when Jen had accused Vicky of being lazy when their creative presentation had failed; in New York City, when Jen ignores with a downturned gaze the kids walking through subway cars selling candy; in her apartment, when Jen's mother calls and Jen turns her phone off because her mother is too much, all at once, all the time—and when this happens Vicky tells Jen *it will be okay*, because it will be, it is better to believe in the future tense, but in the present time, Vicky is furious. She doesn't know if it will be okay because she cannot remember what it *means* to be okay. Because she had tried her best to rush and make it at the cost of her peace and meeting up with Angela, and the loathing devil she's set free whispers to her that though layoffs are scary, maybe Jen should have made the right career decision like she had. Maybe Jen should have embarked on a safer path, a better industry, one that will never die: Death.

Then Vicky watches Jen's guilt dissolve, replaced by dread at what will likely be her boss's anger, the shoot's failures, her inadequacy at leading, and Vicky's bitterness is overcome by self-reproach. Regret over her role in this ugliness on Jen's face—and so Vicky turns away as she always does when things are difficult, intense, too much.

She clomps down the stairs. Trips over the last. Pushes past the gaping photographer, whose camera dangles at the neck, forgotten. Ignores the gawking influencers, the staring producers. Limps out of the park in the wrong-colored fabric of her leggings on the feebleness of her out-of-shape thighs.

## *spiraling*

### JEN

Jen avoids her reflection in the salon mirrors. Her brows are messy; her eyeliner is crooked. She doesn't want to be reminded of herself and her sloppy mistakes. Instead she watches the muted red steadily coat her nails. She can imagine Vicky's jokes about her claws: drenched in her enemies' blood after gouging them to death or in her own blood after being trapped alive, scratching the underside of the coffin roof. Jen finds nothing funny about a violent death. She resents how her best friend's macabre habits infect her brain. Everyone morphs into the company they keep, and she completes her role by becoming more gruesome, but Vicky has somehow never absorbed her relentless positivity. Even if Jen admits to herself that she's faking her optimism 99 percent of the time, why does the osmosis of self go only one way? Vicky should learn from her. Jen is unhappy too, but at least she can get out of bed; at least she can have a normal, wholesome, societally acceptable relationship; at least she's *functional*. Why couldn't Vicky be functional too? Isn't friendship a two-way street? And if it isn't, if the street is a dead end, then did that mean Vicky didn't even *like* her? Sometimes Jen's not sure of Vicky's true affections. She's convinced that Vicky would never remember to text her unless she texted first. How terribly unfair that Vicky doesn't do relationship maintenance, how annoying that Vicky stubbornly entrenches in a depressive attitude when Jen works so hard to get her shit together. And yet *Jen* is the one facing economic stressors at work, not Vicky! *She's* the one under pressure to get her finances in a row, not Vicky!

Coco taps her hand. Once, twice, three, four times, until: "Switch," Coco says, the verbal instruction jolting Jen away from her fuming thoughts back into her neighborhood salon.

Jen exchanges hands, placing one under the UV lights and the other into Coco's waiting palm. "Sorry," she says.

"Everything okay?" Coco asks as she brushes another layer of red.

"Fine. Just busy with work."

"Mmm."

She doesn't blame Coco for not asking further questions.

Coco is there to paint nails and get paid, not to be her therapist. She hadn't lied about being preoccupied with work—friendship is work, relationships are work, and Jen knows better than anyone how other people are pieces of fucking work. She hates worrying over others. Whether or not she is liked. How to shrink herself to fit in. How to please her people. She thinks about her relationships with the same amount of time and energy she's sure other adults think about real work: constantly. Even the black nail polish bottle nestled on the salon wall shelf had reminded her of Vicky, who always wore black—even to her Roller photoshoot! How *dare* she? Jen had seen the color when she walked inside, zeroing in on it despite the rainbow of options, and it had sent her into a tornado of furious racing thoughts and anxiety at the cost of Coco's efficiency.

"Okay, done," Coco says, patting her hand. "Matches well!" She gestures toward Jen's clothes: a longline sports bra and leggings in the precise shade of her new nails. "Very seasonal," Coco adds.

Exactly. Coco had it right. Maybe Coco should be her best friend, not Vicky. Coco, with her pink bow tie and Pikachu-printed nails, who would never show up goth. Jen's intentions in selecting red were not to evoke bloody carnage like Vicky would've believed but to match Roller's autumnal release—she hopes her boss will comment on her dedication to the company products, even through something as silly and small as nail color. She's an art director. She understands the powers of visuals. Hopes it's enough to be excluded from the list of the next round of layoffs.

"Thank you," Jen responds, pulling her wallet out and admiring the flash of red. Her hands, long overdue for a manicure, have returned to stunning. She's one step closer to her original refinement.

Jen pays the rate of gel mani and regular pedi with her credit card, then hands Coco a 40 percent cash tip. She watches the bills disappear down Coco's apron pocket with a rapid flash. She swallows the guilt, the familiar anxiety, that rises in her throat every time she spends money, whether for a need or a want. She reminds herself that threats of layoffs and Eric and her nose-diving credit doesn't mean she should skimp on those who worked harder than her.

Besides, being beautiful makes her feel put-together even when she's cracking apart. Coco did more for her personal wellness than therapy ever could. Because of Coco, Jen still believes in beauty. Still believes in Roller. Still believes in herself.

"See you next month." She waves to Coco.

She walks down the street, small bursts of pleasure in her brain with each winking red nail as her fingers tap her phone screen. No text from Vicky. She hates how Vicky is mad at her, but she tells herself she's mad at Vicky too. This fight isn't her fault. The more she thought about it, it was *never* her fault.

Two texts from Eric. She opens, reads:

> U done?

> Just finished lunch wya ill come meet u

Her stomach grumbles—she hasn't gotten to lunch yet and rarely attempts breakfast other than drinking coffee, blaming her meal omission on forgetfulness and not being hungry in the morning, though the truth she's only ever admitted to herself is that she abstains so she can eat more calories in later meals, ignoring the fact that the lack of food makes her cranky in the hours between waking and midday. She exits out of Eric's text message thread without responding.

She heads into her preferred customizable salad fast-casual chain restaurant featuring various add-ins and mixtures of vegetables, fruits, grains, and proteins ranging in colorways. She selects her usual: shredded kale and baby spinach, mint and apples and carrots and chickpeas and shredded purple cabbage. Roasted chicken and toasted almonds and spicy cashew dressing. 430 calories. Which she tells herself is a manageable amount, that she can burn it all off in her too-expensive Pilates class tomorrow morning.

She reads the total cost on the checkout screen.

Quashes the guilt.

Taps her credit card.

Exits the restaurant with the paper bag in the crook of her elbow.

Wanders down the block checking her phone again. Another text from Eric:

> wyddddddd
>
> Garrett said the met has a cool exhibit up if u wanna go later

Despite the gnawing in her gut, she softens upon reading the texts. She and Eric had woken up late together, but he had left soon after to meet his old college roommate in town for lunch.

No time for the chance of morning softness they both loved on the weekend—a cuddle, a mug of coffee, a catch-up.

She texts back:

Exhibit sounds good.

Im about to sit and eat in WSQ

A quick response: K ill walk over, be there in 20

Washington Square Park is packed with New York University students enjoying the weather, crowding the spotty lawns and pathways. She seats herself on an empty bench, the faint tune of a saxophonist busker and skids of skateboarding wheels drifting over. Starving, she unpacks her salad and begins shoveling greens into her mouth, trying to ignore the youths' audible delights. She hates their laughter, their carefree cheeks, the way they sit in circles in obvious plentiful community, enjoying sheer presence, their bright minds not yet leveled by adulthood responsibility and consequence of choice. They remind her of how she used to be. Especially in freshman and sophomore year. Before junior year hit, bringing about her grandmother's death and her subsequent eating disorder and anxiety, tranquilized by the frequent hit of club drug variations. Cocaine and anorexia, her attempts at reclaiming control of her life, according to her old therapist. Vicky had been both her enabler and her supporter, cutting lines of coke for her one night and rewriting lines of copy for her schoolwork the next day when she couldn't operate because of her immense, insurmountable grief. At the time, she had appreciated the care, but now, bitter over her nearly ruined Fort Greene Park photoshoot, she considers what Vicky had done for her unremarkable. Weren't Vicky's actions required of anyone who believed in friendship as a real, valid form of care? Vicky probably never had her best interests in mind because Vicky was selfish. Though she is vehemently sober now from hard drugs, she knows Vicky would still enter the k-hole with her if she expressed the desire, while Eric would never even allow her to get close to a whiff. Vicky wanted to have fun. Relax. Chill. And when had Jen ever been chill? Sure, the two had different roles in Jen's life: Eric is a partner and Vicky is a friend. Her best friend, but one who had somehow always been able to sail through life so recklessly and end up fine. How was that fair?

How was Vicky so unashamedly Vicky?

*Because you're always making excuses and exceptions for her,* Jen tells herself. Isn't that what love is? To behold someone's worst qualities and still want to be around them? Ever since college she'd been on the receiving end of Vicky's moping, inactivity, and bad decisions, yet Jen had never even once considered giving up on her or their relationship. She'd just charged ahead, checking in on Vicky and being there for her even when it was inconvenient, and Jen suspects her subservience to their friendship is because of the good times—from fire escape cigs to midnight movie screenings—canceling out the bad. The good times were so good that they made her wonder if she should have just dated Vicky instead of Eric.

The first time she'd seen Vicky, locking eyes across the crowded lecture hall and wordlessly agreeing to partner for art and copy, had felt like a scene from a film, where the two protagonists freeze in each other's gaze while the rest of the aimless, loveless world streamed past them. Love at first sight, a cliché that was no longer cliché when it did dare strike. Working together had been electric, their minds not stealing or copying but building off each other into something worth winning—her creativity had never been so buzzy, so charged. Magic, to find an artistic partner who sensed where your ideas were headed, following them down the dark tunnel without question to emerge on the other side of luminous creation.

On the rare occasion she and Eric fought, Jen would never be as angry toward him as she would get toward Vicky. Wasn't this incendiary passion indicative of something *more*? What was the difference between she and Vicky linking elbows as they strolled through the Lower East Side at sunset after a dimly lit dinner, and she and Eric holding hands upon leaving the cellar jazz bar in the West Village at 2:00 a.m.? Both scenarios were romantic, just one as best friends and one as girlfriend-boyfriend, and both were love, and Jen knows Vicky would say that love is everywhere, not just from a partner but from art, friends, the self, but if love was everywhere, then why couldn't Vicky just stop being so fucking sad? Love was supposed to make you *happy*. And nothing would make Vicky happy. She just sulked in her sadness, dragging everyone down with her, even Jen, who strove to be better, act better, do better, much like Eric, her sunny partner who easily retained his optimistic disposition from childhood into adulthood, so why the hell would Jen ever choose to partner with Vicky, the dark gray cloud? She could never date Vicky seriously, even if she wasn't straight. And Jen detests how, with this thought, she can then hear Vicky's voice arguing against her, that straightness didn't even exist, that straightness was a scam, a compulsion, a method of living, one that anybody could break out of if they just tried. Why couldn't the Vicky in her head just shut the fuck up sometimes? Why couldn't Jen just listen to herself, and herself only?

Her wooden fork scrapes the bottom of the compostable bowl, interrupting her relentless, nonstop steaming. She's finished her tiny yet expensive bounty of health far too quickly in a far too little number of gulps. She's still hungry but convinces herself more food would make her feel overstuffed. She rummages through her tote for cigarettes. Her favorite appetite suppressant. Palms one along with the Hello Kitty lighter—tries not to think about Vicky as she lights the end of the cigarette, but the Sanrio character's black dots for eyes stare her down, shoving aside any possibility of a peaceful smoke. She releases a nicotine-laced cloud, breathes in, breathes out. Again—quicker this time. Again—even quicker, and quicker, and quicker, throat spasming, chest tightening, hot flash, until she's nearly gasping for air, the cigarette dangling from her fingertips—*calm down, calm down, calm down,* she begs herself; she'd been better at managing her anxiety in adulthood and refuses to believe the lurking attack could be generated by thoughts of her best friend—no, her *ex*–best friend, she tries to convince herself. The friendship had never been good for her. They are such different people. Jen enjoys—*believes* in—astrology, while Vicky scoffs at horoscopes and the planets and the rising moon, another pressure point in their relationship that was fun to joke about when things were going well and an easy argument starter when things were going badly. Like now. Fire signs were supposed to be compatible with air, but her Aries temper had always been fanned into blazes by Vicky's Libra breeziness, infuriated by Vicky's ability to calmly jump from relationship to relationship, moment to moment, without spiraling into overthinking. Vicky didn't even shoulder the same amount of responsibility she did! Vicky had no unhinged debt, no threat of layoffs, no partner with an ailing mother—all Vicky has is an obsession with her own sadness. Being sad could make her best friend so very self-centered, unable to see past her sorrow. It was insufferable. Other people with valid emotions existed—like herself!—yet Vicky was incapable of holding space for anyone else.

Sure, in the beginning, the sadness had been what drew her to Vicky. It wasn't just sharing a cultural background or being on the same creativity wavelength. It was that they both saw the bleak emptiness and chose to step in rather than deflect. Even during their first ever brainstorm in college, Jen could sense in Vicky a great abandonment. Vicky, in a high-pitched, fake-casual sort of voice, had hinted how Jen could go pick another partner if Vicky failed to measure up to her standards, which confused Jen, because she was a freshman in college—she had no standards for herself or for anyone in her life. She just wanted a friend. A real friend. She'd never had any true ones growing up, spending so much energy fretting over *how* to be liked by her peers that she never had time to *be* likable. Just clingy. Needy. Anxious. Because she was lonely. And Vicky was lonely and clingy too, so they latched on to each other in mutual fear of being left behind by everyone else. People could ignore, hate, or leave them. It would be fine, because they'd have each other.

Jen realizes only now that the codependency is unhealthy—and that maybe, in college and after, it had been because of Vicky, not her own anxiety, that she'd never been able to have any other friends. Like that time in sophomore year, when Jen had managed to strike up a conversation with a girl she hasn't talked to in years who was named Clarissa—wasn't she working at one of the top agencies now? A talented copywriter—not because of her choice of words but because she didn't mind revising and rewriting until the headline for the banner ad hit right—Clarissa had once complimented Jen's logo redesign, and in turn Jen had praised Clarissa's work ethic, and then Clarissa was in the midst of asking Jen if she ever wanted to partner up for a project when Vicky had barged in between them and pulled Jen away, citing an emergency. Of course, there had been no real emergency, only Vicky's panic that Jen would ditch her for someone cooler, kinder, smarter. Clarissa was rubbing her upper arm where Vicky had shoved into her and Jen wanted to turn back to apologize, but Vicky's pleading, apologetic face begged Jen not to go. *You're my only friend,* Vicky had said, and at the time this had made Jen feel special and loved and warm, and she reassured Vicky that she'd never discard their friendship. That she'd always be there for Vicky. That Vicky would be her number one.

But it was impossible to give so much to someone who promised so little in return. And she could now, in her anxious adulthood clarity, see the statement as rather manipulative even if she didn't want to believe it had been on purpose—Vicky had never been supportive when situations *not* involving her arose. When Jen had first started dating Eric, Vicky had been the most vocal opponent, citing reasonable points for incompatibility, finally throwing up her hands and stating, *If you're happy, then I'm happy.* Maybe Vicky had never been concerned for Jen's wellbeing, only masking her fear of abandonment as care. After all, hadn't Jen and Eric made it this far? Sure, the relationship wasn't perfect, but no relationship ever was, and they'd always been able to work out and talk through whatever happened in a healthy, kind, respectful manner, whereas Vicky bottled up whatever she was feeling until she lashed out, then disappeared in shame, ruining every burgeoning human connection she'd ever been close to making real.

No, it was more and more clear that Vicky had just been jealous when she argued against Jen and Eric's coupling. It wasn't Jen's fault that Vicky was incapable of holding down a romantic relationship. Vicky's explanation of nightmares was the most ridiculous justification for her inability to be in a long-term relationship. Even if Jen *had* seen them. What they did to Vicky. How Vicky would twist the covers until they resembled tornadoes wrapped around her torso. How Vicky would puddle the mattress in sweat. How Vicky would whimper and yelp through the night, if she even *managed* to sleep through the night. Jen had learned to use earplugs whenever she and Vicky slept in the same place. Once, in college, she'd stayed up late at her desk to finish a presentation while Vicky, keeping her company, dozed on her bed, and Vicky had suddenly screamed, *No!* and thrashed about like she was kicking an invisible demon, knocking every cushion to the ground, scaring Jen so much that she had accidentally deleted the entire presentation she'd been working on. She'd shaken Vicky awake, yelling in conjunction, *What's wrong, what's wrong, what's wrong?* while Vicky spluttered incoherently. After Vicky had downed a glass of water, Jen had asked, more calmly, *What's wrong?* And Vicky had said, *Sometimes I just dream about people I know in horrible scenarios. It makes me not want to be close to anyone because I can't bear the dreams.*

*Do you dream about me?* Jen asked.

*Yeah.*

*In a horrible scenario?*

Vicky hesitated. *Sorry.*

*You're still close to me, though.*

*You're the only one I'm close to.*

*What makes me different?*

*Everything,* Vicky said. *Sorry.*

*Can I help?*

Vicky shook her head. *You can't. And I don't want to talk about it anymore.*

So Jen stopped asking, though, come to think of it, she only just realized that the nightmares had mysteriously disappeared around when Onwards had been founded. Vicky had stopped complaining about being tired all the time, and if Jen woke up before Vicky whenever they slept in the same room, she'd see Vicky's body breathing deep under smooth blankets, so peacefully that Jen forgot about Vicky's nightmares. As if finding a perfect company and finding purpose through that job had granted Vicky settled sleep. But Vicky's grim and unpleasant tendency for morbidity and isolation had never left, and it was deeply unfair to Jen, her so-called best friend, to bear the despair constantly while smiling. Jen had her own problems, thank you very much.

But. Fuck. It hasn't been very long since they last talked—fought—and yet she already misses Vicky very much.

She sweats, ablaze, her chest tightening—she fans herself, trying to cool down from the uncontrollable thoughts and the heat flash, knocking the empty salad bowl to the pavement. She clutches her stomach, where hunger-induced nausea collides with anxiety-induced nausea. Closes her eyes and focuses on her breathing like the therapist had taught her in order to corral the surge of panic flooding her system. Her hands grip the bench seat slats. Knuckles turn white. She tries to collect herself enough to interrupt the racing thoughts. She needs to start counting instead. But she forgets her methods of management, because the sheer terror overtakes her—and wins.

Her surroundings disappear.

There is no park.

No saxophonist, no skateboarders, no college students.

Only panic.

Time splits; becomes ragged; goes on. This attack will last forever—she's experienced such raw agitation before. She always forgets that there will be an after.

Her ears ring.

She shakes, a jackhammer, bludgeoning into terror—

A sudden pressure on her back. A violation.

No.

A hand.

Her eyes fly open.

Narrow onto the one face she knows better than her own.

"Hey, hey, what's going on?" Eric takes the bench's empty space next to her and begins rubbing circles on her upper back. "Breathe, breathe, breathe," he coos, leaning in.

"Where the fuck were you?" she spits out. If he loved her, he would have shown up earlier. Before the panic struck.

Thankfully, Eric ignores her venom. He's seen it enough times to know what she's like when anxiety seizes hold of her brain. He knows how she never means the hurled hurt. How she's hurting too much herself, so it has to go somewhere. Latch on to someone else. Him. He'll carry it for her.

"Just breathe. Count to five and down and back up again. I'm here," he says. "I'm here."

Her mind shudders. Clenches. Releases. Counts.

*One, two, three, four, five.*

*Five, four, three, two, one.*

*One, two, three, four, five.*

*Five, four, three, two, one.*
*One, two, three, four, five.*
*Five, four, three, two, one.*

Jen's breath staccatos, then settles.

Eric pats her hand. Stoops down to pick up the bowl and places it on the bench next to his thigh.

"Sorry," she says. She is always sorry.

"It's okay." And it is always okay.

"The fight with Vicky—the Roller shit—it's just compounding."

"Do you want to text her?"

"No."

"It's been a while since you two last talked."

"I know."

"Are you sure you don't want to reach out?" Eric asks.

She pauses. Imagines her phone buzzing, Vicky's name popping up on the screen. She wants it. She misses her best friend. Vicky, who would always be her best friend, no matter how frustrating, no matter how much she denied it.

Jen swallows.

Reminds herself of the taking and never the giving.

"I'm sure."

# *work*

Vicky smokes on her fire escape alone, types out her stupid creative ideas alone, eats her dinners alone—she is used to being alone. Solitude, her natural state. But—not like this. Not without Jen at least a text, a ten-minute subway ride, or a twenty-minute walk away. Now Vicky is not only alone but also lonely. Deeply lonely, and she is bitter that Jen is not. Jen, who revels in the fact that she is Vicky's only friend, has more than just one friend. Jen has a boyfriend. A partner. Eric.

Vicky recognizes the mundanities of monogamy were convenient in certain situations, like support during fights with your best friend or splitting the expensive rent of a decent one-bedroom in New York.

She's horizontal on her bed above the covers, staring at Jen's contact name on her phone. Knows she should text and apologize for fucking up the photoshoot. Or ask about the layoffs. Or send her, along with many exclamation points and compliments for Jen's creative eye, a screenshot of the stunning Roller photos at Fort Greene Park, which had started popping up on her newsfeed. These affirmations were their typical course of action after one of them had finished and released a production. But texting first requires the swallowing of pride, and pride is one of Vicky's few personal qualities left shivering upright in the degrading landscape of twenty-first-century existence. Besides, every photo she's scrolled past indicates that she's been purposefully cropped or photoshopped out, as had been the crypt entrance in the middle of the staircase. *See? You didn't even need me there,* Vicky thinks before throwing her phone onto the mattress and heaving herself upward to stalk back to the kitchen table, on which her laptop is open to a deck title slide reading "The LGBTQ+ Opportunity."

Yawning, she slumps in her chair. Rests her chin on the table and taps through the deck. Cringes at the strategy in the up-front slides stating that queer people were more open to preparing for death because death struck their chosen families more often than straights. The stats listed were bleak: Queers were nearly four times more likely than non-queer people to be victims of violent crime. Four times more likely to attempt suicide than their peers. And how queers confronted death daily in their sheer lack of elders, due to the HIV/AIDS epidemic and the erasure of identity in a time when it had been less acceptable to come out, a slow death in itself. Vicky furrows her brow as she reads. How strange to be reduced to a corporate strategy statistic. Her finger hovers over the delete button. It would be so easy to erase these terrible statistics. But deleting the facts would not change reality. And she can't remove her team's work without facing the wrath of her boss—her boss, who is pinging her about how her day is going, what work she is doing, how she's feeling about the Opportunity. She closes the chat without responding, knowing this will annoy him—she just can't bring herself to care. She'll get the job done in the end, won't she?

She clicks through the slides again, noting no mention of the recent increase in the suicide rate among queer youth that the media was now blaming on Onwards and Urnie. She'd read the op-eds that Urnie had transformed the mere thought of death into an appealing, grand adventure, which in turn made the youth, especially Urnie's fans, strive toward death as a goal rather than an inevitable destination—the sooner they arrived, the cooler they would be. The contagion of suicidal behavior created an Onwards-sponsored suicide cluster: the unspoken, real reason for this LGBTQ+ Opportunity. To erase collective memory. If she thinks too hard about her role as PR machine, the floor starts to tilt. So she decides not to think. To suppress her mind in order to make. Besides, she wasn't a billionaire or a politician or even a boss. She didn't *cause* harm, she was just . . . surviving. Right?

She checks the time on her laptop. She sighs. She could have signed off two hours ago, but Onwards ideation had been a distraction from her empty Friday night. She aches to text Jen. Ask her what she's up to, how her week has been, if she wants to get dinner. Vicky pinches the skin between thumb and pointer finger, the webbing turning white. Releases and watches the blood rush back in. Pinches, releases, pinches, releases—

Her phone dings from the bed.

She stands, furiously, frantically. Her chair scoots backward, mind writing a brief apology to her downstairs neighbor. Then she's striding to her phone with greedy hands. Eyes scanning the message.

From two, instead of one—

Vicky! What are you doing tonight?

# *love?*

Vicky weaves through bodies draped in textures of black and silver—leather, mesh, fishnet, buckles, chains, chokers; skin marked in tattoos and pierced by metals. She gives each their due of admiration. She hasn't had the energy to dress up and go out to a place like this in several years. How she had loved these types of people and these parties in her late teens and early twenties. To sweat in music so intense she can't think, impossible to dwell on anything but her shaking feet.

Come dance out the anger, Angela had replied after Vicky vented about Jen in long blue chat bubbles taking up the entire phone screen, then a short one apologizing for the text spam.

Angela: No no all good! That's what I'm here for. Come meet us at Everydays tonight!

Vicky finds them at the front of the line. She joins and they huddle. Angela kisses her on the cheek; Kevin hugs her. Vicky is amazed at how comfortable she feels with them, already, again. Her limbs relaxed, abuzz. As if the three had been dating for a year rather than about to embark on their second date.

"Thanks for texting. Sorry it took so long for us to get together. Sometimes I just need to disappear."

"Honestly, same," Angela says.

"You self-isolate too?" Vicky jokes.

"Hey. No depresso vibes tonight," Kevin butts in, elbows Angela. "We're going dancing!"

Normally Vicky would find this statement callous and obnoxious, enough to make her leave. But the muffled techno and midnight liminality convince her to stay. Besides, Angela is laughing, and she trusts Angela.

"You look good," Kevin says.

Vicky is wearing a loose black crop tee with attached O-rings, through which she's threaded fabric straps crossing around her breasts to her shoulders, and a loose knee-length black skirt. Black to hide the sweat, black to fit in. And on her feet, black sneakers—she is dressed comfortably because she is ready to dance.

Vicky is happy. Here, there is no work, no fight, no precarity. No death—merely joy.

The bouncer waves them forward. Vicky reveals her ID and flips her wrist out for the stamp. The three are ushered in with a group of four others into a small brick-walled entry room, dimly lit by three glowing pink orbs hung behind an Everydays worker sitting on a stool.

"Hi, guys, thanks for being here," they drawl, their lip ring wobbling.

They sit up straighter, drawl disappearing as they descend into their speech, a collection of sentences Vicky has missed hearing, words outlining why it was worth hopping on the F train then transferring to the M—speeding deep into Brooklyn, a near hour-long journey—rather than walking down the block to the table service champagne-on-ice clubs:

"Being among community is one of the primary reasons for our club and one of the primary reasons many of our patrons come here. Some other reasons include listening to the music, dancing without distraction, and finding a safe space to exist at these hours. So, we have zero tolerance for disruptive behavior, racism, violence, homophobia, transphobia, sexism, and other hateful language or actions. If you want to touch someone, get their explicit consent first. Minimize conversations on the dance floor and keep your phones off so you can enter a transitory, undistracted headspace and not worry about strangers taking a photo of you. If there's a need to check your phone, chat with friends, smoke a cig, or breathe fresh air, we have a large outdoor space that's perfect for any of those activities—just follow the lighted arrows pasted on the walls. And if anyone makes you uncomfortable for any reason at all, please flag any staff behind the bar or our safe space monitors who walk around the club. They wear glowing green wristbands and can help you out."

A door on the other side of the room swings open, and out

unfurls smoke, body odor, lush energy.

"Have fun!" They grin, wave.

Vicky clutches Kevin's and Angela's arms as they enter the ether. Her heart leaps in glee, matching the heavy beat.

"I need to pee," yells Angela into Vicky's ear. She thumbs backward toward the bathroom hallway, lit pink with similar orbs found in the entry room.

"I'll go too," calls Kevin.

"I'm dancing. Find me there," Vicky says.

She squeezes through sweaty bodies to the front, where the DJ, dressed in a black sports bra and yellow velvet pants, nods to their set, right hand on their mixer, left bobbing in the air, air-kissing friends who weave behind the table to say hello before vanishing into the throng. Vicky recognizes the DJ from her years as a club rat—they are an Everydays weekend resident known for their industrial textures and frizzy arrangements. Vicky sways, twists, shuffles forward, backward. Raises her arms toward the planted tendrils in halved basketballs hanging from the ceiling—she can't remember their original length, if the ferns have grown since the last time she came here. She's deluded herself into thinking she's grown in her time away from techno, but returning to the dance floor reverts her immediately to the state of being she's never truly shed. Perhaps, like her, the ferns could not grow either—maybe they too were not real, disassociated from reality, their plastic obscured by darkness, used neither for air filtration nor nature but for an aesthetic assisted by the erupting fog machine, something she had believed would be cheesy, an outdated special effect, now adored for how the dense curtain shields her from being perceived and perceiving others—an evaporation into the music. Which is why she comes here. To be free.

Through the cocoon comes a face she recognizes, then a second—Angela and Kevin, their bladders empty, feet itching. Kevin holds out his cup of amber liquid, but Vicky shakes her head. She does not need substances. She prefers control of her limbs so she can dive into the beat without drowning. Kevin kisses her cheek after she declines. He throws the drink back, begins to shuffle side to side. Vicky smiles because she likes how his body flows. Angela grips her shoulder and she turns. Angela says—screams—"*You're good at dancing*," and she nods and brushes Angela off, because it is as the front worker had decreed: This is not the time for conversation. Angela understands. Angela melts into the other bodies. Vicky loses Angela, loses Kevin, but the loss is preferred, because she is not there to be with them but to be with herself. She closes her eyes and moves for a minute that might be an hour that might be an eternity. The dance floor defies time. She opens her eyes after forever. Catches the gaze of someone diagonal to her. The silhouette offers their hand, and she looks down and sees a bottle of poppers in between their fingers like a cigarette. Vicky shakes her head. The person gestures to the fanny pack slung on their shoulders. Vicky shakes her head again. She does not want the poppers, nor does she want the ecstasy, the ketamine, the coke, or whatever pills and powders and inhalants are carried in the pouch around their chest—she had done enough in college and when she first came to New York City, taking whatever was offered to her by wavy strangers who never clarified the chemical makeup. Crossed, faded, mixed at 5:00 a.m., at crooked warehouses remade for one night, whose locations were not released until an hour before the party's start time, and at clubs whose names she could not remember but whose floors she could feel; accepting powders piled on apartment keys and colorful pills in baggies in bathroom stalls and smoking areas. She wouldn't have minded if she died. A student and then newly graduated, she had been unsettled by the deadening required to ascend to adulthood. So she sniffed, swallowed, and waged war on sleep. Anything to lose her mind. Anything to feel something.

But by now, Vicky's learned how this euphoria had been a deception. A mood elevation, only to collapse and come down. She's confronted, invaded, probed the void too deeply to beguile fullness with drugs or work or fake love. She had once adored these things, especially when she experienced them with—her mind stutters over the pain of the recent separation—Jen. She would've taken care of Jen if Jen sought to revert one night. She recognized the substances were a feel-good solution. Jen had loved them too. But the high was temporary. Never regenerated how she needed. Left her feeling more empty than full. So she learned to live life in approximation, settling for a life with her gaping nothing, for waking up in bed and getting out of bed—two acts enough to accept she is to breathe another day. That to feel dead is not to *be* dead. Yet.

Vicky mouths no to the generous silhouette. She's sober now other than tobacco. She allows herself this one vice.

The person smiles. Nods. Shifts away. Because they recognize another kindred in pursuit of getting lost on the dance floor because they are lost in life—though at least they are alive to hear music that keeps them moving. Their ears thumping, their bodies swaying, during hours when normal people float in dreams, asleep to the world shadowed by death's never-ending procession, and here they are, here Vicky is. Alive. Alive. Alive.

*love*

A yell: "Outside?"

Vicky opens her eyes and sees Angela with raised eyebrows, briefly illuminated between swinging spotlights. Kevin is next to her, eyes closed, swaying, face raised.

Vicky grabs Angela's hand in agreement. Sweat glides between their palms. Angela leads, pushing the gyrating bodies aside.

Everydays's backyard is scattered with picnic tables and woven hammocks on which variations of queers drape themselves to smoke, chat, and make out. Vicky stumbles behind Angela to an empty table. They slide onto the top and plant their feet on the bench.

"Want a cigarette?" Angela digs a rumpled box out from her pocket.

Vicky nods. She's still gathering herself from the dance floor. The music dissembles her enough that it takes time to remember basic functions like speaking. Angela sticks a cigarette in her mouth, then pulls one for Vicky, who takes it, their fingers brushing. Angela taps out a lighter from the box, holds the flame to her cigarette, and inhales, its tip gleaming orange.

Vicky tries to take the lighter, but Angela shakes her head, places it back inside the box, inclines forward. Vicky leans in, their cigarette tips meeting. Vicky inhales, her unlit end catching heat from Angela's. A gift of fire, a smoldering.

Angela grins and removes the cigarette from her mouth to talk. "Thanks for indulging me. That's how I used to flirt with people when I was abroad, narrowing in on a hot target smoking outside. Stupid, but it worked."

Vicky musters her voice because she wants to learn more about Angela. "Where'd you go abroad?"

"Prague. Spring, junior year. Too much beer and too little water. Too much childish stupidity. I wish I went somewhere I actually culturally cared about. But I needed to get away from my life. I hated everything. I was really fucking unhappy."

"Ah. Did it work?"

"Getting away?"

"Yes."

"Does it ever?"

Vicky does not know how to respond. "I like your outfit," she tells Angela instead. A new conversation thread to unravel. An easier one, and true. Angela's cotton T-shirt and loose nylon shorts are understated but correct for dancing, and elevated by silver jewelry: chain necklaces with padlock pendants, multiple hoops in both ears with a dagger pendant on the right, thumb rings she recognizes were on Kevin's pinkies during their graveyard date.

"Thanks." Angela blows a cloud of smoke.

Vicky's hand mechanically moves the cigarette to her lips, to her lap. She shivers, her sweat evaporating as she sits with Angela. Late summer in New York is sticky during the day but brings cooler nights with the pursed lips of an approaching fall. When Vicky is on the dance floor, she is both in her body and out—in to move, out to forget; yet when she leaves, the throbbing toes, the aching temples, the burning throat return. Embodiment is permanent.

"Everything okay with you and your girlfriend? What's her name again?" Angela asks.

"Jen. Her name's Jen. It's—I don't know. Also, she's just my friend."

Angela shrugs. "Well, you seem upset enough that it makes her on par with a girlfriend."

"She's just my friend. Best friend." Vicky wonders if this designation is still true after their fight. "Which, you know, yeah. You're right. Kinda makes her my girlfriend, I guess. She has a boyfriend, though."

"Friend breakups are just as hard as romantic breakups."

"Friend breakups are worse."

"There's no manual for it."

"Exactly!"

"Friendship can be difficult," Angela says.

"No. Friendship should feel natural."

"Friendship means you check in. Reach out. Follow up. Make time. That's difficult for most people, especially if, as you said before we went in the club, you have a tendency for self-isolation."

"You mean depresso vibes, as Kevin says."

"Depresso vibes is the perfect way to put it."

"Well, despite my depresso vibes, Jen and I were easy friends. Easy friendship. And I try my best to be a good friend, okay? Doesn't that count?"

Angela shrugs. "You wanna vent about the fight?"

Vicky turns to Angela. "Can I?"

Angela nods.

"I just—I feel bad that I ruined her shoot for work, but it wasn't really my fault—she had no right to be so mean. Especially since she knows I talk and think about death a lot—if it's really bothered her throughout the years, why didn't she just tell me? How am I supposed to know? It's the stupidest fight I've ever been in. We haven't fought like this since college, especially not about our jobs. Why are we even fighting? Who the fuck cares? It's just work!" Vicky exhales. She's lighter after recounting her frustrations. She wonders if she should thank Angela for listening. Dumping her emotions onto another is a burden.

"Why don't you just apologize?"

"Because I'm not a good person."

Angela snorts, cigarette smoke sputtering. "Shut up."

Vicky frowns. She thinks it true: She is not a good person.

Angela, apologetic, extends her arm and huddles Vicky to her. "You are a good person."

Vicky does not answer.

Angela frowns. "Of course you are! You wouldn't be here

with me, and you wouldn't have a deep friendship with someone, if you weren't. You both just said some stupid shit because of stress."

Vicky untangles herself, stubs her cigarette violently. "I wasn't being stupid! I'm right, and she should recognize it. Why does Jen care so much about her stupid job in wellness? The industry is the antithesis of everything natural. Wellness fights against the truth: that we are going to die. That's why the urn is up there in Fort Greene. And that's why I made the right career choice."

"Not everyone wants to be constantly reminded of death."

"Then they need to get their heads out of their asses. Don't you read the news? What's the point of fighting? We're all dying, and we'll probably die before we even hit retirement. If we do make it that far, we can't enjoy it, because we'll be too old and decrepit to properly move, and there's no way our retirement funds will even be enough. Everything's collapsing." Vicky begins counting on her fingers: "Pandemics, mental health crises, drug abuse, climate change, suicide, gun violence, fascism, disease, war on foreign shores we fund despite our protest. So many reasons to give up, to not give a fuck about wellness, to die. Jen is ridiculous if she thinks pretending the inevitable doesn't exist will make it go away." She clenches her splayed fingers into a fist. "I know my job is dumb, but at least at Onwards, we're realistic. We make death fun. Approachable. Equitable. And a celebration of life, as it should be."

"But," Angela says quietly, "death isn't fun. Well, I guess death is fun for the dead because they get to leave life behind. And maybe death is fun for the old because they can prepare for it. They've had enough of life. Their next great adventure. But for the young? For the loved?"

"Okay, fine. Maybe 'fun' is the wrong word. But at least we can prepare. So we feel better when death comes."

Angela looks down at her cigarette. Then: "Has anyone you loved ever died?"

"My grandfather."

"Was it hard?"

"It was hard. I loved him. But to be honest, we weren't that close. No one close to me has died. Not yet."

"Not yet," echoes Angela. "Not yet."

Both girls are quiet.

"What about you?" Vicky asks nervously. Not that she wants to hear the answer. More that the question is the requisite follow-up.

"Yeah. During the pandemic. My uncle. And Kevin's aunt. Everyone wore masks and stayed at home. Didn't let us visit—not that we wanted to. Well, we *wanted* to, but we didn't, because it wasn't safe. And they still caught it and passed away. Probably from the grocery store. Before the vaccines. We did those video call funerals."

"Ah." Vicky pauses. What should she say? What can she even say? She chooses the easy response: "I'm sorry." What else?

Angela shakes her head like she's brushing off the sorrow and pity. "It's fine. We're supposed to have moved on by now."

"You can still talk about it."

"No, I can't," Angela fumes. Catches herself, steels her emotions, cools down. "There's no time for grief past immediacy. You have the funeral. Then you have to move on. You can't wallow because it's pathetic and because nobody has the time or patience for your misery. It fucking sucks," spits Angela. "It sucks," Angela repeats, calmer. Then: "Maybe Jen doesn't want to wallow."

Vicky recalls the month when Vicky had heard Jen but not seen her, because Jen would not stop sobbing while huddled hidden under blankets after receiving the call that her grandmother had passed away in her sleep. Even the fact that her grandmother had died peacefully dreaming did not alleviate her devastation. Vicky had snuck food out from the dining hall, spooning rice under the table into plastic containers balanced on her thighs, leaving the meals to get cold on Jen's nightstand, because Jen would not, could not, get out of bed. Vicky had completed their homework for the both of them, painstakingly copying Jen's handwriting and marking a few answers differently on purpose to not get caught. She had learned Photoshop and Illustrator too from that time of completing Jen's work, making her a decent enough art director, not that she would tell Dan—he would simply assign her more work.

Angela is correct. Jen doesn't want to be reminded of that aching sorrow. But Vicky, stubborn, a toddler reveling in her temper tantrum, refuses to concede. "Still! We can't just ignore death!"

Angela snorts. "Who can ignore death? No one. I wish I could." She puffs smoke. "I think about death all the time."

"Exactly! Same!"

"No, like—I want to die. Sometimes I plan for it. Map out the method. The place and time."

Vicky chooses to believe Angela is being facetious the way many their age joke about killing themselves. She kids too: "You do seem type A."

"I'm such a planner that whenever I think I could kill myself, I worry about who would organize and pay for the funeral."

"Kevin? He's rich."

"Yeah, but that would hurt him too much. Besides, it's his parents who are rich, not him." Angela brightens. "Hey. Maybe I'll use Onwards to help plan."

Vicky laughs. "Yes. That is why Onwards exists." Vicky takes on a saleswoman affect: "To make it affordable and easy to plan for the death of you and your loved ones." She returns to her normal voice. "I'll give you an employee discount."

"That would be great," Angela says. "I'm not really kidding, you know. To be honest, I wake up and wonder why I'm still alive. Would it be more tolerable if I just died? Every day I have to make the decision not to succumb to the anguish. I remind myself I must live. I think, *I can't die, not yet*. Because *not yet* holds possibility. Not yet, because there's Kevin, there's organizing, there's my friends, and there's nights like these"—Angela gestures to the people splayed before them, laughing and hugging and dancing—"and there's food to eat and food to share. Love to give and love to feel. So that means not yet. Not yet. I have to believe in *not yet*. I have to believe that it doesn't have to be like this. That it doesn't always have to be so aching. I'm always wondering why people decide to keep living. What motivates them? I guess that's what motivates me. The search for some other new reason to keep going."

Again, Vicky does not know what to say. What could follow such naked confession? She is not a therapist; she is not even Angela's friend, because they are . . . dating? Could this be called dating already, on their second meeting, the clock reading 2:00 a.m.? Vicky is confused, but she doesn't want to close down, run away, shut up—not like she normally does. She likes this intimacy. This sharing of space and feelings and time. Likes *Angela*.

Vicky flails for a proper response. Muddles through her tired mind. Decides to repeat Angela's words back to her because echoes indicate active listening: "There's Kevin, there's organizing, there's friends, there's food, and—" Her voice catches, and Vicky realizes how much she wants to be on Angela's list. How much she wants her name in Angela's mouth. "There's me?" She cringes inwardly. She hates asking for love. Hates showing that she wants love even when she rejects it. But revealing vulnerability is her own confession: She wants Angela to live. She wants Angela to live with her—not "live with her" as in the same apartment, splitting rent, arguing over who would clean the toilet and who would cook dinner and who would do the laundry. But "live with her" as in: *Live with me so we can live happier, together. Live with me so our lives can intertwine like tree roots, so we can burst free from this grounding despair and blossom upward toward the sun.*

Angela looks at her.

"There's you," she says.

They kiss.

Vicky feels Angela's hand cup the back of her neck, then drop to curl tight at her hip, and though Vicky is sure she's inflicting on Angela bad tobacco breath, a dry tongue, and a dehydrated throat, *who cares*, because Vicky is having fun—does this mean she is in love?

The thought flits through her mind, and yet—again—*who cares*. The party calls for the now. Never mind the future. Never mind the past. Here they are together, here they are blooming. And free.

*lust*

They call a car back to Manhattan. The price is high from deep Brooklyn, but Kevin pays. Vicky sits between them in the back seat. Kevin's hand grips her thigh. Angela's head rests on her shoulder. The dashboard reads 3:42 a.m. The night over, the night just starting. They zoom over the Brooklyn Bridge. The windows are open. Air screams across their faces. Vicky loves being in a car or bus in the city at ungodly hours because of the wild sprints across bridges and down avenues, unhampered by daytime traffic. She thinks this is how life should be experienced. Careless careening. No obstacles. Sandwiched between people you hope to love. Do love? Why not? Never too early. The sky is a panel of black without visible stars or moon. Nature is unnecessary when there are city lights to stare at and golden windows to peek in. More worlds in those illuminated glimpses than any cosmic galaxies. Vicky tilts her head to rest her cheek on Angela's head. She thinks through her happy, exhausted haze of how small yet expansive this moment is. How lovely.

They arrive, they enter. Like hers, their apartment is a walk-up; unlike hers, their apartment is new, recently renovated, spacious with new appliances. Like hers, their apartment is decorated with personal, quirky taste; unlike hers, the decorations are costly. Hers is cluttered with zhizha, free art gallery opening posters, stoop furniture finds; theirs holds Isamu Noguchi lamps, *Infernal Affairs* signed posters, gold-tooled leather book spines crowded on shelves, arching floor-to-ceiling buoyant houseplants that, if purchased in the city instead of from a trip to a Jersey suburb hardware store like Jen and she had once done, would cost hundreds of dollars.

Vicky takes her shoes off and leaves them at the front door. Follows Angela to the couch, training her gaze on the back of Angela's head. She doesn't want to look around. She often discombobulates around nice things, still gasping in rooms of looted objects in American museums—a habit from college, where she had first learned the meaning of wealth of the generational sort, from kids who drove Ferraris on campus gifted from their philanthropist parents with money earned by their industrialist grandparents.

Angela points her to the bathroom. Vicky clicks the door shut and sits on the toilet. Pees. Flushes. Walks toward the sink, marveling at how many steps she must take within just the bathroom itself. Runs the silver spout and uses the gushing water to wash her hands, splash her armpits.

She opens the mirror cabinet to peek inside—what she always does when she enters a new apartment, whether a friend's or a lover's or a coworker's. She believes this space tells her more about the person than multiple interactions ever could. She's snooped so many times at Jen's that she can visualize without effort Jen's rich moisturizer, Roller-branded facial rollers, and anxiety prescription—3 mg of Xanax.

Inside Kevin and Angela's cabinet she spies two frayed toothbrushes, three lipsticks, an organic all-natural tube of toothpaste, a razor, a half-squeezed Korean brand container of SPF 50 sunscreen, and what she expected to see, because she sees them in every bathroom cabinet she's ever trespassed in, and if not there, then in the bedside table drawer, the handbag inner pocket, the refrigerator: pain reliever pills, those available over the counter and through psychiatrists, therapists, and pharmacists, piled in those ugly plastic boxes sorted by day of the week. Vicky believes drug organizers should be prettier, like zhizha jewelry boxes or hand-painted artisan bowls, because magic is pretty and therefore the holders should be pretty too, cradling candy-like magic: selective serotonin reuptake inhibitors and mood stabilizers, the Zolofts and Prozacs and Wellbutrins, even the extra-strong dosages of sunny vitamin D to ward off seasonal depression, which is just one kind of depression. Vicky's learned through years of existing that there's major depression and premenstrual dysphoric depression and situational depression and atypical depression and even something called "treatment-resistant depression," which Vicky bets, based on its name, is the worst diagnosis, though depression is not a competition; Vicky knows without needing to label her kind of depression that depression is hard enough without the misery of comparison. She's sure Angela would agree, and she's relieved to confirm her suspicions that Angela is an expert sampler of medication cocktails, which to her reads as an act of hope, a belief in a future of feeling better. That things were dark, but not *so* dark. That there was a pill-shaped pinprick of light through the gloom.

Vicky unlocks the door, steps out.

Kevin and Angela sit on their couch muttering quietly, legs tangled. Vicky wonders what they are discussing. She's never been in a romantic relationship with one person long enough to have these sorts of private conversations. Always relegated to the role of the witness, which did not make her feel lonely but rather made her sad—sad that she did not feel lonely like a normal person would. Why can't she ever feel lonely? Why can't she ever feel anything?

Vicky walks over. Sits next to Kevin. Presses her thigh against his hip. Kevin looks at Vicky. She looks at both of them. Realizes the silver rings have disappeared from their fingers. Feels slightly disappointed that she did not get to see where and how the rings were discarded—carefully? Carelessly? Into a shared jewelry box or strewn recklessly onto the kitchen table?

Angela giggles.

Vicky cannot wait any longer. She moves first—she always does, and she does not mind, because that is why she is there. Not to flirt or play hard to get when it is past 4:00 a.m., past patience, past pleasantries. She grips Angela's head and Angela obeys, descends—plunges—their lips meet, endless. Vicky swallows, raises her head. Kevin is there, and he slaps her. Her head twists to the side. He hooks a finger in her mouth, then a second, a third, brings her gaze back to him. "Look at me," he says. She likes the pain. She had told them so over text—her likes, her limits. She is pleased he remembers. Her teeth scrape against his knuckles, the aggression flowing from him to her to Angela, whose hair Vicky fists tight, then Kevin is behind Vicky, a hand wrapped tight around her throat, a finger hooked on her teeth, trailing from her jaw; the other hand snaking up her stomach to where he squeezes, strokes—she moans, and Angela moans with her. Vicky has had awkward threesome experiences before, the garish word "threesome" itself degrading the grouping's possibilities, where one starts crying and two end up ignoring her, but this, with Kevin and Angela, feels natural, like three has always been more than two, better than one. Vicky hikes up her skirt, and Angela props her weight up on her elbows and whispers, "No, take it off," so Vicky pushes it down, and then Kevin grips the hem of her shirt and helps her pull it over her head. She is naked, and she watches Kevin's and Angela's faces transform into the glee of abandon. The wild hope is nearly too much to bear. She fights the urge to grab her clothes and run out the door. Resolves to run toward this lust—this love—instead. Vicky pulls Angela back onto her and opens her mouth, Kevin on her neck, Kevin up her legs, losing herself again.

*love.*

During rare occasions when Vicky manages to keep her head above bleak tides, she has fantasies about tenderness like this: The label of a weekend or a weekday dissolved, no lazy Sunday distorting into laborious Monday, the day simply becoming *day*. A day of the week when she wakes up in bed without work next to not one but two—or three or four, though to count exact would be to constrain the sweet, boundless affection. An interlocking patchwork of boyfriends and girlfriends and lover-friends, sharing the blanket with her—Vicky does not fathom one because she has dreamed of more. And some mornings, like this, she is lucky enough to live many: She rolls over and wraps her arm around Angela's side, her hand brushing Kevin's stomach. Tucks her nose into Angela's nook between shoulder blade and spine. Presses her face against skin, blocking out the sunlight, delaying the waking. She does not want to leave the bed. Who would?

But she hears Kevin's morning clearing of the throat. Feels Angela stir.

The three are awake. They come together in a fleeting cuddle to compensate for the soon-to-be separation off bed, on land. Stumble into sweats, leggings, T-shirts—Vicky leaves her party clothes on their living room floor in favor of an oversize sweatshirt from Kevin and a pair of soft shorts from Angela. They embark in search of food. Kevin first, Angela second, Vicky last. Vicky clomps down their apartment building stairs, the cotton fabric scraping against her sore left butt cheek, where lie streaks of red from Kevin's hand. She had told him last night: *Harder. Harder. Harder.*

They stumble into Chinatown. Vicky inhales the late summer air, humidity stirring. If Vicky was a cheesier sort of romantic, she's sure the gentle euphoria she's currently feeling would bubble out. She'd break into song, catch the wind and leap onto Roosevelt Park's benches to spin, grab the outstretched arms of a tai chi auntie, swing them around (carefully) and then slow dance. Like those scenes in the jovial movies she hates: the musicals, the family-friendly, the romantic comedies—she hates these movies because these movies always end.

Everything good ends. Though everything bad ends too—*forevers* dissolving into questions of *remember when?*

And with each step through Chinatown the euphoria saps from Vicky. She's entering the end. Numbness chomping her in its damp, dark mouth. Swallowing her warm heart and spitting out her cold bones, licked clean of anything alive. She doesn't confess to Angela or Kevin about the encroaching nothing. She does not want to chase them away. Negativity is ugly, and the morning is meant to be beautiful.

The three stop at the Canal Street fruit stands. Vicky squeezes a cherimoya, and Angela slaps her hand. Softly, but nevertheless an admonishment: *Don't touch if you won't buy. It's rude.*

Vicky has never eaten a cherimoya because it is nearly eleven dollars for one, and in the area of fruit she plays it safe. Affordable. What she knows she will like. She's never peeled its scaly green skin to reveal its white flesh, has never spit out the black seeds into a trash can while the sugar melts on her tongue. Kevin offers to buy her one so she can try. He is generous among love. But she shakes her head. He opts for a red plastic bag bulging with clementines. Forks over the cash.

"Xie xie," they say to their chosen seller, who has already turned to weigh the next customer's gatherings.

Kevin peels citrus as they walk, alternating handing off slices. Vicky holds it in her jaw, breaks the translucent skin, tongues out the pulp.

The three stroll past Angela's favorite bakery with the silver-painted exterior and the rust-red font sign. Angela yelps in alert, nearly choking on her clementine, dragging them inside. She greets the grumpy lady with the hairnet and asks for three black coffees and three bolo buns.

Vicky whips out her wallet and offers to pay. She's trying to be less stingy.

They sink their teeth into the buns, marveling over the crunch of the topping, the softness of the yeast. With her thumb, Angela wipes a golden crumb off the corner of Vicky's lips.

They leave the honeyed smell of the bakery and continue down Canal under the hand-painted lanterns of Chinatown's sky, toward Grand Street, where Angela wants to buy fresh zongzi from the ayi who hawks outside the subway station entrance.

The ayi greets Angela by name. Does not hand over the laminated list of zongzi options because she recognizes Angela, the cute girl who only ever wants sugary—the red beans, the black sesame. As if swallowing sweetness could expel sadness, which the ayi can read on the girl's face.

Kevin offers a clementine, but the ayi declines.

Angela piles two of each sweet zongzi type in the stomach of her oversize T-shirt, holding the hem upward to form a makeshift basket, like she's a child in kindergarten class, playing with marbles, picking up her mess.

Vicky breaks away. Three into two and one.

The two face the one. "Would you like to come over for lunch?" Kevin asks.

"No, it's okay." Vicky needs to be alone. To rebuild her defenses against the bleak.

"You'd be welcome," tries Angela.

"I'm good." Then seeing Angela's face fall, Vicky adds, "Sorry. I just need to go home and get my life together. I need to text Jen." Morning love has made her anger cool.

Angela smiles. "I think that's a good idea."

"I think so too."

"Will you text me after you text Jen?"

"Yes."

Kevin fishes out a zongzi from Angela's makeshift pouch. "Wanna take one?"

"Nah," Vicky says. She hugs Kevin, then kisses Angela on the cheek. "But I would love to see you again." Maybe next week, after she's collected herself. Would that be too soon? Too late? She can never predict how she'll feel.

"Us too."

"Text me when you get home."

"I will."

Kevin and Angela descend into the subway to ride it several stops back to theirs, while Vicky walks to her apartment and melts onto the couch and smokes a cigarette and checks her email for no real reason other than robotic obligation. She watches stupid television on her laptop, eats a bag of chips, rearranges her zhizha.

Vicky burrows in bed, her body still wearing traces of the two's touch.

Checks her phone, the screen lighting up her face.

No text back from Jen.

Not yet. Maybe tomorrow.

*There is always tomorrow,* she tells herself before she falls asleep, alone.

# work

Angela had responded to her im home! text with a cowboy hat emoji, but Jen still has not responded to her hi can we talk? Monday, nearly noon, and Vicky buries herself in work as a distraction from her best friend's ghosting. She types hunched over, wrists throbbing, composing a write-up for producers to brief the queer artists Onwards will collaborate with for the LGBTQ+ Opportunity. Her idea is splashy, fun, and stupid. Attention getting. Potential to go viral and erase any negativity surrounding Onwards.

According to Dan, Urnie loves her idea.

Earlier this year, Onwards launched its open-minded vision and strategy aiming to champion a new era of the death industry through accessibility, equity, and inclusivity, including the launch of an urn portfolio specifically designed for marginalized groups. These exciting advancements, paired with Onwards's purpose of helping our community embrace the realities of death, have led Onwards to boost a platform and campaign designed for LGBTQ+ people of all ages. We're hoping to encourage LGBTQ+ people to embrace their identities while embarking on a death journey safely made for them.

This is where you come in!

We love your art. We are commissioning you to create an urn modeled after your art and your queer identity, whether you are lesbian, gay, trans, nonbinary, bi/pansexual, etc. Your specially designed urn will be named after you and your identity. We'll reproduce your urn artwork in limited quantities and list it on our site, with all proceeds going to queer youth suicide hotline nonprofits. Of course, we'd love to spotlight your process and your work outside of our commission, so in addition to your urn, we plan to pitch you and your work to various media outlets and partners for potential interviews and spotlights. We think this will be a great opportunity for

She stops typing. She knows what artists will think of this supposed great opportunity. She herself thinks it whenever the calendar hits June. Logos and products suddenly draped in rainbows. Professional network posts highlighting queer employees whom they would never dare lay off in June. Rainbow washing. No big brand actually cares about queers—just profit, for to pander is to rake in dollars. Superficial allyship. Identity wrapped up in consumption—in spending money, in buying things, in having everything and never enough.

She hits the backspace button. Deletes We think this will be a great opportunity for

Types instead: It's not Pride month anymore. Because Pride is all year.

Vicky knows the artists will scoff at this conclusion. She also knows that the artists will nevertheless accept. They have no choice. Who would be silly enough to reject a fat paycheck and the promise of visibility from one of the hippest start-ups helmed by one of the coolest gay celebrities? Even with the recent alleged Onwards-induced contagion of suicidal behavior, the commission could be worse than for Urnie's urns—it could have been for the lobby of a finance building or for the blank living room wall of a pharmaceutical heir. Still, she'd never blame an artist for stooping to degradation. She gets it. She's in the same situation. Sucking hungrily at the corporate teat so she can pay for her apartment, groceries, zhizha, and the occasional splurge. Creativity and capital have always been married, and like the artists, she scams the company, takes the money, and runs.

*It is what it is,* she thinks.

She checks her phone.

Nothing.

Nothing from Kevin, nothing from Angela, nothing from Jen. Her phone, a silent hand-size deadweight with no connections because voids have no connections. She chucks her phone away. It slides off the table onto the floor with a thud. She wishes she could embrace her anger enough to be uncaring about her earthly possessions. Break plates, punch walls. But she is not rich enough to be careless—the cost of a screen replacement threatens. She gets up and toes her phone to check the screen, and sighs with relief to see the glass uncracked, though still black without a text notification to light it up. She sits back down and tousles her hair with both hands in irritation. Blows her bangs out of her face. Squeezes the skin between her fingers. She's disappointed in herself. She believed herself strong enough to rely only on herself. To never hinge her stability on anyone or anything outside her own person. Far easier to encase in a hard pod so no emotion or violent dreams of death could leak in or out. A solid rock with no softness. She had refused friendship from others out of self-protection, but Jen had shattered her way in and nestled into her rib cage. Now came casual betrayal, which she should have expected all along from someone who cared so much about shallow things like wellness and beauty—

A vibration.

Vicky shifts her eyes to her phone on the floor.

How incredible that a mere text notification from someone she loves makes her heart leap for joy, up from her chest and into her throat. She understands why human connection has persisted despite centuries of war, hatred, and violence. She swallows, settles her heart back into her chest, where it pounds its fists in cheer.

She stands from her chair, toddles unsteadily to her phone. Picks it up. Opens the text from Jen and reads it.

> sure we can talk

Her thumbs type in response, hit send: come over tn?

## *friendship, which is also a kind of love*

They sit where they always sit. A matter of familiarity, together on the fire escape. Facing each other, cross-legged. Passing a spliff between them—smooth, long, round, thick. Jen had brought it, one of her peace offerings, along with a bag of Vicky's favorite snack. She had picked it up from the Southeast Asian grocery store on Mosco Street, the one with the grimy windows hiding colorfully wrapped treasures within. The snack is so popular it never stocked on shelves, reserved instead for Somsak's favorite repeat customers. When Jen walked in, Somsak, the owner, had stood from his stool and entered the back storeroom to pick up a bag of skinny beige dried fish sticks in exchange for Jen's cash, keeping the change. Jen then trudged out the door down the slant of Mosco and left to the entrance of Vicky's apartment building, shivering when she passed by the funeral home signs. Jen avoids the crying eyes of funerary patrons. She hates the reminder of grief, and she hates how she must traverse it to reach her joy: Vicky.

Passing the spliff back to Jen, Vicky digs her hand into the bag and brings out a clump of fish strips tangled like noodles. Vicky opens her mouth, tilts her head back, and dumps the entire ball into her mouth. Mashes the strips into mush with her mouth open, smacking her lips.

"Thanks," Vicky says.

"I'm sorry," Jen says.

"Stop. You have nothing to apologize for."

A brief pause.

Vicky swallows. "I'm sorry. I'm—I'm the one who fucked up." Her muscles loosen. The weed, or the apology? The weed, or the letting go?

They stare at what they can see of the other's face in the night.

Jen takes a too-large gulp of the spliff. Vicky shoves more fish strands into her mouth. They both cough from their respective throat jams, coughs transitioning into laughs.

They do not say anything more. They know how sorry the other person is. How much they had missed each other. How the apologies were not just for the fight at Fort Greene Park but for the guilt, the ignoring, the agony that came after too.

"Stupidest fight we've ever been in," says Vicky once she's swallowed her fish.

"Even stupider than fights over frat boys in college," Jen agrees.

Vicky gasps. "I never!"

"No, bitch, you did."

"Don't tell anyone."

"Who would I even tell?"

Vicky grips Jen's non-spliff-holding hand and squeezes.

Jen squeezes back.

They drop hands. Jen stubs out the spliff, lights another. They are quiet as they sit, listening to the city. A clang from a shopkeeper slamming the metal gate down after close; a cell phone game tinkling at full volume from a kid walking past; a siren wailing from an ambulance rushing down an unseen block. Vicky briefly wonders where the ambulance is headed, if the person waiting at its destination will die, and, if not, if that person can afford the ambulance, if that person has a healthcare plan that would delay, deny, defend—her mind spasms as it always does when she thinks of another's pain. She forgets in order to live. She comes back to herself full-body and shivers. Cooler air has started to descend onto the city and its inhabitants. In summer Vicky and Jen are vivid; when winter comes they will be drained; for now, in the soon-to-be fall, they sit together outside in solitude above the funeral parlor, high in height and high in mind, knowing as seasons shift and time passes that they will stay each other's best friend, because the other option would be to die alone, and where would the fun be in that?

"Here." Vicky's peace offering. She removes her phone from

her hoodie pocket, taps the screen, and hands it to Jen. "Thought of you."

Jen squints at the screen, and Vicky plummets into sudden panic—is her gift too macabre, too strange?

Jen looks up at Vicky, phone illuminating her face from the bottom, making her resemble a villain.

Vicky's breath stutters—

Then the phone screen turns black, and Jen sniffles, wipes her nose with the back of her hand, and Vicky realizes Jen is smiling. Crying.

"Thank you," Jen says.

Vicky looks down at her lap, abashed. "I saw it in the window today. I immediately thought of you."

"It makes me feel like I was there, if only for a second. Like I never missed the funeral."

Vicky shrugs to say it was no big deal. Draws her hoodie sleeves around her fists. Hugs herself. She craves smallness after vulnerability, whether given from her or taken from somebody else.

Downstairs, the paper rectangles announcing the day's funerals had one listed with the name "Rui May Chen." Vicky had been taking out the trash when she read the name, and with a bolt of recognition, Vicky had a frantic vision of a beautiful Rui May Chen in bed at age one hundred, dying peacefully in her sleep surrounded by her loving granddaughters—one of whom wore a mask of Jen's face—and grandsons, all these progenies who were so wildly rich they did not have a boss to inform, simply buying a plane ticket in seconds across the globe without needing to track flight prices. Vicky had whipped out her phone, intending to text this story and a picture of the paper rectangle directly to Jen, only remembering after she had taken the photo of the name that they were in the midst of a fight. "Rui May Chen" had been the name Jen tearfully mumbled herself to sleep every night of the month after her grandmother's death, when she had lived under the blankets of her bed. Rui May Chen had moved to America to take care of Jen the Child while her parents disappeared every day to labor at their restaurant, only to move back to China after Jen the Child became Jen the Young Adult Off to College. Jen still drowned in guilt over her inability to attend the funeral abroad because of high plane ticket prices and the diligence of studying, not that Jen had been coherent in grief enough to go to class anyway, but Jen's mother, forever fussy and strict and difficult, had refused to let her take time off from school. Vicky would have been willing to take care of Jen forever, to let Jen mourn in bed until death came and she could join her grandmother in the afterlife, but eventually Vicky became worried about Jen's anemia and lack of sunlight, and besides, the professors could only take a few weeks of her hastily made-up excuses for Jen's absences. On the last night of that crying month, she had sat by the damp lump in Jen's bed and asked about Rui May Chen, the name she had heard sobbed every night. Her favorite foods to eat, her favorite foods to cook, why Jen loved her, why she loved Jen. What stories, what lessons, what of life, did Jen know because of this woman? It was only after these questions that Jen finally poked her head out onto the pillows. Slowly, at first—just her forehead, then her eyes, then the top of her nose. Then her nostrils, her mouth, her neck, then her body, the covers fully thrown off, as she and Vicky laughed over memories of Rui May Chen's delicious congee that somehow always stuck to the bottom of the pot and the time Rui

May Chen had tricked Jen into eating chicken feet by saying they were tree roots.

Vicky had never known either of her grandmothers. A joy to learn about Jen's, because whomever Jen loved, she decided she would love too.

Jen pulls out her own phone, taps the screen. She holds it up, showing Vicky her final peace offering. "This exhibit at the Met made me think of you. I went with Eric."

"Wow," Vicky murmurs. She takes Jen's phone, pinches the screen, and zooms in, out.

"You need to go. It was made for you. Paintings from different eras and traditions brought together, revolving around the theme of death. The entire exhibit is a memento mori."

Vicky smiles. "And you chose this painting to show me."

"Of course."

Vicky has been brought to tears in front of paintings before, her chest contracting at startling scenes and mournful portraits, shadowy still lifes and airy impressionisms and solid abstracts. Art has always made her come alive. She's never made art, but the sheer act of looking is enough. A phenomenon that the nerve impulses carried through the optic nerve and processed by her brain into images could translate into such strong, stirring emotion. Painters—those renderers of tender sentience. She cannot explain why something as mundane as a brushstroke stirs in her what most human interaction cannot. But it is enough to carry the colors in her chest. The shapes in her veins. The shades in the spaces between her bones. Vicky has never cried looking at a digital photo of a painting—staring at pixels could never replace standing bodily in front of a canvas. Yet her eyes are watery staring at Jen's phone, even with the poor quality of the red spider lilies, because her best friend knows this is her favorite flower, and her best friend knows she loves paintings, and even during their fight her best friend thought of her enough to take a picture of a painting of these flowers. *This made me think of you. Thank you for being my friend.*

Vicky zooms back into the photo to peer at the details. The lilies' lines are pristine, their stamens and petals evoking bones and decay, the stark red against black reminding her of blood. Vicky likes to call them by their nicknames: corpse flower, resurrection lily. Hard to find in America, especially in New York City, though Vicky has heard legends of them popping up in cemeteries on top of fresh graves after long rains in summer heat. With poisonous bulbs growing in hell to guide the dead, the flowers remind her of herself: reeking of death and hard to love. She discovered the flower after seeing illustrations of it glowing prettily in the credits of her favorite childhood anime, re-looped from episode 26 back to episode 1 up to 26 again, the one where people died constantly to the point of frivolousness because of two boys ego-fighting over a death diary. Perhaps the show had ushered in her early fascination with death. If people could die so easily from the whims of a narcissistic young man flourishing a pen in Death's diary, then wouldn't it be better to face death head-on and embrace its motifs—the urn, the corpse flower, the all-black wardrobe?

"Who painted this?" Vicky asks.

"I think it was a contemporary Japanese American painter. I didn't write down the name, but you should go to the exhibit and check it out." Jen pokes her. "Invite Kevin and Angela?"

"Yeah, maybe I will. They'd like to go. Hey—do you know if the painter had a loved one pass away recently? Is that why they painted these lilies? In mourning? Do you remember what the description said?"

"I'm not telling. Go with Kevin and Angela and find out yourself."

"Fine." Vicky sips the spliff, rolls her eyes.

"Okay. Your turn."

"Was my apology not enough?"

"You know what I'm talking about. Don't leave any details out. Tell me."

Vicky snorts. "What do you wanna know?"

"Everything!"

"We went dancing, then I went back to theirs. The apartment is gorgeous, Kevin's parents are definitely helping to subsidize it. It's actually pretty close by. Tribeca, near that cathedral with the catacombs underneath—" Vicky breaks off when she realizes she's talking about death again.

Jen interjects: "So you'll always go to theirs, then?"

"You know I hate having people over at mine. I hate stupid questions about my zhizha. Although, if we keep seeing each other, maybe I'll invite them over eventually."

"At least the sex was good?"

"It was the typical sort of threesome." Vicky thinks for a second, clarifies: "Well, no—it was actually much nicer than normal. We were all satisfied. 'From each according to his ability, to each according to his needs.'" Vicky giggles. "Maybe it's because Angela's an organizer and apparently a fervent communist, at least according to her bookshelf. So her beliefs translate to her performance in bed," she jokes.

Jen laughs. "That's so stupid."

"I wonder what Angela studied in college."

"You're dating her, and you don't know that?"

"It's only been two dates! And we talk about other things! Besides, college was a long time ago."

"Well, it's impressive she's an organizer and has read the theory too. That's rare."

"I wonder how she sustains her hope. I have barely any left," Vicky says.

"Why don't you ask?"

"I will, next time."

"Seems like you already feel comfortable around her even though it's only been two dates."

"I think so. Maybe? She's pretty open, which helps me feel open too."

"About everything?"

"Most things. I'd like to talk to her more. I think she has interesting things to say. Three a.m. at Everydays isn't exactly conducive to depth." Vicky feels soft. Warm. Serene. Not from the weed but from sharing details of her life with Jen. She feels tender because she is talking to her friend, and a friend is tenderness itself.

"So you definitely want to see them again," Jen says, wanting confirmation.

"Of course. They're both pretty busy, and I have the queer urn campaign going into production soon, which means I'll have to work late. But I'd like to make the time."

"Will I get to meet them?"

"They have a big Halloween party every year since it's their anniversary. You should come. If you promise not to embarrass me."

Jen giggles. "Ooh, yes. I'll be good. Can Eric come?"

"Yeah, of course."

"Yay!" Jen claps. "We gotta figure out costumes."

Vicky passes the spliff to Jen, who inhales, exhales a cloud, hands it back.

Vicky smiles, continues: "I really like them. Angela especially. You know I always like the girl more when I date couples. I feel very . . . gooey? . . . toward her. More than I've felt for another person in a long time."

"It was bound to happen eventually," says Jen.

Jen means well. Jen truly believes Vicky has a heart. While Vicky knows it's impossible for her to love one person the way love seems to come so easily to others. She's tried before, only to feel even worse that she couldn't love normally, that she couldn't give someone the love they needed, the love they deserved. Her heart, incapable; her heart, dead. She wants too much and she wants nothing at all, and she disappoints everyone, eventually.

"Enough about my stupid love life, or lack of it. What about work? Is everything okay?" Vicky asks.

Jen sighs. "Give me the spliff."

Vicky hands it over.

Jen puffs.

Vicky waits for her response.

"I just feel bad for my coworkers—well, ex-coworkers. I know work isn't life, but work means you can pay for your life, even if life is unaffordable. One of my ex-coworkers just bought an apartment. Another is here on a work visa but can't return to his home country, and another's wife just birthed a child. It'll be hard for them to find a new job in this economy. Now we're on a salary and hiring freeze—which I guess is fine. 'Cause it could be worse. I should be grateful I didn't get laid off, but I just feel anxious."

"There won't be any more layoffs, right? You'll be okay."

"That's what management says. But it's always the same bullshit. Just one round of layoffs of people who deserved it anyway. The family is still a family!"

"Diversity commitment, yet a sea of white faces in every meeting," says Vicky, thinking of Dan, Dean, and Derek.

"Record-breaking profits, yet not enough to raise wages."

"Pathetic."

"Extremely."

Vicky smokes.

Jen continues: "I know I'm not broke, not anymore. And my debt isn't, like, an astounding six figures. I'm supposed to pay it off reasonably within my lifetime. I just—I want to be able to afford something without thinking or checking the price tag, you know? Like, to book a plane ticket across the country to visit home for the holidays without feeling demoralized over the credit card charge. Or to use the grocery store at the corner instead of walking to the far one across the city just because it has slightly cheaper produce. Shouldn't going home always feel good? Is it so privileged of me to want these things?"

Vicky shrugs. She doesn't really go home, not in the Thanksgiving, Christmas, two-parent-household-in-the-suburb sort of way. She just stays home in her crumbling apartment above a funeral home in a high-cost-of-living city.

"Of course not."

"How do I manage to make a good income in the richest country in the world and still feel so fucking poor?"

"Richness is subjective," Vicky says.

"When will the precarity go away, then?" Jen asks.

"I don't think it ever will."

Vicky brings the nearly over spliff to her mouth. Inhales. Stone settles in her veins. She closes her eyes and breathes in Chinatown. Musky air with a trace of raw fish and trash and chicken, fried oil and noodles and rice. She breathes in and breathes out. Decides she will ignore the precarity tonight and settle for living, because it feels good to be alive, for now, even though she knows she will die—until then she knows she must live. To live; to smoke; to have lovers; to sit on the fire escape with her best friend before a dawn of headlines and extinctions and work. She hears the crinkle of the plastic wrapper as Jen reaches a hand in for a tangle of dried fish. Vicky reclines against the bars of the fire escape and smiles and thinks about her stupid, unlivable life.

## *interlude: life*

Time passes. Sleep, wake, work, fuck, die. Maybe, if lucky: love. Love in restaurants, parks, apartments, bars, cafés, shelters, kitchens, museums, galleries, theaters, bookstores, libraries; walking sidewalks, riding trains, hailing cabs to reach these places where we might find love. People to love. We think love will fulfill our lives, lengthen them, and maybe love will, but maybe love won't. We try, and try, and try again, losing meaning through repetition. Different curation but same museums; different riders but same subway trains; same daily bullshit, same cops bullying the churro lady, same trash piling up on the tracks. Different meals but same restaurants. Different cafés but same blocks—blame gentrification. Rent going up, real estate lines redrawn. Neighbors dying, neighbors moving out, temporary neighbors moving in for a summer internship, neighbors evicted. Cycle of the city until cut short by climate change. Don't worry. The city is resilient. The city bounces back. Nevertheless, maybe during our lifetime, or during Vicky's lifetime, the city will flood. Burn. Raze into a developer's wet dream. Banks and Starbucks and chain fast food. It won't be the same city, like the neighbors always changing into different faces, same expressions. Happy, sad, tired, joyful—joy! There is joy because there is love despite the disasters. Wildfire haze, rightful protests taking over the streets, mass death—death, always death, and yet, *I can't live without you so you can't die,* thinks Vicky when she looks at Jen. When she looks at Angela. Vicky would punch Death in the face if she could. Rip his black cloak to shreds. But Vicky isn't stupid. She's deranged, but she's not stupid. She knows Death will come, eventually, for her and for everyone she loves—hasn't she been dreaming about Death ever since she'd been young? Death's endless pursuit, her exhausted legs running away from his jaws. So she wakes up as much as she can so she can embrace another day of living, even if no matter how much she wakes up, she'll still die in the end. Yes, the end will come. She will die. The people she loves will die. They'll die someday. Maybe tomorrow, maybe next year, maybe in fifty—if she's lucky to have that much time, but she's been lucky to love in her own way, so maybe she'll be lucky enough that the love will last for her lifetime. A life that she spends dining with her best friend and waking up with Kevin and Angela, chugging coffee and opening the laptop and watching some television and trudging around the city ignoring the fake monks who want to give her wooden bracelets and dropping coins in the open erhu case of the serenader and cursing the MTA when the train's late. *Stand clear of the closing door.* Showtime. Sometimes she imagines her life moving like the view out the window on the 2/3 express from 42nd to 72nd. Flashing by, indistinct, until something remarkable or strange grinds the journey to a halt. An ending. A death, again. But death has not struck this group of friends and lovers, not yet. So Vicky goes to techno with Kevin and Angela, splits a spliff on the fire escape with Jen, buys a zhizha of a mansion and a luxury car and a set of fancy silverware, ideates urn campaigns, replies to emails, writes presentation decks. Goes into production, works late. Texts back. It's a busy life she leads. But she makes time. Carves out time from her calendar. Chops, gouges, wounds it like the shadow grooves on the sidewalks—the sun is setting earlier. Time jumps forward. Autumn already! Where did the time go? When would Vicky stop being surprised that time passes quickly, that she is getting older? When would she stop asking herself these questions? She forgets that she forgets. Shocked to find it is her birthday again. Here is a new year, and to celebrate, the friends and lovers go to a dim sum palace in Flushing. Eric gives her a book on Chinese funerary traditions he picked up at a secondhand art book store on the Upper East Side; Jen knows Vicky loves giving presents but hates receiving them herself, preferring people just show up as an act of care, so she hugs her for so long that Vicky has to extricate herself in embarrassment; Kevin and Angela show up with an Ube Overload Cake from the Red Ribbon in Woodside, the chiffon cake filled with so much ube halaya that Vicky wishes her entire being too was bright purple and as delicious as the yam. Bizarre that last year's birthday she had not known these two, and that for this year's birthday here they are, cherished, lugging a sugary mass of sweet, laughing with Jen and Eric like the four had known one another since childhood. Who would Vicky meet next, who would come to next year's celebration? Would there even be a next year? Is it presumptuous, ridiculous, futile, to waste hope for a next year? The friends and lovers go to the top floor of the big mall for karaoke at the lounge with the leopard-print walls and mirrors and disco balls. So campy and kitschy and glorious. They order the drinks and the most expensive platter (it's Vicky's birthday, they can splurge for one day). Vicky thinks this might just be the best time of her life. So many ways it could be worse and no way it could be better; if she was allowed to repeat one day out of her entire life, it would be this. She knows she'll never be truly happy and that she'll never be so *nearly* happy as she is now, among friends and lovers who sing and dance and revel, together, because to revel needs more than one. She suppresses her fears of the future. Grips the microphone, sways her hips. Better to be in the now. Vicky and Jen sing the song they always sing together, "Umbrella" by Rihanna. They do their classic dance where Jen places her palms above Vicky's head in a makeshift umbrella while Vicky shimmies and belts out, *"AY AY AY AY."* Kevin and Angela choose a Cantopop classic and it passes without notable incident, because Kevin has too good of a singing voice for proper karaoke and Angela is too self-conscious to dance freely. Eric settles on a new BTS release, a song about good times yet to come. He had learned the choreography at a workout class and performs it as he sings off-key in mispronounced Korean. The rest of them holler and clap as they sway on the soft couch, abs working to keep themselves upright. Then the hour they booked is over. Done. The karaoke worker peeks his head in, tells them to get out. An hour, so fast. Gone by so quickly, like the summer. Like her youth. Vicky has so much of life left and yet so little. At least she has Jen and Angela and Kevin and Eric. Together they ignore time's inevitability. Let the death fall where it may. Too busy to pay attention to nothingness because there are cakes to eat and songs to sing and people to love, for when the world ends, love is what will linger on.

# work

The black business casual sheath dress rides up her thighs and into her ass as Vicky strides across Canal Street, impatiently rushing past the slow tourists. She tugs it down—she's borrowed Jen's dress, two sizes too small for her, but her own wardrobe is too dark, too mesh, too cutout, too fishnet, too *queer*, for a work party. Not that she believes in dress codes, but she does believe in fitting in with the workplace to lessen the chance of being fired. She did not want to spend money on a new dress, nor did she want to spend time hunting through thrift stores in New York City, so she had raided Jen's closet, despite their difference in size.

She's late to the party. Past fashionably late and now in *where the fuck were you?* territory, not that she had been doing anything of use before, just lying on her bed after her shower, mustering the energy to simply get up. Get dressed. Get out of the apartment. She's disgusted with herself. What was the point of wearing a dress to blend in when she would likely walk in during Urnie's speech? All eyes would be on her. Dan would have to splutter out an excuse for his inferior's rudeness. He'd find her after the party and fire her for disrespect. She'd lose her health insurance, hold her breath when swiping her credit card, stalk the discount grocery store aisles. She'd get hit by a car while running late to a job interview, then wake up in the hospital slammed with a bill labeled with so many zeros that she'd still be counting them by the time the first payment date arrived.

Anxious, she unwinds her scarf to cool down as she power walks, sweating in the brisk late air. The city is always chilly during the last week of October, but this year's late fall has been colder than usual, her exhalations visible in puffy clouds, the parks' tree leaves long since disintegrated, the city's gray winter filter permanent until next May—yet she still overheats when she walks because she walks fast. She does not know how to saunter because she is always late. So she does not stop to raise a fist with the group of activists outside the Chinatown Museum protesting the board's acceptance of city funding in exchange for a concession to build a jail in the neighborhood, or the construction workers beside the giant inflatable union rat that's been parked for the last week outside a half-built office building, or the picket line of restaurant workers, fired after the landlord raised the rent so high that the iconic dim sum banquet hall was forced to close. She does not join, she does not march, she does not protest. She rushes past. Ignores. Forgets. Turns away in favor of the office, a building she's been to only a few instances before. She didn't mind the space, a trendy corporate design with the employee—no, *family member*—in mind: wood floors, open plan, floor-to-ceiling windows, stacks of coffee table art books no one has ever opened, kombucha on tap, and a kitchen stocked with snacks, though most employees did not go into the office regularly—were maggots proliferating within the brightly colored wrappers like they had been found several times already?

She weaves past the handbag sellers. Dodges the outstretched laminated pamphlets of pixelated Prada and YSL leather fakes. Steps over the mats of Coach and Gucci knockoffs. She gives a glance to the Chinatown storefronts plastered with faded mooncake details and lavender boba drinks, but no. She does not have time to indulge.

She arrives at the building on Lafayette—and halts in surprise. Gawks at the mass of hip people tapping on their phones and taking pictures of each other. Despite the emails crowing about the success of the first Onwards store opened underneath the company offices, she's unprepared for the magnitude of the winding line. The store had been designed not by real estate investor hive minds but by ENBY, with each urn displayed like a work of sculptural art, given its own white platform with square footage around each perimeter for the peruser to examine and enjoy from every angle; with walls plastered with mirrors, supposedly so visitors could confront their immortality through self-reflection, but really so visitors could take selfies and post themselves in the coolest concept store of the coolest brand. The store itself was a work of art too, with an experiential room designed after death: a James Turrell Dark Space and Doug Wheeler Synthetic Desert soundscape partnership, a once-in-a-lifetime collaboration spun into reality by their friendships—patronships—with Urnie. Groups limited to four were allowed to experience Dark Space x Synthetic Desert: a lightless, soundless room to emulate a void, a vacuum, a death. Vicky had seen endless write-ups about the room on everything from fine arts media outlets to tourism must-do lists, while social media bragged about the epitomes experienced—like ayahuasca but better, claimed the video reviews, though she had sat alone in the room before it was open to the public, granted special access as an Onwards employee, and had merely thought repetitively, *What exactly am I supposed to be feeling right now?* She had been utterly bored. She had felt nothing special. But maybe that was death in the end: nothing.

"Take my picture," insists a woman near the end of the line. She flips her hair over her shoulder and hikes up her shoulder bag to make it visible for the photo. Her boyfriend crouches, tilting the phone up for a more flattering angle.

"Looks good, babe," he says.

Vicky smiles. She's not cynical enough yet to hate people who take photos of everything for screen consumption. She gets it, even if she shuns it: the desire to be seen, to be known, to show off. How else is one to be reminded of their existence?

She bypasses the line. Waves to the security guard. Holds up her key card to buzz into the smaller side door next to the main entrance. Enters the elevator and presses P for penthouse. Zooms upward, away from the store, away from the death room, away from the office floors. She closes her eyes. Braces herself.

The elevator dings.

She exhales. Opens her eyes.

Forces herself to step out.

The party assaults her: red lusters from heat lamps hung from the veranda, jagged electronic dance music, the horrific sight of her boss dancing in a banana costume, one hand clutching a PBR, the other gripping the hand of a woman Vicky recognizes from HR dressed as a cowgirl—the company party is the day before Halloween. Death Day. Vicky refuses to dress as a character. Her happy attendance is enough costumery.

Her phone buzzes. Jen.

> hows the party are u surviving
>
> i still have ur extra key card. do u want me to crash lol
>
> ill show up in roller gear!

She texts back: i can survive a night without you

Jen: idk if u can:/ HAVE FUN THO

"There you are." Lani sidles up next to her. Vicky turns her phone screen off. "Thought you'd never arrive. Anthony and I are *so* bored."

Vicky had met the two other newly hired creatives on her first day at the office: Anthony, a much-older, graying alumni of her university, tired of the hustle, who had transitioned out of hectic agency life for what he'd hoped would be a better work-life balance in-house; and Lani, a goth slicked in all black who had confided to

Vicky her real name was Ana, but that she wanted to go by Lani, inspired by the famous-but-dead-at-twenty-seven melancholic lo-fi artist named Lani Screeches from her parents' home country of Argentina, whose posters she had hung on every inch of her bedroom growing up, dreaming of her twenty-seventh birthday eve so she could join Jimi, Janis, and Lani in the 27 Club. Lani was now twenty-eight and no longer wanted to kill herself, but she had never relinquished her interest in death—hence her job at Onwards. They liked each other, not only because they were the sole non-white creatives, but also because of their respective answers during the creative team meeting icebreaker question of *How would you like to die?* It had been meant as a joke, but the three of them had taken it seriously: Lani the goth wanted to die by choking on her own blood, without elaboration on how the blood fountain gushing out her throat might occur; Anthony, the cynical salaryman, wanted to die drowning in a pool of hard cash after reaping the benefits of an early retirement and financial independence; Vicky, answering snarkily, stated she could not die because she was already dead inside. Her coworkers had shifted nervously in their seats, but Anthony and Lani had giggled, and Vicky marked them as her workplace allies. They promised to be friends—work friends—who would alert one another of raises and gossip, but after they scattered to work on their respective campaigns from home, their communications whittled down to volleyed messages in their group chat during company-wide monthly meetings when Urnie presented Onwards's latest wins and business plans:

> Did Urnie get a haircut?

> I'm gonna fall asleep.

> If revenue went up by 8% then we better fucking get a raise.

Vicky hugs Lani. "Damn. You look good. Maybe I should've dressed normally," she says, scanning Lani's outfit of leather pants with silver chains hung from belt loops, black T-shirt, and mesh elbow-length gloves.

Lani laughs. "What is this boring office dress you're wearing? You look like a nun, and not the sexy kind."

"I wanted to play it safe!"

"Just say it's a Halloween costume. You're a CEO. Or a funeral-goer, to stay on theme."

"Fuck the theme," interjects Anthony, joining the conversation dressed like a normal dude in loose jeans, a gray T-shirt, and Nike Dunks with a New York Knicks hat slung low over his forehead. He clinks his beer bottle against Lani's flute of bubbly gold liquid and turns to Vicky. "Happy Halloween. Long time no see. Congrats on the campaign."

Vicky's queer outreach had been a wild success, every artist excited to be granted such a lucrative opportunity, sending over pretty designs, sketches, and illustrations perfectly fitting the urn specifications she had provided, and when produced into reality they looked even better: the bisexual urn with purple-, blue-, and pink-painted handprints ornamenting the surface; the yellow nonbinary urn crisscrossed with white and black leather harness O-ring straps; the transgender urn with polymer 3D-printed clouds and a blue, pink, and white rainbow pasted onto its body. The campaign had been boosted by the deployment of Onwards-sponsored drag queens and deathfluencers alike, taking selfies with the urns matching their queer identity; fans in the comments endlessly raving about how hot their idols looked and how they couldn't wait to get their own.

"Yeah! Congrats! The urns were so pretty," Lani adds.

"Very rainbow." Anthony snickers and swigs his beer.

Vicky shrugs, parries. "Loved the Black History urns. Weren't they a hit?"

"Yeah. A bit too much of a hit, if you ask me." Anthony rolls his eyes.

"You should be happy they did so well." Lani elbows him.

Vicky grins. "Yeah. It was your idea. You only have yourself to blame."

Like with Pride, the Onwards strategy team had argued that Black History should not be constrained to one month—moreover February, the shortest month. Anthony had been tasked with a campaign celebrating Black History *Year*, Black History *Life*, rather than a Black History Month, and his idea had been to create a limited-edition line of urns printed with the last words of famous Black leaders, activists, and artists, such as James Brown's "I'm going away tonight." Black History Life had, alongside Vicky's queer campaign success, driven Onwards's profits upward.

"You should've heard Dan's stupid comments during the first round of ideation. Shit like"—Anthony raises his tone and emphasizes his consonants—"*'Black Lives Matter'? Well, we don't want to alienate our customer base. These urns are for everybody. All people. Why don't we say 'All Lives Matter'?*"

"They're a parody, I swear," says Vicky as Lani shakes her head.

"Wish we could quit," moans Lani.

"Can't," Anthony says. "Need money."

"Till death do us part," Vicky says, and the other two laugh.

Lani flashes her phone screen. "I'm on the warpath. Swiping

through the finance dudes. My ideal man: making a ton of money, too busy to bother me. Trust fund. Tall. Just give me two more months. I'll get the ring and the lifetime financial safety net along with it." Lani cocks her hips. "Who could resist me?"

The three huddle in the corner, discussing Lani's dating stories and Anthony's scathing comments about their coworkers' costumes. A half hour ticks by without Vicky checking the clock. She's distracted from time by warm conversation and good people.

Vicky is giggling at Lani's recent dating anecdote about a fintech entrepreneur who had dove in for a gaping open-mouthed kiss after dinner, only to miss and lick Lani's cheek, when she catches Dan's eye. She immediately pulls her dress down and looks away, looks back—he's waving at her. She swallows her annoyance and waves hello because she doesn't have a choice.

Oh no.

He's heading her way.

The tip of his banana costume bobs with each step.

"And that's my cue," Anthony says, melting into the crowd.

"Good luck," says Lani, stomping away in her black boots toward the bar.

"Vicky!" Dan says, arms open for a hug. Vicky grimaces, steps in, brushes her body against the banana fabric, steps back immediately. She doesn't understand why Onwards's workplace parties call for hugs between boss and worker, but again, she does not have a choice.

"So—what are you?" Dan scans her. "Is this a costume?"

"Oh, I'm, uh, Death's secretary," she fibs quickly.

"Nice!"

Vicky congratulates her brain for the creative answer. She's smarter in quick thinking—given too much time, her brain sinks, dragged down into spluttering anxiety by the many possibilities of response.

"Are you having fun? Aren't these decorations amazing?" Dan waves his arms. "Urnie always goes all out." His voice drops in volume to impart a secret, and Vicky leans in grudgingly. "He's amazing—he never cares about building management rules. Or any rules! He's a rule-breaker! The best in disruption. Wait until you see what he planned for the party. It's gonna be the *bomb*." He winks. Vicky cringes.

"What is it?" Vicky asks, trying to feign interest. While true this is the first year the company party has been held at the office rather than at a swanky hotel venue, she couldn't care less about the party specifics. She cares more about when she can leave.

"You'll see! It's even better than last year's," Dan says, then winks again, forcing Vicky to school her features from reactive disgust to what she hopes is eager anticipation. "Just make sure you stay," Dan adds. "Lots of surprises you shouldn't—can't—miss."

Vicky tries to hurl an excuse of why she needs to go home soon. Cat dying, sister sick, stove left on, anything, but before she can speak—

The dance track stops.

The workers hush.

The lamps flicker. Shut off.

A red beam bursts alive. Shines its power at the elevator for the star of the night:

Urnie.

Raucous applause as he struts into the space, his long, shapeless cloak dragging behind him. He is dressed in a costume of Death, hiding his muscular body, and Vicky experiences an urge to stomp on the trailing fabric to reveal . . . what? A corpse, a skeleton, a black hole? What did Death look like underneath his cloak? But Urnie is not gathering up souls or carrying a scythe. Urnie smiles and waves elbow, elbow, wrist, wrist like royalty among his applauding subjects.

Urnie stops.

The center follows him.

A grin plays around his mouth. It opens, voice booming:

"As a kid, I'd summer on my grandparents' estate in Oregon. I'd run around meadows, get lost among the trees, splash through streams with my grandfather. Smell flowers and bake bread. Listen to birds with my grandmother. While my parents worked. Busy flying around the world. Acting in blockbusters, accepting industry awards, doing press interviews. They were busy being famous. They were good at being famous. You know them, and because of them, you know me." Urnie inclines his head, the crowd giggles. Addressing, rather than denying, his nepotism: endearing.

"I grew up and decided I wanted to be famous too. I stopped summering at my grandparents' because I had to do what my parents were doing. Memorizing scripts, networking, bowing to publicists' whims. Instead of spending three months with my grandparents, I began to see them three times a year. I knew they were old, but I did not know they would deh—" Urnie stutters, his flow broken by grief.

He takes a breath.

"—die."

His shoulders tighten underneath his cloak.

"I grew up and stopped visiting my grandparents. I was busy. I believed I had to focus on my blossoming Hollywood career. I was in love." Urnie exhales. "Yes. Love." He shakes his head as if disappointed in himself for ever believing love could fight when love would lose. Death's tsunami bore destruction despite love's seawalls and high points.

"I met the love of my life. And then he died. The day he died was the same day my grandparents died. The same day my parents died. And it was the first day I had seen any of them in months. I was busy. He was busy. My parents were busy. My grandparents were retired, but they were famous, so they were, of course, busy. Until they weren't. Until my parents weren't. Until he—" Urnie chokes.

He bows his head, goes quiet.

The workers know this cue. They bow their heads too.

A moment of silence.

Vicky follows the motion but cannot turn off the thoughts in her head. She thinks of how she has never heard Urnie say his lover's name since the day of his departure from earth. What kind of love insists the beholder keep it close to the chest? Wouldn't it be better to share? Is Urnie unable to say his lover's name out of pain or out of performance? She's never been in love the way Urnie seems to have been in love. She cannot fathom treading above that depth of feeling, of holding a dead lover's name inside, unspoken.

Urnie clears his throat.

"If I had known of death, I would not have chosen busy. If I had known of death, I would have respected time."

Urnie slowly rotates, locking eyes with each and every employee around the room.

"Time. It's why we're here today. To raise awareness about death, which is to raise awareness about time. And to be aware of time is to be aware of how to spend that precious time. So, thank you, my friends. Thank you for gifting me, and us, your valuable time."

Urnie raises the champagne flute that has suddenly appeared in his hand, placed there by an employee rendered invisible by the blinding force of Urnie's presence.

"Six years ago, my family went Onwards. I stayed put on this plane of existence to build Onwards in memory of them, and in honor of you. Together, in this life—we go Onwards."

The workers follow their boss's lead, raising their glasses too. Vicky spies Anthony from across the circle, halfheartedly lifting his empty beer bottle with a cocked, skeptical eyebrow.

"May our time go on and on. And Onwards."

"Onwards," murmurs the crowd. Vicky stays silent. Sees Dean beginning to clap, then falter after Dan glares at him to be quiet. Urnie is not done. He will never be done.

Urnie: "I want to take the time today at this party to recognize one person, one creative, who built a beautiful campaign for people like me."

Silence. Bated breath. Urnie smiles.

"Vicky. Our very own Onwards copywriter who ideated Rainbow Bridge. Where are you?"

The light swings around the circle, searching.

Vicky dissociates.

She's seized with the impulse to run into the elevator, bash the lobby button, and sprint past the line of Onwards selfie-taking fans, down Canal Street, down Doyers, up the stairs back into her apartment. Strip her body of the ill-fitting work-appropriate dress. Jump into bed. Throw the covers around herself. Pick up her phone. Text Jen to come over. Text Angela that she misses her. Send an email to Dan, Dean, Derek, and Urnie:

*Hello, find my resignation letter attached.* A document with four words reading: *I quit. Sincerely, Vicky.* No lies like *I loved working here, but I can't turn down my next opportunity,* or *Please keep in touch, I am truly so sad to leave,* or *It's not a goodbye, it's a see you later. This industry is small, so who knows, maybe I'll see you again.* Nothing but: *I sincerely quit.* How satisfying would that be? To not offer a chance of reconciliation or pave any avenue of rehiring possibility—just burn, burn, burn all the bridges. But she leaves neither the company party nor the company itself, because she is still an active participant in the economy and needs something other than her friends and her lovers and her void to fill the time and earn the money she never seems to have enough of. So she stays still. Exits her mind and body and goes numb to survive.

The spotlight finds her, drenching her in blinding red.

Urnie enters her ring of light. He offers a hand. Vicky stares at the nearing palm, panicking—what could he possibly want, and what could she, a mere mortal, a mere employee, give him? She has no riches or resources to offer that he does not already have.

He wiggles his fingers.

Vicky snaps back to semifunctional.

He wants a handshake.

She takes it. His fingers are thin. His skin, papery. For such a heavy presence, there is nothing substantial about him. Vicky's armpit glides as they pump hands; she notes her self-disgust—she'll have to wash Jen's dress before returning it.

Urnie rotates, still holding her hand. Raises it like he's the referee and she's the winner of a wrestling match. The room erupts for her hard-fought victory, the cheers deafening, and suddenly, adding to the racket, comes explosions of searing light, hot bursts, loud cracks—fire?

Panicked, Vicky jerks backward, but Urnie's grip is tight. She shuts her eyes in fear. She can't escape the inferno. The sweat she's producing bursts out in even greater gallons. Flame is not how she wants to die. She realizes she does not want to die, not yet, not now, and not at work—if she must, let her die in Angela's or Jen's arms. Through the flame crackles, she hears her coworkers stampeding, their footsteps drumming, but why are the beats staying within proximity, why are the partygoers not fleeing?

Somehow, then, the air cools—has the fire department arrived already?

Vicky opens her eyes. She sees the last firework sparks splutter out.

The building had not caught fire—rather, Urnie had somehow released rainbow fireworks to celebrate the queer urn success. Through the hazy smoke she spies Dan across the circle nodding with a wide grin, believing Vicky to have closed her eyes in ecstasy, to savor the colorful display on her behalf.

Urnie drops her hand and Vicky's arm flops back to her side. He claps her on the back, a visible, camaraderie-like show of *this company is a family*, but the impact is so hard that Vicky stumbles forward, out of the red spotlight and into the black, absorbed into the masses of the average employee.

She trips toward Anthony and Lani.

Anthony raises a hand to high-five, ready to congratulate, but changes expression when he sees her face. "You okay?" he asks.

Vicky is shaky. Draws breath. Tries to speak but only whimpers. Musters herself again, tries a second time, then a third, only the fourth reaching coherency. "I guess that's what Dan meant by his winking when he said the party would be the bomb," she says. "I think I would have appreciated a heads-up."

"Yeah, you shouldn't have been thrown into pyrotechnics without warning," Anthony snorts. "Typical Urnie hubris. It wasn't safe. Remember those gender-reveal parties in California that set off wildfires for days? What happened to fire codes? You could've been burned. The building could've caught on fire."

"I think it's cute," Lani says. "It's not like we're on the drought-ridden West Coast, and who cares about fire codes?" She lowers her voice conspiratorially. "Dean told me Urnie ordered extra. They're all in the storage room on the fifth floor. I might steal some to take to a Halloween party later."

"Lani, that's a terrible idea," Anthony says.

"I'll just take a few!"

Vicky turns to Anthony. "Why didn't he honor you? Your campaign performed just as well."

Anthony shrugs. "Urnie's gay, not Black. People relate most to their own reflections—Rainbow Bridge probably meant more to him." Seeing Vicky frown, he slugs her upper arm in consolation. "Hey. Don't look like that. It's fine. You should be proud. Seriously."

"Yeah!" Lani says. "Congrats, Vicky!"

Vicky looks down at her feet. "I guess."

An awkward pause.

Anthony grunts. "I need a drink," he says. "Anyone else?"

Without waiting for their answer, he turns and walks to the bar. Lani follows. But instead of joining, Vicky uses the opportunity to exit. She backs away from the party, slowly, with shifting eyes to make sure nobody catches her leaving and penalizes her for an early departure. In the center of the room, she sees Dan, Dean, and Derek engrossed in a conversation with Urnie—four reflections, relating to one another.

Quickly, she pushes her spine into the fire escape bar door, then slips inside the concrete column to run down, floor after floor after floor, her legs mechanical and burning, spinning so fast she nearly trips on the last three steps of each staircase. And then she is free, blessedly free, and she gulps in the cold night air. Like in her panicked dream, she sprints down Canal, her dress hiking up and her kitten heels clicking as she hurtles across car-choked lanes, their horns blaring when they nearly run her over, but she does not care, because she needs to escape to her bed before she is lost completely.

*can love last?*

"Congrats!" Jen attacks.

Vicky staggers two steps, giddy. Returns the hug and pats her best friend's upper back. "Okay, okay. Thank you."

Kevin glances between them, confused. "Congrats about what?"

Eric follows Jen into the party. "Vicky's boss congratulated her performance last night in front of the whole company, fireworks included. It was a big deal."

"What does that mean?" Angela asks, wide-eyed. "Why didn't you tell me? Are you getting a promotion?"

"Um, no, not really," says Vicky, relinquishing Jen to brush down the black sequins on her jacket. "Maybe eventually. Not sure."

"A raise?"

Vicky shrugs.

"We'll have to go out to celebrate. In a few weekends?" Jen asks.

Vicky nods, confirms.

Jen turns to Angela. "Wanna join?"

Angela beams. "Of course."

Both women then turn to Vicky, whose insides begin to sing because she loves them both. Not in the way that love is written about in movies and in fairy tales, but in the way that love is a warm feeling spreading through her body when she looks at them. When she dances with them. When she hooks arms and elbows with them while walking around the city. The kind of love that she's capable of. Love that is care, tenderness, warmth, and hope—hope that no matter the bleakness of the future, that she'd be there suffering with them. She had told Angela this, at their last date two weeks ago, after they had fucked sweaty and Kevin was in the kitchen retrieving glasses of water and Angela was rummaging through their closet for a sweater Vicky could borrow before she left for her own apartment—Vicky hates sleeping over places. She always leaves, but she swears it's not because she's an asshole. She's a tosser and a turner, and she needs to be alone to get any rest. Maybe she's just too prickly. Maybe she's just too okay being alone. Nevertheless she opened her mouth to confess, *I love you both*, paused, and then: *But let me caveat, let me explain what love means to me*, she said frantically, before Angela and Kevin could panic about her feelings, yet Angela merely replied with: *I love you too. Don't worry. I understand.*

*I understand you.*

"How'd we do?" Eric raises his arms and spins slowly, showing off his outfit. After a complete revolve, he flourishes his limbs toward Jen and Vicky, who mirror his action.

Like every Halloween since their college days, the three of them have decided on a theme, with Jen and Eric in coordinating partner costumes and Vicky falling under the umbrella. They have always made an effort for Vicky to feel included without their being overt. She is the third wheel without feeling like the third wheel. She knows and is grateful.

This year they have chosen Leslie Cheung—iconic, queer, devastating. Vicky re-created her favorite Leslie look: an outfit from his '97 concert series collaborating with the designer William Chang Suk-ping. Leslie in '97 and Vicky today are dressed in a shimmering black suit, a white button-down, a black lace mesh corset, and red sequined heels. She hates heels, and her toes holler in agony, but she would suffer them to cosplay as Leslie. She had found the red pair in the basement at the Abracadabra costume store in the Flatiron District, her and Jen's favorite spot to discover campy treasures.

Jen and Eric are dressed in loose, mandarin-collar white button-downs tucked into flowy pants, though the star of their outfit is the makeup: Jen with dramatic pink eyeshadow slathered up to her eyebrows and to the sides of her forehead, lips slicked in red; Eric with a face coated in paper-white paint interrupted by curvy black lines reminiscent of cellos. Separate, Jen could have been the Leslie playing Chan Chen-Pang, the opium-smoking son of a wealthy family who longed to be an opera actor, in Stanley

Kwan's *Rouge*. But Jen is not the doomed Leslie in *Rouge* but the doomed Leslie in Chen Kaige's *Farewell My Concubine*, dressed as Dieyi, with Eric as his doomed, but less doomed, partner Xiaolou, played by Zhang Fengyi. Eric and Jen are embodying the dressing room scene in which Leslie paints on Fengyi's half-done makeup, the intimacy found not in the action but in their shared liminality, the in-between of actor and character, witnessed only by the other. No reality of audience, wife, or war.

*Farewell* is their favorite film, yet one neither Vicky nor Jen can rewatch. The heartache—they love Leslie too much. Can never relive a story in which he dies at the end: no *Farewell*, no Wong Kar-Wai's *Days of Being Wild*, no jump off the twenty-fourth floor of Hong Kong's Mandarin Oriental hotel. Instead she pretends Leslie is acting and thriving like his costar Tony Leung; living and loving with his partner, Daffy, who still posts a picture of Leslie every year on his birthday.

"You guys look hot," Angela says. She's dressed in her typical witch outfit, repeated every year, partly because she is too tired for effort and partly in homage to how she and Kevin had met at that fateful first Halloween.

"I love your black lipstick," Jen says.

"I'm sure it'll rub off onto my teeth by the end of the night," Angela says.

"I could have dressed like Leslie too—don't I look like him from that boring Wong Kar-Wai wuxia movie?" Kevin piles his hair, which has only grown since their first date at Green-Wood, into a bun at the top of his head.

"Not even half as hot," Angela says. "And it wasn't boring."

Kevin lets down his hair, pouts. "If you were nice, I would've let you be my long-lost Peach Blossom."

"Nah, I wanna be Leslie too, even if I'm not dressed like him," says Angela. "I practiced." She closes her eyes and bends slightly. Shakes her hips and juggles her hands. Spins, witch hat flopping. She claps, doing the famous mambo the way Leslie does in *Days of Being Wild* when he puts on a Xavier Cugat record and admires himself in the mirror wearing his white undershirt and boxers. Vicky watches Angela as Leslie and thinks of Leslie as Yuddy the playboy, who loses his mother, and then loses his adoptive mother, and then loses his lovers too. Loss after loss after loss. Leslie as Yuddy claiming he is the bird who must fly and fly but cannot land until death. Leslie as Yuddy searching for love and trying to get happy for ninety-four minutes. Leslie as Yuddy who says, while shrugging nonchalant and disbelieving, *You think I've been happy? We'll be unhappy together.*

Watching Angela, Vicky feels a sadness that is not fully sad. A happiness that is not fully happy. It is a feeling that is merely hers: neither light nor heavy; teary, but not weepy. A sensation on her chest, winged, with pretty markings and hollow bones. The body of a bird landing on her heart, flying to stronger branches before she can note its shape, size, and sound. The bird will not stay. The sensation will not stay. And the tears will not stay, collecting behind her eyes for a brief second only to disappear when Angela stops swaying and fist pumps instead, an anachronistic move that jolts Vicky back to a New York City Halloween party beating with bubblegum pop, away from a blue-tinted bedroom in 1960s Hong Kong. Kevin and Jen and Eric applaud Angela's dance as she bows, but Vicky stands still. Does not move. She is trying to grasp the sensation, now gone. What was it—sorrow? Nostalgia? Love? Where did it fly from, where has it gone? Nothing lasts, neither grief nor joy, intense because of their temporality, carried away by the winds of time, leaving nothing in their place.

"Shall we dance?" Angela asks.

Vicky looks at her. In the eyes, behind the eyeliner, behind the party fervor. Vicky wonders if this is how Urnie felt when he choked up during his speech at the party. When he could not bear to say his lover's name, moving on to the next sentence like every person in pain must do. Learn to move on despite the ongoing apocalypse. Move Onwards.

Had Urnie choked because the bird had landed on his throat? Was it the same bird she had just felt?

Vicky grips Angela's hand. Pulls her through the hallway. To move, to forget, to fly.

Vicky pushes through the teeming mass of revelers, wondering how Kevin and Angela will explain this party to their landlord or neighbors, though she supposes with the price of their rent, the walls are thick, residents allowed to do whatever they want. She doesn't know anyone else except the hosts and her own guests, all of whom she's lost track of in the gyrating throng. She searches for Jen, Angela. Cringes at the sweaty backs she presses against. The music thuds against her skull. Though she knows this is a celebratory holiday anniversary for two people she deeply cares for, she's miserable, wishing the night was enjoyed by the five of them and no one else. The five of them in their weird little friend-love-romantic-love-multi-love huddle, enjoying steamed fish and gai lan, dining by thrifted candlestick light, cuddling on the couch in a heap as a Leslie Cheung movie plays.

She bumps into a damp T-shirt and ricochets off in disgust like a trapped pinball, backtracking into Kevin, who's bouncing to the thudding techno with the friend from his school whom she had been introduced to an hour ago, whose name she recalls being surprised by—some shade of beige? Tan? Fitting for an art school graduate.

"There you are!" Vicky says.

Tan waves. She ignores him.

"What?" Kevin yells.

She gets to the point: "Where's Angela?"

"What?"

"*Where's Angela?*"

Kevin points upward, jabbing the air repeatedly in rhythm with his bobbing head.

"The roof?"

Kevin furrows his brow, cups his ear.

Vicky shakes her head. *Thanks*, she mouths. Nods in acknowledgment to Tan after achieving her objective.

She elbows through the mass toward the apartment entrance. Exits in relief as the hallway sucks out the clamor. Rests against the wall for two, three breaths before mustering the strength to climb the staircase. Parties of this sort exhaust her more than revive.

She climbs four floors, then finds a door propped open by a ragged combat boot—half of an old pair of Angela's.

And then Vicky is outside.

"There you are," she says.

"I needed some space." Angela squats on her haunches, smoking a cigarette whose tip glows orange in the darkness. Empty bottles of beer scatter around her, one half-empty and resting upright next to her calf.

"Want company?"

"When it's yours."

Before Vicky joins her lover, she detours to the edge. She loves being up high. It is late, in the single digits of a morning still considered night, and below, the streets are empty but for a few silhouettes. She has always found the designation of New York City as "the city that never sleeps" to be rather silly, as any dweller who has ever ventured out past respectability knows: that the eyes on the street must close to rest. The silhouettes are solo or in pairs, perhaps stumbling home from a bar or an apartment party like the one she's at now. She wonders how the silhouettes would react if she were to fall off the roof and splatter her guts over the concrete. She'd dreamed about it happening before, to Jen and to herself. She'd break her skull, spill her brain juice. Would they dial 911, or would they step over her bloodstains like how every New Yorker minds their own business? If she plummets from this rooftop, would she hear Angela's screams? Or would she hear Angela's congratulations? Nice to think death could be so easy. Death merely a step away, an obligation to gravity.

"Come back from there," Angela says. "You're making me nervous."

"Sorry," Vicky says to the sidewalk. *Not tonight.*

She turns and plops down next to Angela, ignoring the gravel, dirt, and other strange phenomena collecting on rooftops. Angela shakes out a cigarette from her pack and hands it to Vicky, who sticks it into her mouth.

Angela bends forward to light hers with her own cigarette, but Vicky shakes her head and brings out Jen's Hello Kitty lighter from her pocket, flaring and taking a drag. With the other hand, she removes the cigarette from her lips, carrying it between her fingers so she can talk.

"I like your lighter," Angela says.

"It's Jen's. She gave it to me tonight to carry—she didn't wanna be tempted. Said she smoked too much last night already."

"It's cute."

They exhale clouds. Face the city together. Mirror their poses as lovers do.

Vicky experiences what she suspects others would define as bliss.

She decides, for this specific moment, to be happy to be alive.

"So, was it a promotion or not?" Angela asks. "It wasn't clear."

"Not a promotion. Just a congratulations that might lead to a promotion."

"Do you want a promotion?"

"Of course I want a promotion, because usually it comes with a raise."

"If you want it, then why don't you just ask for it?"

Vicky sighs, finding the conversation exhausting. How can she explain the difficulty in asking for what she is worth? How her boss's answer, even if she musters up the courage to ask, would likely be instructions to wait for the next promotion cycle? Could someone like Angela, brilliant Angela, understand self-defeat?

"Sorry. You just—you just work so much. I barely get to see you as much as I'd like."

Vicky giggles. "Don't you have Kevin?"

Angela shrugs. "You're not Kevin."

Vicky leans over and kisses Angela on the cheek. "Listen, if I could quit and get paid by fucking around with you, I would."

"Instead, you get paid to make urns for queers." Vicky had texted Angela the press release link with a rainbow emoji and an emoji sticking its tongue out. Angela had replied with a laughing emoji.

"It's my job," Vicky says, defenses raised.

"Yeah, but you have to admit the whole company is kinda absurd. I mean, you're basically telling people that it's cool to die. And everyone just goes along with it."

"Death is scary. We're just making it easier to accept."

"Yeah, but—"

"I'm sorry it's not making a better world like yours is," Vicky interrupts, angrily.

Angela scoffs. "Don't tell me you believe that shit. My job is just a job. I'm just one cog in the wheel."

"So am I. I'm just a passenger."

"And how's the driver doing? Probably lost, consulting the map, asking for directions, scratching their head, because their destination doesn't exist."

"Wow. Cynical," Vicky says, surprised. She hadn't realized Angela didn't fully prescribe to hope.

"Nah. Just realistic." Abashed, Angela corrects herself. "Sorry. I mean, you're right. My job is good work. It's needed work. And I'm not working half as hard as the people I'm working in service of. I'm just tired of driving around, talking to people, being ignored—but you're right. I shouldn't be so bitter. I believe in the work. I believe in the people. I do. I'm just . . . tired."

"Yeah. Same."

Angela grins. "I'm stressed, I'm depressed, but I swear, the war between capital and labor is worth fighting." Angela nudges her. "Which side will you be on?"

Vicky snorts at Angela speaking like a poorly written propaganda poster. "The working one," Vicky says.

"The winning one?"

"Whichever side you're on will be the winning one. That's just the type of person you are."

Angela discards her cigarette butt and pokes Vicky in the upper arm, laughing. "Thanks."

"I'm serious."

"You guys at Onwards should unionize. Everyone should unionize. I can help! Doesn't have to be complicated. Simple asks like a salary floor—you might've been making more money sooner," she coaxes.

Vicky squirms under the pressure, pebbles carving craters into her butt. She doesn't want to say no to Angela. Because she loves Angela. And neither does she want to expose the limits of her own uncaring. Because sure, she could scroll past injustice, discuss injustice, *see* injustice, but no, she could not actively fight against it, because—"Angela, I'm just trying to get out of bed every day. I can't risk getting fired." True, yet, she knows, not enough. Depression is a mere excuse. A common affliction. Not a reason. So she continues. Tries to explain: "It's not like I was always 'successful.'" Vicky raises her fingers and makes air quotes around "successful," because success is temporary, success is hazardous, success could be yanked out from under her to expose the bottomless pit she'd tumble down if she dared to stick out, organize, speak up against management. She knows success hinges upon the ever-degrading sprinkle of luck, no matter how hard she works, and oh, how hard has she worked: "I *worked* for this!" She's bitter now. She's an alum of an East Coast liberal arts college, she lives in New York City—she's been stuck in too many conversations at parties filled with people whose heads were too stuffed with dreams of proletariat revolution to remember that their parents had paid their full-price tuition while she accumulated student loans. She's earned her material comfort of living alone with her zhizha, hasn't she? Not like them. Not like Angela—"Not that you would know," Vicky adds nastily. She immediately regrets it. "Sorry."

Angela laughs. "No. It's fine. I get it." Angela pauses. "Before I met Kevin, I lived with three other roommates in a literal closet. I know it's not the worst thing that could happen to someone new to the city, but it wasn't very good for my mental health. I don't think I would've stayed in New York if it wasn't for Kevin. Can't afford it. So, I get why you're angry—Kevin understands the anger too."

"I'm not trying to blame him."

"I don't blame him. I love him. He loves me. He works hard at his art. You know he does. And he's good at it too. His situation is not his fault, the same way mine is not my fault, the same way yours isn't your fault either. He's doing his best, just like me, and just like you. All I'm saying is . . . it could be easier. It doesn't have to be like this. It didn't have to be like *that*!"

This, that—harder than they seem. Waking then sleeping then waking again, wondering all the while about the meaning in between. "That's so cheesy."

"It's true!"

"No. I think it's unfair. It's unfair that the burden of change falls onto me and you."

Angela opens her mouth to retort, and Vicky can predict her response, something about how it's not a burden, it's a battle—Vicky cannot stand to hear any more, needs to eject herself from this topic.

"What could be better than this, right now?" Vicky waves her hands toward the city lights. The night sky. The littered cigarette butts, each a discarded conversation. "What else could I possibly need? I don't want to change a thing. I'm sitting on a roof in my favorite city with my lover while my best friend dances below. I'm having a great time. I *was* having a great time. Until—" Vicky chokes, not daring to fully shove the blame onto Angela, because though she's angry at Angela's superiority, she's even angrier at herself. Angry at the cheap meals of rice and beans, the windowless room that was really a converted closet in an apartment shared with four others, the extra mile walking instead of paying for another subway ride, how all those inconveniences when she was just starting out in the city were just that—inconveniences. Minor. No big deal, because it could have been worse, it could always have been worse. Unhoused, uninsured, at risk of deportation—at least she had had a stovetop to cook those rice and beans. Vicky hated her own bitterness more than she hated those who made her bitter. Why was she so ungrateful to be bitter at all?

"Vicky, I'm not trying to make you feel bad. All I'm saying is that you deserve better! Graeber once said—"

"I don't care about what any of them said. You think knowing whatever Graeber said about mutual trust being the true meaning of communism, whatever Marx said about capital dripping from every pore, makes it easier when you lose your livelihood?"

Angela is silent. Vicky wants to gloat about how, yeah, she read the books too in college for her elective classes, though they had the opposite effect—the books had only taught her it was better to dedicate herself to herself rather than to a cause or some dead man's ideas. Because the cause could fail, and the cause could turn on you, and the dead man was likely a terrible father and a terrible husband, so why should she listen to him? Angela is still wordless, and Vicky thinks about how she could brag that the opponent's silence is its own form of victory, but then Vicky shuts her mouth, cutting herself off. She sticks another cigarette in her lips for something to do but can't bring herself to light it. To lift her arm and click on the flame of the Hello Kitty lighter Jen had lent her for the night requires energy that she can't muster. She's neither half-empty nor half-full—simply drained. Gravity seduces her again. The edge, still there. She could hurl herself off the roof. Maybe then she'd feel something. Her body twitches, understanding what she craves. Her calves tense. Feet flex. Only Angela interrupts the impulsive urge to hurt herself. Angela speaks: "Vicky, I'm sorry. Let's talk about something else."

Vicky shakes her head. She is tired of talking. She throws her cigarette onto the ground, unlit, unsmoked. Useless trash, like herself. Wobbles upright, brushes the pebbles and dirt off the seat of her pants. "I'm gonna go downstairs."

"Okay. I'll see you inside—"

"No, no. It's late. I should head out. From the party," she adds, for clarification, so Angela knows she's leaving more than just the roof.

"Oh. Wait. Already?"

Vicky knows that in this moment, she could apologize. Make a joke. Wave the disagreement away like it had been nothing, because it really had been nothing, and then they could continue the same as before: as lovers, comrades, and confidantes. But what if she hurt Angela further by trying to explain why she'd been upset? And what if she hurt Angela again in the future, when the same topics come up in conversation, as they surely would? It would be safer to end it now. Before more fights and further hurt could come. So, her options: communicate or stonewall. Vicky chooses what she always chooses. The latter, which is the easier way. To deflect. Avoid. Self-sabotage.

"Bye," Vicky says.

She turns away without a kiss. Without a touch. Without meeting Angela's pleading eyes.

She limps away on her perilous heels.

"Text me when you're—" Angela calls out, but the door slams behind Vicky, sealing off the "home."

# *the void*

If she knew why it happened then she could stop it from happening. Decipher the root of the problem so she could dig out the ugly. But if she could figure out why it happened and how to stop it, she'd be heralded as a medical marvel. She could become a lifestyle coach who instructs sad, anxious women how to meditate for twenty minutes every morning with a side of lemon water, no caffeine; how to boot the ass off the couch across the marathon finish line; how to win friends and influence people. But she is merely a depressed person. Sometimes the plot is that there is no plot. Sometimes the reason is that there is no reason. No devastating life event like a death, but simply a matter of faulty brain chemistry and a fight with a lover. Darkness festers inside her, rotten and putrid. Was her depression why she felt nothing when she stepped inside the Onwards Dark Space x Synthetic Desert? She already embodied a nothing, her bleeding heart dyed not a light rose but a near-black maroon.

She lies on her side. Stares at the wall with corpse eyes. Her limbs, so heavy. No need for a phone or book, her brain passive in its separate reality. Acting dead is never as satisfying as being dead. After a minute, or an hour, or an unmeasurable chunk of meaningless existence, she hauls herself upright, wobbly, and walks to the fridge. Opens the door, yellow light glowing on her unwashed face. Stares at the carton of eggs and the gallon of milk and the slimy, spoiled spinach leaves she purchased when she had greener ambitions of iron, calcium, and vitamin C. Here is sustenance. She could boil water. Drop in eggs. Watch the pot for six minutes. Ladle the hard-boiled eggs out, run them under cold water, smash and roll them against the counter to crack and peel. Pop the protein into her mouth for sustenance. Minimal effort in exchange for reasonable nutrition. Instead, she shuts the refrigerator door. Slouches to the window. Looks down at the funeral crowd with colored bands around their waists, mingling on the sidewalk, holding hands, smoking cigarettes. Around them, pedestrians, with earphones and sunglasses plugging their senses, clutching tote bags of produce and notebooks, stepping off the sidewalk to bypass the mourning. She's separated from the grievers and the street-goers—the outside world—by a glass pane as impenetrable as a concrete wall. Like she's a guppy zipping around a tiny fish tank at the doctor's office, so common and uninteresting that she's not even worth tapping the glass to agitate, the patients immersed in their phones and magazines.

She trudges across her apartment to the fridge. Returns to the sluglike spinach. Opens the door. Shuts the door. Heads back to the window while brushing her hand over a zhizha along the way—the hood of the car, the roof of the mansion. She wonders if she should pop downstairs and purchase a zhizha of a smiling face atop a fit body. An expression that would indicate a brain well-adjusted to adulthood, a countenance of someone who swallows the correct amount of antidepressants without throwing up or descending into brain fog. An aspiration for the afterlife: to be happy. But this purchase would require her to go outside, and the outside is daunting, fatiguing, unreachable.

She returns to the sofa. The sky turns dark. She closes her eyes, acting dead, and then shudders alive two hours later. She manages to drag herself to bed and lies motionless under the covers thinking about how it would be nice to fall asleep and not dream. Insomnia is not pretty, and neither are the nightmares that come when she does muster short-lived slumber: those long-since-shoved-away recurring visions of those she loves dying. In the few hours of sleep Vicky snatches she sees Jen suffocating under the sand on Coney Island after she agrees to let Vicky bury her on the beach for fun; Eric breaking his neck after slipping on a banana peel in a smoothie shop; a strange shadow in a bathtub wearing a mutated mask of Angela's face drowning from fluid buildup in her lungs, empty containers of sleeping pills discarded around the bathroom floor—and in all these visions, in the periphery, a bat-like figure in a rippling black cloak similar to the one she had seen Urnie wear floats above the bodies. Vicky suffers. Tries to return to her old comfort show, *Ten Thousand Ways to Die*, but the depictions are more gruesome and mean-spirited than she remembers, and she turns it off, queasy after watching the episode about a man who went down a makeshift Slip 'N Slide with an unseen nail poking upward, which cut open his stomach, spilling out his entrails. Her self-disgust and nausea after this disembowelment is her first acute emotion in days. Vicky turns to the recommended method of counting sheep, but the sheep she imagines bleat and bleat and bleat. She can't quiet the endless baaing in her head, so she abandons the tried and true and begins instead to tick through a list of everything she's ever lost in her life: her favorite stuffed manatee from the Natural History Museum, accidentally dropped onto the highway because she liked to stick it out the car window to ride the wind, pretending it was waves; her coziest black sweater, which she'd left draped on a chair after an all-nighter in the college library; a healthy sense of fun; a consistent relationship with her parents; a relationship with any of the good people she's ever dated; her grandparents; even the majority of the semblance of devotion she had felt for Angela—loss after loss after loss, telling herself that the never-ending pile of losses in her life, whether from death or depression or neglect of what Jen calls "relationship maintenance," should indicate that she'll be fine, she'll know how to cope, when death, real death, strikes her life. The hours of loss tick on and then night departs and light dawns and she emerges from haunted dormancy with bruised under-eyes to repeat: the fridge, the window, the sofa, the fridge, the window, the sofa. Until: her bladder.

The bathroom.

She sits and gapes at the expanse of the white wall long after the last drops of urine have trickled free. She stands when her ass numbs. Pulls up her sweats over her pressure-induced red butt cheeks. Flushes. Exits the bathroom to repeat: window, fridge, couch. No thought, mere mechanical muscle movement. Like how she knows without reading the signs which subway entrance heads uptown to Queens and downtown to Brooklyn, or which Canal Street fruit vendor has the sweetest clementines in the winter months when every citrus option looks the same.

She's slinking toward the window when her phone vibrates, screen down on the table. An arm's-length distance, short enough to pick up without effort:

A text from Dan. Her boss has her phone number because he had asked for it on her second day of work, and so she could not say no, though she'd rather be unreachable, unknowable, on mental health days off—a privilege she's earned because of Rainbow Bridge's success and an allowance because they are between creative campaign deadlines. Lucky, because it's been harder and harder as the months go by, as winter approaches, to pretend the abyss isn't yawning inside her. Her boss notices too, noting her passivity, her camera off, and her lack of energy. He calls her "room for improvement" "opportunities for initiative" instead, to avoid direct insult.

> Heads-up to enjoy the downtime for now bc Strat is preparing a brief for you. Will be next week or week after. You're leading because you're the perfect fit. Great opportunity!
> Looking forward to your initiative.

She scoffs. Swipes left and deletes the notification.

There are other alerts she must've forgotten while in her daze. It happens. She loses track.

A text from Angela last week: I'm sorry about what I said. Want to grab a drink this week?

Another text from Angela yesterday: is work busy? Can u talk?

Another, today: ?

The persistence! Wouldn't it be easier to give up? Vicky scoffs. To be ignored once did not mean to then reach out twice. Didn't Angela have any semblance of self-respect? Angela had always been clingy, relying on someone else to make her feel better. Vicky shakes her head. Angela would never learn.

Vicky has no desire to rehash the argument. Though her anger has faded, she can't motivate herself to respond. She's demolished every relationship she's ever had with her dissociation. Love into indifference. How quickly a body could spring back to its original form after molding itself around another.

She wishes to disappear from New York City. Reappear halfway across the world with a different name and a new face. No lover. No responsibilities. Just herself.

Her phone buzzes in her hand.

Her gaze wanders toward the window.

Another buzz.

She ignores.

A third buzz.

Another.

She sighs. Checks the screen, reads the new texts—not from Angela but from Jen. Always checking in. Always easy. Always never letting her go.

stop ignoring my texts

celebratory hot pot tn?

i promised at the party and we gotta celebrate u

u better be out of bed. vent to me at dinner abt the fight?

angela looked upset.

k ima come over and pick u up then lets go to flushing?
bitch i know ur at home i have ur location on my phone

plssss. i want the good hot pot in queens not the manhattan ones

Vicky sucks in a gust. Holds the air in her lungs. Could she suffocate herself if she tried?

She relinquishes. Breathes out her nose because her chest hurts.

She can show up musty and miserable and Jen would understand. Food in Flushing would fill her up, and hot pot would help her sleep tonight.

She texts back.

k. ima hop in the shower

# *friendship*

Transferring to the 7 at Grand Central. Then a ride on outdoor elevated tracks past the darling Silvercup sign with its serifs, Citi Field, and the tops of Queens shingled houses and brick apartment buildings—the joy of journey underlining delight of arrival. The last stop on this train. Chinese advertisements for casinos and city services greet Vicky and Jen as they climb out of the Flushing–Main Street station. They push their pelvises into the turnstiles and trudge up the stairs, following the current of people into the chaos of the Roosevelt Avenue and Main Street corner. Bakeries, boba shops, and tofu pudding stands accompany pop-up stalls selling knit hats, gloves, and scarves for the coming winter threat. Vicky and Jen love Flushing's disorientation upon emergence. A teen with a dangly cross earring hurries to the bus, shunting Vicky aside. Jen grabs her elbow to not lose her in the crowd. Despite the bodies in throng, the November air is chilly. Vicky wraps her black wool coat tighter around her core and tucks her chin into its collar, receding into herself. Jen hooks her arm around Vicky's and pulls her back out. They merge, joining the flow of people in search of home, work, food. Vicky's limbs lift lighter, reanimating. She feels alive again. It could be so simple to feel alive.

"Want anything before we get hot pot? Boba, egg tart?"

Vicky shakes her head. Her stomach rumbles. "After. For dessert."

They head up 39th Ave., dodging aunties dragging carts stacked with produce and ropey men hauling cardboard boxes off trucks, toward their favorite spot: the Chinese chain with outposts in New York and on the West Coast, notable for its flavorful soups, fresh ingredients, and terrifyingly impeccable service. Located on the second floor of one of the newer glass-and-metal-style buildings introduced by the overseas real estate developers beginning to infect Flushing, the restaurant is so large that they do not have to wait long for a table despite its popularity. Patrons are spread around the waiting room, scribbling on free notepads and crunching on mung bean snacks. A waiter with a perm and silver-rimmed glasses leads them to their table. He bows when they sit. Vicky had read online that the waiters at this chain underwent arduous orientation processes mirroring the absurdity of the Disney employee cult, taught to bend over in every direction to keep customers like her happy, recruited from rural areas whose only economic opportunity was to leave. To serve. What would Angela say?

"Spicy?" Jen asks.

"Of course."

Vicky and Jen tap the screen for the reddest broth, luscious with so many peppers stewing on top that it looks solid. The spice will force them onto the toilet tomorrow with regret, but the tingling of the tongue and the sharp bite of the cooked vegetables, seafood, and meat are worth the burn. Then, hot pot etiquette: They take turns to retrieve sauces. Jen stays behind to watch their things while Vicky goes first. She grabs a curved white bowl and opts for her classic mix of sesame paste, black vinegar, soy sauce, smashed garlic, and chili oil. Takes another white bowl for chopped cilantro and spring onion. She'll sprinkle in these greens with each bite. She never deviates. Why try the mushroom-flavored soy sauce, the chunks of black bean sauce, the diced chilis, or the preserved pickles, when her go-to has never gone wrong? True that the restaurant's combo recommendations line the back wall of the sauce buffet and tempt her to try something new, but whenever she arrives in front of the many ladles, she cannot help but reach for what she knows she likes. An indictment of her personality. Her inability to grow. Stagnant in her stupid choices. Yet she would take her dipping sauce into the afterlife if she could. She'd have it drizzled onto her corpse before being thrust into the crematorium flames. She'd have it as a zhizha, printed and constructed from the finest Chinatown funerary supply shop. Was this not evidence of eternal devotion?

No other sauce mixture or human being could invoke such a pledge of loyalty from her.

Vicky returns to their booth balancing the two bowls. Jen departs for her own. Vicky stares into the bubbling soup, the jumpy spices. Left alone, without distraction of company, she wills herself not to cry. The broth is salty enough without her tears dropping in. Attempting to force her mind elsewhere, to more appetizing regions, she shovels the free snacks into her mouth: roasted peanuts, marinated seaweed, boiled edamame.

Jen slides back into the booth, clutching her dipping sauce, hers much less viscous than Vicky's—Jen prefers less oil, less paste, less fat. The waiter follows, pushing a cart of their requests: meat, fish balls, potato chunks, prawns, seaweed knots, mushrooms of wood ear and shiitake.

"I am so happy," Jen declares, dropping three slices of rib eye into the broth, the pink marble shifting to brown.

"That makes one of us."

"Why don't we eat here more often?"

"Because Flushing is far away."

"Which is what makes this meal so special." Hot pot is their friendship tradition. To celebrate promotions, ridicule Vicky's exes, banish depressions.

Vicky clacks her chopsticks in response.

Jen leans forward: "Guess what I learned recently from social media. You'll love this little fact. I meant to send you the video, but decided to share it in person because I wanna see your reaction." Jen pauses, waiting for Vicky to burst in with a guess, but Vicky stays silent, unable to fake excitement. Jen hurries to fill the blankness: "Did you know that in French, the nickname for the orgasm is 'la petite mort'? Translates to 'little death.' That feeling after a good orgasm where you kinda faint and go black and leave your body. 'Cause the pleasure is unearthly. Isn't the phrase just so lyrical?"

"I've heard of it."

Jen wiggles her eyebrows. "Death shit, horny shit."

"Horny death. Yes."

"Okay. What's wrong? I'm trying my best to cheer you up, but you're not giving me anything."

Vicky shrugs.

"Everything okay with Kevin and Angela?"

Vicky doesn't answer.

"Tell me."

"Nothing's wrong."

"Something's always wrong."

Vicky chews a string of enoki.

"Tell me what happened," says Jen.

Vicky opens her mouth, closes it, opens. Shoves a turnip inside. Swallows.

Jen: "Just apologize or reach out. This time is different, I can tell. You're happy with them. With her. Just enjoy it and keep it going, okay? Let yourself be happy. You are allowed to be happy. It doesn't make you special to be sad."

Vicky stabs a fish ball with her chopstick.

"Just say sorry. Do what you did with me when we were fighting. You know how to apologize. Or invite her to that art exhibit at the Met—it's closing soon."

"Which exhibit?"

"The one about death, remember? I told you about it on your fire escape when we made up."

"Right. That one." Vicky frowns. "I'll just go alone."

"No, go with her. Or—" Jen sucks against her teeth. "Come on, Vicky. Just text her."

Vicky extracts a roll of tofu skin, now soggy. Grumbles another excuse. "I'll be busy soon, okay?"

"Bitch, with what? Aren't we all busy? You said it yourself: You make time when you can. Doesn't have to be every day."

"This project at work is gonna start soon. Dan says it'll be a great opportunity. I'll probably have to work late. Weekends too. As it goes with these sorts of projects."

Jen gasps in sarcastic horror, a stem of something green between her teeth. "Work late? We've been doing that shit our entire career. You can make it work."

"Do I want to, though?"

But Vicky knows she does. Just . . . doesn't know how. Running away is easier than staying.

Jen tilts the last of the mushroom plate into the broth. "I think you do."

Vicky fishes out a wood ear, dips it in her sauce, places it on her tongue.

Jen decides not to push Vicky. She has said what she can. She moves toward the easier choice of the two topics. "What is the campaign about?" she asks.

"I don't know yet. But he says it'll be the perfect fit for me."

"They'll promote you and give you better pay *before* they force you to helm the campaign, right?"

"After." Vicky does not inject the adverbs of uncertain promise: hopefully, probably, ideally.

"How shitty. It's like a dangling carrot, and you're the rabbit thrust into the harness of capitalism. Straps too tight, binding you, cutting into your skin as you strain for escape. Scars across your limbs—"

"Okay, okay, enough. Since when did you start talking like that? You sound like Ange—" Vicky chokes off.

Jen raises her eyebrows.

Vicky coughs, pretends a peppercorn is stuck in her throat. Pivots: "I'm just worried about the workload." She thrusts her chopsticks into the soup and seizes a piece of kabocha, only for it to crumble, mushy, plopping back into the broth. Like her. A solid whole broken into pieces, crushed by pressure. "I'm worried about fucking up. At work—and with Angela."

Jen sighs. "Vicky, you're doing fine. You just want to feel worse off than you actually are, so it justifies the sadness."

"Just because you aren't as sad doesn't mean I can't be."

Jen collects her near-empty sauce tray, frustrated. "I need more sauce." She scoots out and heads toward the buffet.

Vicky pulls out a soggy noodle from the bubbling cauldron. Dips it into her sauce. Winces when it comes with a peppercorn, cracked by her teeth, releasing a concentrated buzz. Thinks about Jen calling her out on her trying to justify her sadness. Why be so miserable? She had neither kids nor any real responsibilities; rather, she had neither direction nor destination, and could not even enjoy the ride. She knows she's pathetic, she's annoying. She should apologize to Jen. That Jen was only trying to be her friend. She sighs. Why were relationships so exhausting? She'd opted out of most for a reason.

Vicky dips her chopsticks and circles the perimeter of the broth, swirling the overcooked debris. She stares at the whirls and thanks the hot pot for reviving her into a semblance of aliveness. No, not just the hot pot—also Jen, dragging her here. Always Jen. Vicky slams her chopsticks down with more force than she intends. Pinches skin from her thigh. Picks at her nails. Runs her fingers through her hair, uncaring that her hands are slick from splashes. Hot pot is messy, its odor lingering on skin and fabric even after washing, but she considers it a mark of honor. A mark of delight. She tries to convince herself that pushing for equitable access to death ceremony, achieving a higher salary, and leaping along the traditional career path trajectory are worth it, even if she is miserable, even if its lack of meaning is scraping her insides raw. She tells herself she can do it even if she remains despondent. Bang out another script for an urn commercial, vomit out three urn launch ideas—easy, right? What other choice does she have? Quit? She can hear Angela's voice: *You could unionize.* Angela, Angela, Angela, silly Angela, who thought the answer to Vicky's melancholy could be so easy. Vicky had always thought unions were for farmworkers and construction laborers and teachers, all of whom deserved more pay, not workers like her who had offices in tall skyscrapers and expensive salads for lunch. She believed unions meant burly men in suspenders and loose trousers and pageboy caps, crowding smoky basements close to the shipyard or the factory. Bushy mustaches collecting spit from fierce arguments over the Boss, the Man. Applause and stomps as they break out in song *Les Misérables* style. *Do you hear the people sing?* And yet—Angela. Someone Vicky cannot respond to because she is exhausted, so how can she ever have the energy to start a company movement? She can hear Angela's chiding: *That's how movements fail.* Angela is hard to please, hard to measure up to. Vicky barely remembers how she felt around Angela—hadn't she loved her once? Yet she'd never had straightforward dreams about her death, only a strange shadow wearing a mask with Angela's face. There had been feeling before, though, she's sure of it, feeling that has now fled—it scared her, how her love could flip into indifference. Not a slow descent but an instant switch. How she could go to sleep one night dreaming of someone, then the next morning never need to see them again. She is heartless, unfeeling, selfish. She's heard it all from her exes and absorbed the hurled hurt. It's true. What kind of heart could pivot so quickly? A heart in despair, for despair is the victor of a one-sided war.

"Hey. You okay?"

Jen eases back into her seat holding a filled sauce bowl. Some of her mix sloshes over the rim as she settles, landing onto the table in dark spots. Vicky stares at the new stains, thinking of bruises and decay.

Jen waves her chopsticks. "Vicky. You there? You're not eating."

Vicky looks at Jen. "Yeah. Sorry. Just thinking."

"About what?"

Vicky looks into the bubbling broth. "Nothing important."

## can an artist who loves their work also love people?

**KEVIN**

Kevin never understood why people talked about romantic love as if it were the only passion worth seeking. He had grown up hearing the common laments from song lyrics, television episodes, and his sisters plucking flower petals: *What is love? When will I find love? Do they love me, do they love me not?* When the only questions he had ever asked himself were about his art. A kind of love, yes, but not the same.

It wasn't like he stayed home shut in his bedroom playing

video games, messaging on incel chat boards, and participating in No Nut Novembers. He had a multitude of options for falling in love, or, at the very least, falling into whatever semblance of human connection everyone around him seemed desperate for. He was good-looking. Smart. Rich. Kind. Caring. A good listener. Introverted, or, as the girls and guys and theys in his circle of proximity labeled him, mysterious. Sure, he had a general disregard for romantic convention, but his dates left his bed warm with an afterglow of good orgasm and good conversation, which canceled out his reputation as heartbreaker, fuckboy, serial cheater—labels that, yes, could be true, but it all depended on how you looked at the situation. At least he was honest about his drifting around, dating around, fucking around. He would have preferred to be the type of person his exes wanted him to be, with steady eyes, not wandering—it was exhausting to meet new people. But then he would not have been himself.

Besides, his libido demanded it—if he did not displace energy into sex, his concentration for his art began to slip, along with his output too. Anything negatively affecting his art had to be taken care of. Because his art was the greatest love of his life.

Was he defective? Or merely so moored in artistic love that his heart could not spare room for any other kind?

During his figurative sculpture exploration in college, he'd cradle the clay with his palms, giving it life. A rough lump transformed into something worth devotion—wasn't that essentially love? And love was never easy—the gap between his ability and the art he craved to make never closed. Whatever his hands produced was never what he imagined it to be, compelling him to try again, and again, and again. During late nights and early mornings in the university studio, lampposts twinkling outside the large windows, he'd hallucinate taking off his clothes and lying in the divot of the body molded by his own hands to thrust, ejaculate over the clay, and work his fluids into moisturization. He'd blame his depravity on his lack of sleep and overcaffeination, but hadn't all the famous artists been erotically charged by their own art? Pollock climaxing on his canvases, Picasso sketching his lovers' curves, Dalí pouring his sexual anxieties into paintings with titles like *The Great Masturbator*.

After school, his cohort moved to New York City to achieve their artistic dreams. Which meant they became baristas, white cube gallery attendants, and underpaid, overworked nonunionized artist assistants whenever they weren't drinking their asses off at apartment parties in Bushwick, basement music shows in Bed-Stuy, and warehouse raves in Ridgewood. Kevin was seldom directly invited, rarely showing up when he was. He could sense his peers resented him and his parents' money. He coped with the ostracization by reasoning that if they spent less time socializing and more time in the studio, they'd have just as much of a chance as he did.

Not that he finished many pieces. The translation from energy to reality now frustrated him more than sustained him. As if however many years he had gained in age since he first realized he wanted to become—could *only* become, as he had no other choice; it was compulsion, really—an artist, he had lost in gallons of attention span and craft ability. He had begun to tell himself corny reminders like *Love the process; trust the process*, even writing the phrases on Post-its stuck on his bathroom mirror to read every day. Until he tore them off in disgust after a particularly terrible session in the studio reverting the same canvas he'd stared at for two years back to white gesso, erasing the black lines he'd brushed all over like a wannabe Lee Bae. Square one. Wasted effort. The shadowed, textured curves he pictured in his brain refused to become real.

His mother had offered well-meaning consolation on the phone: *Just take a break. You need time and space away from the studio. Isn't it Halloween? Dress up, eat some candy, go out with your friends. Relax.*

Friends. His mother didn't know that he never really had any real ones. Either they liked him because he had money or he ruined the friendship by fucking them.

Yet his mother is right—Kevin can't face another futile night scribbling and scratching. He hadn't checked the alumni group chat in weeks, but there would be a party invite somewhere if he scrolled up. Art school alumni *loved* Halloween.

"Jackie Chan. Make me a drink?"

Kevin looks up. Performs his artist scan of the radiance addressing him. The radiance is composed of black curves—his painting? Could it be?

Black hat. Black dress. Black eyeliner.

Black lips, speaking a name not his, yet he would have tried to murder the action star he'd been mistaken for with his own fists if it meant she'd address him again—

"Um?" the lips ask. "Wait, was that offensive? Sorry—"

"Oh, uh, yes." The rum he'd been pouring sloshes out of his now-full cup, past the brim and down his wrist. "Fuck. Sorry. No. Not offensive. And, yes, I'll make you a drink."

The lips part. New curves. Different meanders. He'd like to traverse them. A laugh. Bells peal.

"No worries," she says.

*Many worries,* he thinks.

"Here," she says. Picks up a stack of orange napkins printed with cobwebs—stupid and ironic in the art school way.

She wipes the alcohol from his skin, each smear of her touch vibrating through him. His fingers are so shaky from nerves that he drops his drink onto the table, amber liquid made of mostly rum and little Coke. Terrifically embarrassing. His hands wield paintbrushes and belly rakes; they are supposed to be strong and steady like a surgeon's, yet here he can't even grip a red Solo cup.

Bells again. Blame those black lips. Curves. She's laughing. He blushes. Notes that she jumped toward him to avoid the spill rather than away.

"I am so, so sorry—" He's frantic.

"It's fine! It's fine." She grabs more napkins. Dabs. Pats. Gives up. Drops them into a ball, where they sag into a wet clump. "It's a party! Tan will clean it later. Occupational hazard of being the host."

He chuckles, gags on the third note, botches the cough. Oh. She's funny. "You know Tan?"

"*Tan*gentially."

Cheesy. He slips her a giggle.

"My friend who's a friend of his friend invited me. I don't know many people here," she says.

"You know me."

"I guess I do. How do *you* know Tan?"

"We went to school together. One of the few people I can tolerate—who can tolerate me." He's gaining back his natural confidence as the conversation winds forward.

"You're difficult to be around?"

"More like too easy. They say my company is delightful."

"Who is 'they'?"

"You."

Those black-painted curves, twisting in delight! He longs to see them again and again. And again and again. And so on, forever.

"Actually, so far, the company has been just a drunk mess." She waves her hand toward the glob.

"Stick around. I'll be better."

"Give me a reason to?"

He raises his eyebrows, impressed. "I will." Weak volley on his part.

"What did you study in school?" she asks.

"Nothing real. Went to art school, like everyone else here. That's why we're so try-hard. Artists. Wannabe, at least. But craft matters." Though he's the least dressed up among his cohort in a suit and red tie left over from his graduation ceremony. "How'd you know I was Jackie Chan?"

She lifts her hand. Catches the end of his tie. His breath stutters, neck prickles. He dares her to pull him close.

"It was a guess, but also, this red tie! Obvious sign. Where's your Chris Tucker, though?"

"Oh. Somewhere. Dancing," he lies. He doesn't want to admit that he doesn't have any friends.

"*Rush Hour* is my dad's favorite movie. We rewatch it together every holiday."

A vision: He joins her and her father on the couch to laugh at Tucker and Chan, his hand snaking unseen to hold hers. Jokes with her father over bottles of beer and bowls of peanuts. Asks her father for permission for her hand in marriage.

He frantically pulls his mind to the present.

What is he thinking? He doesn't care for peanuts. Doesn't want to crack open a cold one. Never plans to be married. One tremble of his heart and he's suddenly a mushy, gushy romantic? He has artistic dreams, goddamn it.

*Focus, Kevin.*

She drops his tie, a divot appearing between her brows. Kevin exhales.

"I like *Rush Hour*. Racism can be funny when white people aren't involved," he says.

She giggles, nods. Her hand rises again and stretches toward him, and he forgets his imagined museum acquisitions, because she is going to touch him again and this is the most important thing that will ever happen to him in his life—but her fingers land in the candy bowl filled with chocolate balls covered in bloody eyeball foil and black licorice in plastic wrap. She sorts through. Picks a piece. Twirls the stick of black licorice the way he used to spin his pencils in math class, bored out of his mind. Is he losing her?

"Do you like sweets?" he asks in panic, fumbling for a new topic like a loser who cares too much.

"Of course." She begins to strip the plastic off.

"So do I. You seem . . ." He swallows his *sweet*. The pickup line is too easy, too cringe.

"Seem what?"

"Never mind. Wait. I don't even know your name."

"No, no. I'll tell you later. What were you going to say?"

His brain spits a line even worse: "Does your black lipstick taste like black licorice?"

She scoffs.

He tries again: "Is that why you're eating it? Reapplying?"

"Do you want to find out?" she parries. The dark curves approach. Amplify. And he's . . . lost.

His cold doctrine on romance dissolves after the second date. His prior beliefs are unfamiliar—they had belonged to someone who had never been him. Because he hadn't been truly alive until he met her.

How remarkable, love.

He is endlessly curious about her. Asks questions, then asks questions about her answers because he wants to know her and because he senses she shields. She reveals she hides because she believes her sadness toxic, that she does not want to inflict it on anyone, and he chuckles and tells her he will hold her darkness for her, then expel the shadows onto his canvas.

They sit on a bench in Prospect Park sharing a bag of sweet-and-salty kettle corn they had selected together while browsing the Foodtown aisles on Vanderbilt. She asks about his art, and so he tells her about his mean opinions of others' work instead of his fears about his own because he is not ready to share. He knows she knows he is avoiding, and yet she does not pry, and he loves her for this, among other reasons. Many other reasons. And even if his opinions are more malicious than true, she neither agrees nor disagrees, but discusses. And he listens. Because he wants to know what she's thinking, always, about everything.

He loves her the way he loves art: through feeling and

desperate need. He makes art for that brief, terrible moment of feeling alive; with her, he realizes the moments are not terrible, and that they could last forever if he tried.

He can create again. The black curves burst from his mind to his sketches to his paintbrush in grand, sweeping gestures no longer derivative of Franz Kline and Lee Bae but wholly his own—or hers, because he sees in those lines her smile from that Halloween night. The wall blocking him from his practice simply needed her—love—to crumble down.

To call her his muse would be patronizing. She is not a flash of inspiration. Passion always dies. What remains is the art. The work. The love.

Still, he is loyal most to his first love, art. So he agrees to nonmonogamy because, unlike his own, her love for him is indivisible. Her love does not cut in half but multiplies. Abundance. She deserves to feel the love she can give. She had been born with the ability to love many. He is fearful, sometimes, that she will awaken to the unequal force of their emotions and leave him.

She swipes on the apps, texts back, sets the times. Informs him. Shows him the photos and the bios. Allows him to agree whether he wants to come along. His yes is less because of the attraction to the date and more about whether his art is going well.

He finds he doesn't mind nonmonogamy. He likes sex, and the erotic, and the experiences of more than one. Though he does feel occasional flares of anxiety and insecurity when Angela is with other lovers, he reminds himself that Angela's love for him will not decrease. And that it is revolutionary to share. So he returns to his self, his canvas, his clay.

He likes Angela's lovers anyway. He admits she has good taste.

Not as an ego boost because she's also into him, but because it is true. They are his preferred type of people. Aware enough to be irrevocably sad, but optimistic enough to try for happy. He's liked Vicky the most out of everyone. Partially because she likes to talk a lot and eat a lot and look at art a lot—he's pleasantly surprised by her opinions on art. But mostly because she makes Angela happy—as close to happy as Angela can get. Because Vicky is like Angela in a way that he is not. Vicky and Angela have nothing but each other. While he has his art. He'll always have his art.

"I can't decide if I'm actually medically depressed," Vicky says, staring into the trash can, foot heavy on the lid pedal.

"Happy people don't have to decide. They just are," Kevin says.

The two relax in the kitchen. Angela had dashed out saying she needed a walk since she'd been in bed all day, promising to return in twenty minutes with Canal Street cherries for dessert. Kevin had cooked maeuntang for dinner; now, Vicky cleans, emptying the bowls of leftover rice.

"You can just be . . . happy? Just like that?" Vicky lifts her foot up and the lid snaps shut.

Kevin has had this same conversation with Angela before. Futile to convince somebody of their despair. Impossible to be dragged out of the gloom—one must confront it oneself. Learn to embrace it, like Angela has, over the years. He returns to flipping through the Wangechi Mutu monograph Angela bought him as a present recently. He had been pivoting away from sculpture and into collage. "Yes," he tells Vicky absent-mindedly, turning the page and landing on a full-bleed photo of a bronze mermaid sculpture. "Depression is only one facet of who you are. It can be a good thing sometimes. Like, it probably contributes to how you and Angela get along so well." He wonders how Mutu had made the decision to pivot from paper collage to sculptures, so heavy and dense. His trajectory is the opposite. He is lighter now.

"Is that why you two work so well?"

He looks up. Vicky is frowning at him.

He shifts on his stool, considering. "No. But . . . we take care of each other, you know?"

"I feel like you're a sad person too, though."

"I am. But our sads are . . . different. I don't know how to describe it."

"Try."

Kevin pauses. "I don't think I can. But. I do think the love I need is the love Angela gives me. And vice versa. I need space to make my art, and Angela gives me space. I like to take care of people, I'm good at taking care of people, and I take care of Angela. Because she needs it. I take care of her the same way I take care of my art, and I know my art is love, so I know I love her."

"Maybe that's my problem."

"What is?"

"That I don't know what kind of love I need. Or the kind of love I can give."

Kevin snorts. "Most people don't. Most people want one kind of love and never realize they need something different, and most people want love more than they can give it."

Vicky is silent.

"Why are you bringing this up? Because of what we talked about at dinner?"

Vicky shrugs.

"It was just a silly discussion," Kevin says.

Vicky and Angela had been arguing over whether a random

nap constituted exhaustion or depression; Angela made a flippant comment on how Vicky should at least *try* therapy because Vicky is obviously sadder than she thinks. Which made Vicky drop a clump of rice into her lap, visibly annoyed. Kevin had attempted to broker the awkwardness by pointing out how a nap could be both.

Vicky stares at the closed trash can lid. Then she snaps up her head. Their eyes meet.

"Yes?" Kevin asks, disconcerted by her stare.

She shakes her head. Looks away. "Nothing. Just ... take care of her, okay?"

"So you don't think I do?" he asks, annoyed.

"I'm just making sure."

Irritated, Kevin clenches his hand into a fist over a Mutu reptile photo. Then reminds himself to relax. His fingers straighten. Vicky doesn't know, and besides, how could she understand? His reminders to Angela to take her medication even if it isn't working; his cleaning after her depressive stasis; his encouragement to eat. It hurts him when Angela is hurting, the same way it hurt him when his art languished unformed, unrealized, unmade. He takes care of Angela because that's what partners do. Not like Vicky, whose refusal to admit to her own sadness meant that she'd never be able to figure out how to show or accept love that could patch her up. He judges Vicky because she deserves it. Vicky, who disappears when things get difficult. Vicky, who hasn't yet learned that love meant you stayed.

"Go," Angela says.

"Are you sure?"

"Of course I'm sure. This is your dream." Angela waves around the acceptance letter. He'd handed it to her in wordless shock after he'd furiously ripped open the envelope. "I believe in you," she adds.

Kevin wonders if she rather meant: *Don't let me hold you back.*

The residency is prestigious, offering every artist's dream: uninterrupted time and space to make their vision come true. Extremely limited access to wi-fi; no cellular connection. A private retreat in nature. Seclusion, not isolation. The hour-long communal dinners with other artists who know to leave each other alone after dessert. The protective bubble, allowing the mind to play. To wander. To escape from the demands of normal life.

Not to attend to depressed partners.

Kevin and Angela have been . . . discussing. Insisting their strung-out, heated conversations are discussions rather than arguments in hopes that the label would soothe the antagonism. Angela has not been doing well. A mixture of factors: upcoming seasonal depression, a drawn-out strike she's co-organized with no response from management, Vicky drifting away. The typical depressive ups and downs, waxes and wanes.

"I'll be fine. Stop babying me. I can survive without you. I have before." She says the last sentence rather nastily. He understands she is tired of herself, of her reliance on him.

"Never for this long, with little contact from my end. And I'll miss you," he says. Which is true. But he would regret missing the opportunity more.

"I'll miss you too. But you can't pass it up." Because she understands she'll never forgive herself for not letting him go.

He emails the residency coordinator his confirmation. Before he leaves, he texts Vicky in disgust. Vicky, who has not replied to either of them in two weeks after she and Angela had fought on their roof.

I'm going away for a bit. Artist residency.

Can you hang with Angela?

She misses you.

He'd be back soon, he tells himself. He always comes back. No one he'd rather return to than Angela. There would be time, always more time, to care for each other. Their agreement: partners for life. As long as life lasts. And how he hopes it lasts—it is worth it, with her.

# work

Vicky's apartment is chilly. The radiator bangs. Her toes flex within thick socks, trying to muster warmth. Vicky turtles tighter into the scarf around her neck. She lifts a steaming spoon of congee and blows gently onto its surface. Congee is easy enough for her to cook—one cup of rice and six cups of water into the Instant Pot. Jen had shown her the recipe—if it could be called a recipe—in college, when they were both drained and broke. Jen would manage to top hers with a drizzle of sauce, an egg, and a pile of herby greens, but Vicky would always settle for the basic no-frill. No energy for more.

Dan's head drones from her laptop:

"... we'll go through three creative rounds over the next two weeks. Final approval before the holiday. In the new year, we'll move into production. Sound good?"

"Um—" Vicky drops the still-full spoon back into the bowl with a plop. She hasn't managed a bite. Her appetite has fled.

"Can we see first ideas this Thursday?"

"I don't—"

"We can do a quick brainstorm sesh now, if you'd like. I don't have another meeting after this."

"So this is ... the ... Asian American Opportunity?" Vicky asks in halting pauses. She hasn't moved past Dan's opening lines: the Asian American Opportunity, in time for next year's Asian American and Pacific Islander Heritage Month—another profit-driven month. According to the brief, the Asian American market had been and would continue carving its slice of the American economic pie, most college graduates spending their high-earning salaries on Costco hauls, collagen plumpers, and ethnoburb multi-bedroom homes, with spare income to waste on what the Onwards strategy team hoped would be urns.

Dan had informed Vicky that she would lead the Asian American Opportunity. Because she is Asian American, and therefore must care about the Asian American Opportunity.

Vicky doesn't care. She finds the targeting perverse. But caring leads to a better paycheck, a better title, a better life. So she'll work the nights, the weekends, the overtime. She'll do it. She could buy Jen a nice dinner and a funky zhizha. And she wants to buy a better coat with the imagined raise—she dreams of double-breasted wool falling to her knees, body bag–like in a sexy way, to keep warm this winter, her most hated and depressive season. Next week threatened December.

"Yes. Like I said. Culturally relevant, but not so specific that we alienate. Something relatable to Asian Americans that is also relatable to everyone else. Like family. Or! Food. Always food. There has to be one thing that ties everyone together, you know?"

He continues: "Look at Anthony's Black History campaign. We need something similar. But less revolutionary. A more . . . homey feel. I was thinking . . . I dated a Korean girl a few years ago. She loved Korean dramas and would force me to watch them with her. I was fascinated by how these sixteen episodes would begin with the most basic coziness and end with gut-wrenching tears thanks to the funerals. Why does every K-drama have a funeral scene?" He pauses and stares at Vicky expectantly as if Vicky—a Chinese American who's never visited Asia and has never been Korean—has coached every Baeksang-winning screenwriter in melodrama. "Is that something we can lean into? Famous funerals in Asian television to evoke emotion? Are there any unforgettable deaths in anime? Isn't suicide common in entertainment over there? Maybe we can try gathering footage from real funerals for Asian celebrities—no, no, no, sorry. That would be too gauche." Dan taps the end of his pen against his cheek, frowning. "Just throwing out ideas. Take what you need. You're being quiet. I hope brilliance is marinating in that head of yours."

Vicky is still processing Dan's Asian ex-girlfriend.

Dan continues his suggestions as if merely listing cuisine options for dinner. "Can we create a way for Asian Americans to reconnect with their heritage through funerary rites?"

He slams his palm down against the table, trying to capture his flash of inspiration. The echo bangs through Vicky's laptop speakers; she flinches.

"Oooh! What if you write a script where the daughter and mother fight daily because the mother's expectations are just too high? The daughter leaves for college and never calls home, but then the mother dies. The daughter regrets their lack of reconciliation and attempts redemption by purchasing an Onwards urn. The tagline can be something along the lines of 'honoring your dead because you couldn't while they were alive'? Sorry, terrible copywriting—I'm just spitballing—come on, Vicky. Are there any Asian death traditions we can discuss?"

Vicky attempts to speak but chokes. She could wax poetic about the zhizha but refuses to soil its goodness with her job. She'll keep her zhizha to herself, while everything else in death, from tomb sweeping to ancestor veneration, is a blank. Her parents are second generation, and she is the third. For her, there had never been another language to learn—no Canto or Mando or Hokkien or Fuzhounese. Jen had once asked her if she wished she were more Asian, as if the level of Asian could be scientifically measured by a thermometer held to her forehead. Vicky had scoffed that the endless catcallers in the street saying *ni hao* had no problem confirming her as Asian, but, seriously, it wasn't that she wished she were more Asian—a ridiculous measurement, because if you were Asian, then you were Asian—but that she still had her people. It would have been nice to have older relatives to talk to and learn from. For death was a severance not just in person-to-person but in person-to-home, person-to-memory, person-to-story. What last name lore is she ignorant of because she does not have elders to ask? Death is a loss of a person, and a loss of a person is a loss of everything that person knows, experiences, and believes. Could teach.

So Vicky is not Asian in the way Dan thinks because she cannot tell Dan what the Asians do. But she can pretend, so she opens her mouth to tell Dan she needs some time to think. That she'll come to the first-round review with a fleshed-out deck of ideas perfectly targeted at the Asian American community. Because in corporate America, what is a community if not a bull's-eye for profit? A community is worth deeming a community only if it has money to spend.

"Fine," Dan says, both optimism and disappointment in his tone. "I'll put the meeting on the calendar. Talk soon. Reach out if you have any questions."

Vicky hits the end meeting button. Slumps over frustrated at her own impotence, furious at the so-called opportunity being more like an offense. Bends forward and bangs her forehead against the table three times. The spoon rattles against the side of her bowl of congee. She picks up her phone to reduce brain activity—distract, distract, distract. She does not want to think. Scrolls through her social media feeds, full of profiles of people she hasn't talked to in years, who have more money, looks, and charisma than her. Exits in frustration. Opens her texts full of people she should talk to but doesn't. Sees Angela. The name.

Opens the thread. Spaced out by different times, more texts she has not read:

> i miss you how are you?

> you working?

　　　　　　　　　　　　　　　can you talk?

She should have responded, she knows.
She extends a peace offering:

hey.

sorry.

jen told me about this death exhibit at the met

wanna go this afternoon? i'm playing hooky

She shoves her phone into her hoodie pocket. Tilts her head, her neck screaming. Becomes a statue. An hour or a minute passes. Three work email notifications in cheery chirps—ignored.

She takes out her phone, checks the screen. No response from Angela, just the time, 10:32, in front of the background image: an aerial perspective of her and Jen's feet dangling off the fire escape, Jen's slim fingers in the corner clutching a half-smoked cigarette, the sidewalk below a tiny strip. She returns to her texts, scanning her desperate attempts to reconnect. Cringes. She always does this. Pretends as if everything is fine, everything is okay.

Clicks open the unread texts from Kevin:

　　　　　　　　I'm going away for a bit. Artist residency.

　　　　　　　　　　　　　Can you hang with Angela?

> She misses you.

Vicky closes the texts, annoyed. No specific dates of departure and return? No *hi, how are you?* Typical Kevin, floating around. Vicky checks the date of receipt: over a week ago. She wonders if Kevin has returned yet. How long do artist residencies last anyway? And why is she responsible for Angela? Why is Kevin begging for company on Angela's behalf? Vicky doesn't owe either of them anything. She can barely rein in her own sadness—how can she be expected to corral someone else's? She is not a partner. She is not a girlfriend. She avoids these labels precisely because labels imply behavioral expectations she can't shoulder. She is no one; at most, she is what she is. Nothing more. She emphasizes this distinction in every relationship she's ever been in, because she is not so thoughtless as to accept burdens she's unable to carry.

Her phone, silent.

Vicky scoots back her chair, stands up, stretches. Slams her laptop shut. Yawns. She would go by herself to the exhibit. She doesn't need Angela to accompany her. She's never needed accompaniment. She has herself, though herself does not even have herself—depression is a separation from the separation, reality twice removed. When she walks with Angela or Jen, she is walking with herself, which is that she is walking with nobody. She's nobody, and nobody means nobody there—alone. Always. Again. Alone.

## *remember you will die*

The representation of life in paintings gives Vicky more life than life itself. Because she feels that she's never experienced life fully immersed—more a robot, trapped in a laboratory as scientists attempt to teach it how to live, forcing it to watch through a glass pane an identical twin who laughed and cried and convinced people to tell it *I love you*. For Vicky, to look at art is not just a lesson in how to look but a lesson in how to understand. How to live. And to have someone next to her as she studies paintings would be like whenever Jen would whisper to her about a party during a lecture in college, so that she heard only the professor's every other sentence, a jagged half-formed education. She hated being with people when learning. Only in solitude can Vicky stare at a painting and float into feeling. Once, an ex-girlfriend who wanted a million photos of herself in front of whatever they were looking at, while also having a million questions *about* whatever they were looking at, accompanied Vicky to the Whitney for the Jennifer Packer exhibit, and Vicky had broken up with her by the time they had hit the third painting, *The Mind Is Its Own Place*, featuring two figures with conflicting poses, depicted in hushed grays. The perfect backdrop to end a relationship. The ex had accused her of being a pretentious snob, and Vicky had shrugged and agreed. It's true, and therefore, it's perfectly fine—the preferable outcome, really—that she ascends the grand steps of the Met without Angela. A weekday afternoon meant majority tourists and school groups, scattered around the staircase taking photos. She weaves around each huddle, looking back with every other step to admire the fountain's enthusiastic bubbling and the saxophonist playing renditions of popular songs Vicky can hum along with but can't place a name to. At the top of the staircase, she pivots to take in the view of Fifth Avenue: the yellow taxis, the veteran hot dog king, the opulent architectural flairs of the Upper East Side buildings. She still finds restorative magic in looking at the city vista—this is how she knows she can't leave.

The line through security moves quickly. Vicky opens her tote for the security guard, who offers a cursory glance to the debris inside. Before she enters the Great Hall, she snakes her arm over the velvet divider rope separating the exit/entry lines and pulls off a ticket sticker from the THANKS FOR COMING sign, on which tourists place their used stickers when they leave the museum. Her stolen mark goes on her shirt, over her heart—she's never entered the Met legally, but why should the act of looking at beauty cost so much money? She tells herself that if Western museums could show off their plunders of colonialism, then she, descendent of a traumatized country, deserves free, speedy admittance. If the museum was close to running out of money, then it shouldn't pay its president and director over a million in total compensation every year. True, she could get into the Met free as a New York resident, but she's too impatient to wait in the long line to show evidence like an electric bill or library card. She could die tomorrow—why spend her last day being patient? Impossible, also, to pay the twenty-five-dollar tourist entry fee at the no-wait digital ticket kiosks, though she might have been more willing to wait if it meant the money would actually go to the workers.

She follows the signs for Momento Mori to the left of the Great Hall staircase, through the modern and contemporary art wing. She's come to this section many times for fashion anthologies and career retrospectives, but never to an exhibit so proudly exclaiming the theme, DEATH, in dramatic black block letters painted onto the wall above the entrance door.

She steps inside—the opening room is nearly vacant, with only a security guard pacing and a teen typing on his phone. Had the bold proclamation driven away guests?

She scans the exhibition description: "*Memento mori* is an artistic category acting as a reminder of death, the most common motif being the skull accompanied by bones. . . . Throughout history, artists have explored the impermanence of life through memento mori paintings, whether in the symbols of still life ('dead nature') or in canvases draped in the deepest black.... In the spirit of *omnia mors aequat* (death makes all equal), this exhibit is a rich, groundbreaking selection of memento mori across time, place, and style brought together by galleries, collectors, and museums around the world. For only in the acceptance of death can we emerge as victors over our inevitable erasure..."

Frowning, she glances across the first room, thinking about how the acceptance of death as a victory over death sounded like an Urnie speech, her eyes skipping over the teen to land on the contemporary Japanese painting she recognizes as the apology offering Jen had shown her months ago. A rendition of her favorite flowers. The spider lily petals' red gashes contrast stark against the white wall, reminding her of bleeding wounds. Her skin bristles. Though she had looked forward to seeing the painting in real life, she's unnerved by the perceived gore, the room's emptiness, and the introduction's similarity to the Onwards motto. The spider lilies pulsate and enlarge within her gaze—she cocks her head and squints, trying to end the distortion. She feels faint and overly hot. She tips to the left, stumbles to catch her balance.

"Are you okay, miss?"

Vicky fixates on the lilting Guyanese accent to bring her back to her body. The guard has approached her, a worry line creasing his brow. His name tag reads MR. SINGH.

"Yes, sorry." She musters a smile toward the guard, who has his hands out as if to catch her if she collapses. "Just... overcome. By the art."

Mr. Singh chuckles. "Yes, I know the feeling. When I am feeling empty, the art fills me. When I come to work sad, the art reminds me of joy. When I tire of standing, the art revives." He tucks his hands behind his back. "Are you sure you would not like to sit? There is no shame in resting. There are benches over there for you."

"No, I'm fine now." She is. She's always enjoyed speaking with the museum guards. The guards spent time with the art to protect rather than to display or own, and this different approach had always appealed to Vicky, who thought of art not as something to show but as something to love.

Vicky straightens. Mr. Singh's insight reminds her of why she is here. "Thank you."

Mr. Singh nods and returns to his post. Vicky waves at him as she hurries into the next space.

This room is more crowded, mostly retirees on an afternoon date soothed by the more accessible European oil still lifes and Asian ink scrolls. Vicky drifts to a work empty of onlookers—a dim oil painting of a woman holding a skull in her lap as she peers into a candle, shadows encroaching from the corners, creating a dramatic contrast. Vicky swallows and reads the name: *La Madeleine à la veilleuse*, or *Magdalene with the Smoking Flame*, by Georges de La Tour, c. 1640. She relates to Magdalene, obsessed with the weak flicker of warm brightness that eventually, no matter how hard she stares, will burn to a stub and go out, leaving her in the dark with nothing but the clutched skull representing death—if only she, and Magdalene, could stand and search for more candles to dispel the demons.

Vicky turns away.

The next painting is a hanging scroll—遊仙圖. *Daoist immortals in a landscape.* Her eyes trace the cliffs, branches, and rocks animated by inked lines fading into the paper. She can almost hear the clack of weiqi stones against grid boards and the murmurs of the immortals whenever a stone is expertly placed. Her nostrils flare, trying to grasp the damp fresh air. Invigorated by the sensations, she remembers what she learned in her college elective Chinese art history course: how the 仙 character translates to "immortal" and could be split into pictorials of 人 (person) and 山 (mountains), implying that those secluded in the mountains can live forever, because being in refuge from the everyday life below renders mundane concerns like death irrelevant. Vicky stares at the group of friends playing weiqi under a tree—they remind her of her former tender desire: Angela and Kevin and Jen and her, living together, their weird little friend-love-romantic-love-multi-love huddle in harmony, sharing a meal and a movie without any notice of the outside world, and this reminder of what could not be, never be—not when she has ignored them for weeks, not when she is so fundamentally alone—pains her. Causes a burning throb in the left side of her chest. And so she moves onward. Leaves this room for the next.

The new gallery is empty of spectators. A guard stands against the wall, her black suit breaking the white and matching the black squares of art. Vicky stands in front of a Pierre Soulages *Outrenoir*, his "beyond black" work more effective than any Onwards death room. The ache inside her deepens. A dark cavern where her heart used to be, just like Soulages's single-pigment black surface paintings: light removed. The painting reminds her of death, and the details of its inevitability slowly reveal the longer she stares, a *luxurious* looking, for time is luxury; though it meant also that the longer she stares at one detail, the less time she has to look at another, because time is limited—as in, there are always details she will miss. How she will never be able to step back and see the painting, the life, *her* life, for what it is as a whole. And the inability to see the future, the powerlessness to understand everything all at once, causes her to further descend into panic, her breath shortening, and she runs from the Soulages into the next room. She moves on and on again, running away, yet luckily, this time—the final room—hope:

HOW MIGHT WE CELEBRATE LIFE? reads the exhibit wall in the same block letters that had graced the entrance with DEATH. Vicky rolls her eyes when reading this question. Celebrate is too strong a verb for a noun so undeserving. Life? Life is not meant to be celebrated but endured.

She scans the walls. Figurative contemporary paintings here—she recognizes many of the artists on display through their distinctive touches. There's a green-toned Salman Toor, his wavy paint portraying a circle of gentle-souled men helping one another put on makeup, and Vicky can nearly whiff the sharp cocktail of smoky cologne and masculine scent. She taps her feet in rhythm looking at the Louis Fratino painting of thick-limbed revelers kissing and dancing in vibrancy under a disco ball; she smiles at a tender Jordan Casteel of two kids sleeping on each other's shoulders on the subway—in her mind she hears the crinkle of their winter coats rubbing against each other and the conductor's warble of *the next stop* over the speakers; she tugs both earlobes in delight at the rainbow-hued Devan Shimoyama of a high-top fade in a glimmering barber shop; and she craves to join the table in the Amanda Ba painting of four naked sisters smoking and drinking and eating watermelon, staring defiantly back at the gaze. Each frame a glimpse into proof of life, each frame its own mundane swirling world, allowing Vicky to stop and gaze and feel. And then she comes to an artist she doesn't know, not yet, not intimately, whose canvas portrays faces resembling hers, and despite the separation between each body leaning against a brick wall, they are clearly cohesive, a group, for they are laughing all at once. Vicky rubs her elbows and leans closer. In the painting, the sun shines, the wind soothes, and all is well because the friends are together. Vicky guesses one of them has just told a joke—her eyes shift to read the description: "*Ning Dai in Person Having a Laugh* by Liu Xiaodong, from the 2021 solo exhibition called *Your Friends*, which features Liu's gaze on those closest to him for over three decades—his childhood friends and his best friends—meditations on the shifting definitions of 'friend,' perhaps simply an intimate relationship blossoming over time . . ."

Overcome, Vicky begins to cry, the tears flowing down her cheeks. Here are her emotions. Because though she and Jen have not yet reached even a decade in their intimacy, they are friends. Friends! Friendship! How important, important enough to warrant this painting, this room, these frames, this exhibition, this celebration of life. Without human connection, art and life are a mere sketch. An unfinished outline. Yes, she can feel it now—her heart, her poor and heavy heart, a freshly beating weight where there was nothing before. She walks toward the far wall, which holds two paintings by Alice Neel, whose work she adores for its close dialogue between the sitter and Alice herself, who always painted her friends and lovers and collaborators in mirrored poses and mutual gazes, for to paint—write, sculpt, film—a person is to conduct an act of love. An act of remembrance. The first Alice Neel is a portrait of Jackie Curtis and Ritta Redd, bright colors for bright subjects, their legs overlapped as they huddle and glare forward, united in challenge at the spectator who dares judge their queer love; the second is a muted-color street scene of the Uneeda Biscuit Strike, union demonstrators fighting for better working conditions while being trampled by cops on horses. But Neel paints on the canvas witnesses too, standing rapt on the sidewalk, noting the brutality. And these two paintings, placed together, remind Vicky of her own lover, the one she loves—Angela. Angela. Angela.

She shoves her hand in her tote. Scrabbles her fingers around the debris of lip balm and receipts and hair ties. Finds her phone. Opens her messages. Types, hits send:

sorry again. you deserve an explanation.

ive been swamped with work and too sad to reply tbh lol

not just to you, to everyone.

obviously thats not fair to you tho

i'm sorry

i have a terrible habit of spiraling into existential despair. it's not like the numbing of depression!!! it's literally a spiral. like a fall into a deep pit. and i need to figure out how to climb out. so i isolate myself thinking its the only way to help me find my footing. i read an article once about how avoiding human interaction is a coping mechanism that lets me bypass the cognitive processing of distress.

but what the fuck do i know?

also tbh i think im terrified of abandonment. i am terrified of the people i love leaving me, so i leave them before they can leave me, because it gives me a sense of power or control or whatever.

but death is the one thing i cant control. if the people i love die, then they're gone forever and i cant predict when or how it'll happen. just that it'll happen. and it kinda makes me panic. so i think about death all the time because i cant think about anything else but also it sorta helps me cope? sorry. i know thats weird

and im sorry for this novel of a text

anyway i want to stop leaving people. and i want to stop thinking about death

i hope this apology makes up for my idiocy a bit

i went to the exhibit i texted you about and it reminded me of you. especially these:

She raises her phone and leans backward to fit both Alice Neel paintings into a photo, which she texts to Angela.

i miss you.

can i see you soon?

She flips her hair around her shoulder.

Looks up at the paintings.

Taps her thighs.

Looks down at her phone.

She frowns. No immediate response like she'd been hoping. She reminds herself that she's hurt Angela with her absence and therefore should allow some more time.

Drops her phone into her tote—

It buzzes as soon as it leaves her grasp.

She thrusts her hand back into her bag, finds the phone, checks the screen.

Angela!

Her fingers shaking, she nearly drops her phone trying to open the text—

This is Kevin. Need to talk. I'll come to you. Lmk when/where

## *she'll wait—*

### ANGELA

A therapist had once asked Angela to pinpoint the beginnings of her fondness for bathtubs, but Angela could not. There had been no beginning because beginnings imply endings, and she'd never end her bathtub habit, not while she still lived. She knew after hearing the question that this therapist, her ninth in two years, would never understand her. She cut the session short. Never tried therapy again.

Kevin said she gave up too quickly. That the antidepressants she attempted every so often needed consistency, rather than sampling to stimulate the neurotransmitters; that it took time to find the right therapist; and that therapy was not a quick fix but a pathway to a greater sense of being. Her boyfriend sometimes spoke like a cult member, which she privately believed was the same thing as being an artist—an opinion she'd never dare admit to him. Besides, she found his optimistic proclamations on human nature and creative expression endearing. She hoped he found her own manner of speech charming too, even if she didn't think herself as appealing whatsoever. Too foolish, too naggy. Too angry. Too depressed. Too many abnormalities in her brain chemistry. Too many empty serotonin tanks.

Her thoughts had a tendency to run rampant. If she molded her inner demons into reality the way Kevin claimed he could with his own through his art, then she'd construct a bathtub, one of the stained, rusted, antique cast-iron claw-footed tubs with layers of grime and chipped paint in desperate need of repair and refurbishment. The sort of tub an urban explorer might photograph shoved onto its side in an abandoned former tuberculosis sanatorium, overflowing with darkness in the shape of a million uncontrollable Susuwatari—those spiky black spherical soot-sprites in *Spirited Away*—though her Susuwatari would be neither cuddly nor helpful. Hers would be vomiting out the bathtub in the form of anxious thoughts, unstable emotions, and depressive behaviors.

She doesn't know why she is the way she is. She had a relatively trauma-free childhood. Her parents were loving and emotionally available, able to display affection while maintaining stern yet reasonable discipline in their small yet comfortable home in Milpitas. Sure, her father worked too much, and her mother even more, but she knew the efforts were to support the family, and it wasn't like they were never around—they ate most breakfasts together, tucked her into bed most nights, and celebrated every one of her birthdays with a decadent, thick sans rival cake. She had been a happy child. The photo albums her parents flipped through during every visit from her and Kevin were proof enough of her genuine baby joy.

Where had it gone wrong?

Teenage Angela spent her days wearing long sleeves and heading to the bathroom post-meal. Self-cutting and bulimia were easy enough to conceal. Her parents never noticed the small scars scissoring her arms or the constant toothbrushing to get rid of vomit breath. They believed she ran cold. Had an overactive digestive system. That she maintained good dental hygiene.

Only the internet and emo music understood her angst. Forums where aspirational skinny limbs were reblogged and lyrics like *Your demons and all the nonbelievers* and *I'm in the business of misery / Let's take it from the top* showed her she wasn't alone, that her pain wasn't special. If everybody was suffering, then what would be the point of seeking help? Everyone had an eating disorder; everyone cut at least once just to try it out. Weren't teenagers supposed to be angsty and hormonal anyway? She settled for the coping mechanism of having a boyfriend, usually someone who had never had a girlfriend before and therefore thought it was normal for girls to cry every other day for no reason other than unexplainable sadness. They always held her hand and asked her how they could help. They were sweet—but she wasn't. She broke up with them whenever she got bored. None of them interested her.

Nothing interested her.

She'd been dating Dustin the longest. She was a high school junior and he was a senior off to college next year. She couldn't say she was passionately in love with him the way movies and television shows depicted romance, with all those sweeping gestures and fancy dinners, but she knew she loved him. A lot. Probably—definitely—more than the others. Because he didn't comfort her in that false way others tried when she was sad; he just held her and let her cry, rather than ask her how to fix it. And he was nice to talk to—she liked his brain, how it cared about reading poetry and drawing flowers more than getting boba and playing basketball. Dustin liked her too. Their relationship was comfortable, kind, and constant. What she wanted love to be. She was happy with him.

Yet, somehow, she noticed she still felt drawn to Jung-hee, her lab partner in chemistry. She couldn't explain the connection, only that it felt good—really good—to pass notes during class about their after-school plans, to send texts about homework that somehow then shifted into texts about sleeping well and sweet dreaming, to dissolve into a huddle of close giggles whenever Mr. Leeway raised his arms in excitement over ionic bonds to reveal the sweat stains on his shirt. Whenever she and Jung-hee waved goodbye, Angela felt a wrenching pang of disappointment combined with eager excitement for the time she would see her next. They were friends—maybe more? She wasn't sure. But. She was sure that it was easy and lovely and fun.

One day, Jung-hee passed her a note: *I'm craving cookie dough. Come with? I'll drive you home afterwards.*

Angela looked at Jung-hee and nodded. She was free anyway. Dustin couldn't hang out because he had Yearbook Club after school. And both her parents were at work.

Jung-hee ordered a scoop of chocolate chip cookie dough in a cup while Angela got three scoops of her favorite—Graham Central Station, vanilla with graham cracker crumbs and chocolate chips—in a waffle cone because she was always starving and because calories didn't matter since she would throw it up later anyway. They sat on the hood of Jung-hee's car while they listened to each other chatter because to listen is to love. Angela vented about how chemistry was her worst subject, how intramolecular forces evaded her understanding; Jung-hee jabbered about how she wanted to get her PhD at one of the University of California campuses, ideally Berkeley, though she couldn't figure out if this was her own goal or simply borrowed from her mother's failed dreams. Jung-hee, waving her hands as she talked about her future, had devoured her ice cream long ago, while Angela still had most of her waffle cone remaining. Angela, self-conscious, hated to eat when the other person had already finished, so she offered the rest to Jung-hee, who declined, claiming her stomach was stuffed with cold treats, but that she'd be happy to use her warm mouth elsewhere.

Jung-hee leaned in.

Angela did too, so preoccupied that she dropped her cone onto the pavement, where it landed cone point up, leaking out beige sludge.

The car ride to Angela's was awkward, silent, other than Angela opening her recently kissed mouth to give one-word directions: *Left. Right. Left. Left.*

Jung-hee pulled into the driveway and turned to Angela, but Angela was already out the door and into her house before the car had even come to a complete stop.

Angela ran up the stairs and into the bathroom. Locked

herself in and sat on the toilet and began to cry. Woeful not because of the realization that she might be bisexual—being queer was not a big deal to her or her family, as she had an uncle with a boyfriend who made family reunions more fun. She cried because she knew she had hurt people she loved: Jung-hee, bewildered at her escape from the car, and Dustin, who didn't know yet about her transgression. She hated hurting people because she hurt all the time and would never wish how she felt on anyone else. How could she commit such a mistake? Why couldn't she just exercise some self-control? Why was she so fucked up? Nobody else seemed to have the same issues she did. It would get worse, she reasoned. She'd grow up and keep fucking up, she'd never be happy, she'd keep hurting other people with her own stupid unhappiness, she's toxic, she's a virus, she's a curse, she's a horrible person whose only way out would be to die—

Those spiky demons. Overwhelming and uncontrollable. She wrapped her arms around herself and tried to squeeze, to hug, to be held. It wasn't enough. She slunk like an eel off the toilet and descended into the closest thing resembling a full-body cradle.

The bathtub.

But the porcelain was hard and cold against her heels, elbows, tailbone, and the back of her head. She sat up and turned the hot water on without taking her clothes off, her jeans immediately dampening and sticking to her skin. But instead of shying away, her skin welcomed the warm gush. The tub filled quickly with less available volume from her body and clothes added in.

She shut off the faucet and fell back, the action sloshing water over the sides. Her ears filled—she could only hear a gentle buzz. Her breath slowed from a panicked hurry to a gentle monotony. She floated, carefree and blank. Here was what she craved: nonexistence. A quiet head. No black spikes.

The therapists were wrong. The bathtub was not the beginning. The bathtub was the return.

Somehow college was worse. She had hoped it would be better because she'd be away from her parents, whose unconditional regard for her when she embodied everything conditional suffocated her.

She spent the four years cheating on her tests, especially the STEM-related mandatory electives. She couldn't study because she was too sad, preferring to lie unmoving on the floor of her dorm room than to sit at a desk. The only class she tolerated was Introduction to Tang Poetry Themes and Contexts. The romantic yet tragic lines reminded her that sorrow had always been an undeniable facet of the human condition. Like how emo bands and her online mutuals had shown her, she wasn't alone.

And she spent the four years cheating on her partners. She couldn't remain loyal even when she wanted to, because she was too stupid, too slutty, too cold, according to all her exes. Fine. She might be stupid and slutty, but she was definitely not cold. She lived the opposite. She owned too *much* warmth, too much love, which is why she simply found herself loving everyone. How could her exes say she was cold when the only true thing about her was her ability to love? *I love you, I loved you, I still love you, I do,* she wanted to blurt out every time she ran into an ex on campus. She couldn't help it. She loved to love, to fill up her emptiness with love. And because everybody she loved left her in the end, she sat in the bathtub instead.

Once, during finals week after an all-nighter not in the library but in her bed, trying to convince herself to *go* to the library, she had dragged herself into her dormitory's bathtub in the hopes of comfort. Exhausted, she told herself she'd float for ten minutes, then dry off and head to the stacks to read the textbook. But the warm water lulled her to sleep within seconds. She dreamed of her mother's pancit, her father's woodsy cologne, her teenage car rides driving a hundred miles an hour with the windows open blasting Lea Salonga just to feel something, anything. Like the stories and scientists always said: In the moments before you die, your brain explodes with memories of life.

She finally awoke to the frantic yelling of her floor's resident adviser, a blond twink named Gary. The dorm's entire hallway carpet was soaked because she hadn't turned the faucet off while sleeping near drowning—*But never mind the damage, you could've drowned and died,* reprimanded Gary. *Get some rest, okay? Finals are hard on everybody. Here's the school therapy hotline. Don't be afraid to call.*

Undeterred by the near-death experience, Angela had enjoyed her mind's conjuring. She wondered when she'd watch it again. The before-death trailer of her life had been comforting, just like it had been to black out and be blissful, unaware of disturbances like her exams and shitty grades. If death felt as lovely as a bathtub, she'd welcome it in relief.

The recruiter's hands reminded her of her mother's: dry, chapped, and raw from constant washing in her previous life as a nurse, now raising signs in the air to mobilize networks in support of caregivers across the healthcare continuum. It had been the recruiter's hands that convinced Angela to accept the flyer, and it had been the job's location that convinced her to apply. She resolved to run to the East Coast after graduation, as far as she could get from her childhood. She prayed going somewhere new would refigure her brain into thinking new too. Positive, happy thoughts.

She'd scrolled through New York City open room listings, looking not at the roommate descriptions or the bedroom she'd be taking, but the photos of the apartment bathroom. Only places under her budget of $1,200 per month with a full-size clean bathtub were considered, which meant there were nearly no options at all. She finally settled on a place in deep Bushwick with three other roommates, who banged impatiently at the locked door whenever she floated between her union shifts. She didn't care. Ignored their desperate texts in the group chat. Whether they needed to shower before their date or pee before they left the apartment, no need of theirs was as important as her bathtub time. Didn't they understand she would have killed herself without it?

She learned to adapt to the hectic city and demanding job. The hours were long and irregular, including frequent tasks on the weekends and holidays, but the collective nature of her job gave her a warm feeling that had previously only been found in the bathtub. And she liked how her daily activities were in support of workers to improve care and create safer staffing—workers like her mother. Maybe if Angela worked hard enough, other mothers wouldn't have to work as much as her own did. A sense of purpose enlarged in her chest, edging out her need to float in the bathtub, making the bathroom more available, to the relief of her roommates.

And the need disappeared almost entirely after she agreed to move into Kevin's beautiful apartment. Only after the change in her living situation did her mental well-being boost so drastically that she understood how money really could be the key to happiness. The only people who claimed otherwise had so much money they didn't have to think about it at all. Like Kevin. Her center of gravity. Kevin, who loved his art but who she believed loved her just a bit more. Kevin, who understood that the love she had for others did not reduce the love she had for him. Kevin, who accepted her and her depression and her nonmonogamous ways because she was his muse—though she knew Kevin would argue she's much more than that to him, because to be a muse separates her from her personhood, whatever that meant.

She doesn't mind being a muse. She finds it romantic. Another reason to live.

It is true that the bad days never fully disappear. There would always be bad days. Sometimes the reason is as terrible as a street harasser during a picket line or a disagreement with Kevin. Sometimes the reason is as simple as the weather turning cold. The sadness is unsolvable. Nonetheless, the number of bathtub floats does decrease—once a month, once every two months, then once a quarter. Her life continues unfurling with her work and Kevin and their lovers, and then:

Vicky.

Vicky, more than an occasional date, not yet a partner. Whom she had met through a dating app, which she considers absurd considering how little luck she had when presenting both Kevin and her on one profile. Whom she fell in love with during their first date at a cemetery, a location she found utterly, deeply romantic. Simply, Vicky. A deep intimacy. Whom she loves more than she loves herself, because she has never truly loved herself.

Loving Vicky reminds her it's okay to be loved despite her sadness, because Vicky is sad too.

The bathtub becomes a place to wash.

Angela thinks she's recovered. That she's all better.

She deludes herself into thinking it is so easy to be better.

Angela and Vicky in bed. Kevin at his studio.

Angela tucks her hand behind her head, posing like someone lying in a meadow to admire the shapes of clouds. She begins to hum, not a recognizable song but an expression of contentment. She loves fucking Vicky. The sheer exertion, the retreat of reality.

Vicky kicks the covers off. With the arrival of autumn, Angela and Kevin have switched their summer linens for heavy cotton duvets. "It's too hot," she complains. "You make me all sweaty."

Angela gathers the ditched blankets toward her own naked body. "Give me yours. I never feel warm when it's colder out."

Vicky laughs. "Not even after that?"

Angela stares at the ceiling. Easier to confess to a blank wall than an expressive face. "I never feel good when winter is on its way."

"Because?"

"Winter is freezing, gray, and apocalyptic, frankly. There's no sense of saunter like in the summer."

"Sense of saunter?" Vicky turns to her side and props her head up on her elbow. "That's very poetic."

"Thank you."

"I feel the same way in the winter. I think most people do. I just wanna stay home and watch bad movies."

"Yeah. SAD. Seasonal affective disorder. But, like, it feels way more than that." Angela cringes at her honesty but can't stop herself. Sex unzips her mouth.

"I know what you mean."

"Like, I love Kevin, but he's just not fucked up enough to understand, you know? He doesn't feel sadness the same way I do. It's like I'm lying in a coffin and the stone lid has been slid over me. I know New Year's Eve is still two and a half months away and that it's supposed to mark new resolutions, but I feel dread as it gets closer, because it means there's a whole 'nother year I have to contend with. It just means I have to live more."

Vicky frowns, opens her mouth. Closes it, wonders what to say. Fumbles. "Well—I—I want you to live more," she decides to say.

Angela exhales and turns to her side away from Vicky, who scoots over and presses against Angela. Vicky wraps her arm around Angela's waist and begins rubbing the soft drooping of Angela's stomach.

"I'm just glad we met in the summer," Angela says. "Falling in love is hard in the winter."

Vicky buries her nose into Angela's hair—the odor reeks of a packed subway car on a hot summer day. Angela sweats profusely when they fuck, and the nonstop bleaching and re-dying of her damaged hair only makes the essence worse. But Vicky sniffs because she loves how Angela smells. She loves Angela.

"It was a lovely summer," Vicky whispers.

Angela shifts, turns around to look at Vicky, tucking her hand underneath the pillow. They face each other.

"What do you think happens to us when we die?" Angela asks.

Vicky scoots toward Angela, not touching, but close enough that the bed dips them into the center. "Why do you ask?"

"I'm just curious what you think. Give me your wisdom."

"You go first."

"I think we reincarnate. Like, Asian style—"

Vicky laughs. "Asian style? Are we a buffet?"

Angela frowns. "Don't interrupt."

"Sorry."

"I think we get reincarnated. Not into one being but into many. Our souls dissolve into a million pieces, like the seeds from the flower of our original self. And then we sprinkle into the wind that then blows us into other forms. So, when I die, I don't want to be reincarnated into one human. I want to be a tree and a jewel-like beetle and a cat basking in sunlight." Vicky giggles, though Angela seems serious. She continues: "But if I'm forced to choose one form, I'd like to be a butterfly in my next life. Like the butterfly lovers in that Chinese legend. The lovers who were forbidden to be together, so one of them died of a broken heart. And the other jumped into the grave, and their spirits transformed into dancing butterflies, so they'd never be parted again. So a butterfly is someone's soul, because the beautiful wings and colors mimic the soul rising above the mortal earth."

"I think you're more beautiful alive than as a butterfly who's dead," Vicky says.

"That's not the point."

"Can't I just be nice?"

"Okay. Thanks. So, what do you think?"

Vicky's answer is bleak. Perhaps the opposite of what Angela needs. But she is nothing if not honest: "Reincarnation sounds nice. But I think it's slightly ridiculous. I think we become nothing. Our flesh vessels are burned in cremation and shoved into urns, while our souls—these strange intangibilities that make us *us*—" Vicky gestures to the space between them. Angela grabs

Vicky's hand and twines their fingers. She almost wants Vicky to shut up so they can kiss, but she lets Vicky go on because she likes to listen to her thoughts. "—our souls just die. Blank out. Stop existing. There's no heaven, no hell, no cycle of rebirth. Which is why I do agree with Urnie and the Onwards vision. It's easier to face the onwards of nothing when you expect nothing."

"I think that's sad," Angela says.

Vicky throws herself up and tackles Angela. They wrap themselves together, Vicky pinning Angela. She peppers kisses around Angela's collarbone, digging her tongue into the divot. Angela, ticklish, squirms and giggles.

"Well, according to you, I'm a sad person," whispers Vicky into Angela's skin.

Angela settles, brushing her hand through Vicky's hair.

They lie sandwiched in a short eternity. Angela wishes for a never-ending.

Vicky playfully smacks Angela's right butt cheek and hops out of bed, out of the room.

Angela, alone. She experiences an immediate comedown. Shivers. Burrows deeper into the mattress, pulling the blankets atop her like a mound of dirt.

Angela, falling, falling, falling—

"I brought you a present," Vicky calls out, unseen. "I like giving gifts. Sorry, I meant to give it to you right when I arrived, but you distracted me. Hold on."

Vicky, holding something behind her back. With her return, the room's luster reasserts itself.

"Hold out your hands," she says.

Angela scoots upward eagerly, stacking the pillows against the bed's headboard. "Should I close my eyes?"

Vicky shakes her head. Sits on the edge of the bed. "No, it's fine. It's, uh, not that big of a deal. Here. I put it in a box so it wouldn't get crumpled in the subway." She opens the lid and pours the contents into Angela's waiting palms.

"Wow," Angela says. "It's you." She brings the six-inch paper doll Vicky closer to her eyes, cradling her.

"I commissioned it for you from a zhizha maker near my apartment. She said I only needed a photo, so I emailed her a full-body mirror pic of me, and then I picked it up the next day—do you like it?" Vicky says in a rush.

Angela looks up, startled—sees Vicky picking at her nails, nervous. Scooches closer to Vicky. Kisses her cheek. "I love it. Thank you."

Vicky lets out a breath, her body deflating in relief.

"Wait. Sorry. So, what's a zhizha? Is this a doll? Do I tuck it into my pocket so you're always with me? Or is it like Elf on the Shelf, where I'm supposed to place it in a different spot in the apartment every day to freak Kevin out? Or should I rub certain places when I feel a little"—she jabs Vicky in the side, who falls over giggling—"you know. Make you feel it too?"

Vicky sits back up, grinning. "No, silly. Huh, I guess you've never been to my apartment before. I'm always coming to yours."

"You never invite me over!"

"Well, your place is better than mine."

Angela shrugs. "I'd still like to see it."

"Yeah, you can come over sometime. You know I live in Chinatown, above a funeral parlor, and there's a lot of funerary supply shops on my block where I buy these—they're my apartment decor. Have you seen them before? They're everywhere in the windows on Mulberry."

Angela shakes her head. "Haven't noticed. But haven't known to look."

"You can buy zhizha from these shops before heading to the funeral next door. Burn the paper so whoever you're mourning receives what it shows in the afterlife. I just think it's an interesting death tradition. Especially to consider what people want when they're dead. Like high-tech phones, fancy cars, expensive alcohol. It's just weird. Why can't we dream bigger for our deaths? Why do we settle for burning meaningless objects and not themes like happiness or love or rest?"

"I guess we believe those objects, which are luxuries, will give us those themes. Not that I agree. They say death is the great equalizer, but if anything, I think it just widens the difference."

"Well, that's what Onwards is trying to fix. Equal-cost urns for everyone. Equity in death."

Angela opens her mouth, and Vicky hastily steamrollers because she knows Angela is about to argue:

"So you don't think my zhizha appreciation is weird?" She lowers her eyes, fidgeting with the mattress cover, hating her own embarrassment.

"I like you because you're weird. If you're weird, I'm weird," Angela says. The zhizha Vicky rests in the divide between her hands—Vicky as the butterfly abdomen, Angela's cupped palms as butterfly wings. Angela muses that this is perhaps what the butterfly lovers had tried to teach: that a love can be its own kind of death, that to fly away with a lover on jeweled, paper-like wings can be its own form of surrender. She wonders if souls are concentrated in the abdomen, the wings, or the entire butterfly body. The entirety would be too risky, she thinks. And a love like theirs would never center in delicate wings that could be so easily torn, trampled, or dampened. Better to remain knotted in the stem. The thicker armor.

"I wanted to give you this because I hoped it would remind you of me when I'm not around. I might be pretty busy at work soon."

"Oh. It's okay." Angela hurries to impart how she'll be busy too. That she's not overly dependent on Vicky's presence. That she doesn't hate being alone: "I have to travel to Baltimore soon to join picketing." But because she would rather hope, she adds, "I'll be back in a few days. You can come over late. After work. You know I don't sleep much."

Vicky laughs. "You should sleep more. The bed is a good place to be." She pauses, then, in preemptive explanation, adds, "Thank you for the offer. I love spending time with you, but when I have a lot on my plate, I just want to keep my head down and be alone and get it done."

"Right. Sorry. Of course." Angela looks down at Vicky's paper self. Wonders how she managed to fall in love with two people so okay without her. Kevin and art, Vicky and work and sadness. If Vicky disappeared, would she be forced to return to the bathtub? Angela wonders if Chinatown sells any bathtub zhizha. She'd check the Mulberry storefronts next time she's in Chinatown. If in stock, she'll buy one and jokingly tell Kevin to burn it when she dies, even if Kevin has confessed how tired he is of her flippant kms text messages and *I'm gonna kill myself* statements whenever she experiences any sort of minor discomfort or inconvenience.

Angela begins to cry.

Sometimes she cries when she's with her lovers; sometimes she cries when she thinks about Kevin; always it is because she feels misinterpreted. It's not that she *will* kill herself, more that she accepts the possibility of killing herself exists, and to joke about it makes light of the heavy desire. Yet Kevin has stopped laughing, instead groaning whenever she teases suicide, as if her humor discloses itself in a foreign language Kevin has only half learned. The person she loves, the people she loves, who supposedly love her back—weren't they supposed to be the ones who would never need a translator for what she actually meant? Weren't they supposed to want to spend time with her? Didn't *to love* mean to witness, to accompany, to comprehend, to *know*? She has never been understood. Has never been wanted. And so perhaps she has never been loved, not truly, and she feels very alone even in the company of a lover, this lover, and so . . . she cries.

"What's wrong?" Vicky grips her hand.

"Nothing, nothing." How could she confess?

"I can come see you! I just didn't want you to expect me—I'll be busy. Sorry, I—"

"No—I'm sorry—I don't mean to be a burden—I cry sometimes randomly, no matter if I'm happy or sad. I can't help it. I'm surprised this is your first time seeing me cry." Angela wipes her tears and looks to the empty side of the bed. "I'm okay, I'm okay! I love the zhizha. Thank you."

"Are you sure you're okay?"

"Yes."

Angela tucks the zhizha Vicky under the blanket with the head sticking out. Leans in and kisses the paper forehead. Then turns to the human forehead wrinkled with worry and kisses there too.

"Now I have two Vickys. Lucky me."

How could there exist both a Vicky next to her and a Vicky who won't talk to her? Angela floats in the bathtub staring at the zhizha Vicky she's propped up on the faucet, protected by distance from wayward splashes of water. She can't understand how she'd received her six-inch paper Vicky before Halloween, only for the sixty-three-inch flesh-and-blood Vicky to disappear after. Was it really so easy for somebody to disappear with zero warning? In her previous relationships, there had been a separation period. A break. A relaxing of daily communication until the complete end. Never this—never such a nothing. She must never have been anyone significant to Vicky after all.

She hates herself for that conversation at the Halloween party on the roof. She doesn't resent Vicky for angrily leaving. She nagged too much, Kevin said when she told him about the conversation. He knew this because she nagged him whenever he did not eat enough, sleep enough, or spend enough time with her. But why couldn't Kevin and Vicky see her behavior as care? Why couldn't Vicky just text her back once, even when busy with work?

She can't convince someone to respond to her. She can't convince someone to love her if they didn't want to.

And why would they want to?

Kevin had been spending more time in his studio. Which meant less time with her. He was close to unlocking a piece of his art, he had said in explanation, as if his art were a door and he'd been searching for the key for years. *I thought I was the key,* she wanted to retort, but she kept quiet. Tried to show support. Being her partner was exhausting, yes. Kevin was always reminding her to take medication, go for a walk, call Vicky because Vicky was good for her—Vicky, who acted like she had flown off the edge of the Empire State Building, into the sunset.

And then Kevin had been accepted to the artist residency he'd been dreaming of, and because she didn't want to be the burden she always was, she encouraged him to go.

*It's fine*, she tells herself as she sinks deeper into the bath, her nostrils filling with water. She closes her eyes so she only sees darkness, the punch of it that has stalked her for her entire life.

Kevin is always leaving. Vicky had already left. Everyone would leave. Though her bathtub never would. The bathwater, always nearby.

She descends farther in. Her forehead, her scalp, then all of her, until no part of her body touches the lightness of air. Only the suffocation of depth.

She'll wait until she polishes off the last chip in the family-size bag Kevin bought for her before he left—
    She'll wait until Kevin returns from the retreat—
    She'll wait until Vicky texts her back—
    She'll wait until the bathwater goes cold—
    She'll wait until—
    She'll wait—

She can't wait. She can't remember how long she's been alone in this cage of an apartment. Only that she's been isolated her entire life. A being without relation—lonely and ostracized, like a deserted island atop an ocean of fish; a weed thrusting itself unwelcome through cracks of abandoned concrete; an insomniac wide-eyed and hunched over at 3:00 a.m., their window the sole golden rectangle among darkened panes of occupants long since snoozing. She hasn't slept. Hasn't eaten. Can't remember how Kevin loved her, can barely remember who he is. Even the bathtub's warmth has failed to chase away the misty gray fog creeping around her ever since he left. She hasn't texted him—she's too much of a bother already, and limited phone connection at the retreat, he had said.

He won't miss her too much.

He isn't missing her now.

She leaves the note on the kitchen table along with the Vicky zhizha. Runs the bath. Steps into that inviting water. The resolve to return to that brief burst of memory. And then . . . nothing. Finally. Free.

# *take care*

Vicky had sprinted to Second Avenue, away from the Met. She now waits for the downtown Q, but the sign indicating the next arrival blares DELAYED. DELAYED. DELAYED. She shifts her weight to her left foot. Her right. Her left again. Bites her nails. She steps forward and glares at the dark, empty tunnel. Nothing. Hurtles up the stairs out into the street. Who cares about cost when in a desperate rush? She charges into a taxi, shoving aside the person who had flagged it first, ignoring their protests. "*Step on it,*" she tells the driver like she's chasing a villain in an action movie. Stares out the window as they head south, tapping her fingers rapidly against her thigh every time the cab trickles to a slowness from traffic. How long has it been since she talked face-to-face with either Kevin or Angela? She can't remember. She tells herself if there had been an urgent issue Angela would have called, silencing the nasty, honest voice in her head that she wouldn't have picked up the phone. The guilt tsunami rushes into her stomach, a panic she recognizes. Something is wrong. She doesn't know what. She could ask, but . . . she's terrible at communication. Always running away from conflict. The Halloween party wasn't the most toxic fight she's ever been in with someone she'd been dating, and yet it had felt the worst because of the opponent. She resolves to apologize. Grovel. Beg. Anything to return to good graces, to things being fine, to love. Vicky throws cash at the driver. Clambers out. Sprints up the stairs. Takes out her phone and types a text to both Kevin's and Angela's numbers while still stepping out of her shoes.

im home

Vicky enters. Drops her keys on the floor with a clatter. Collapses onto the sofa, her phone on her stomach screen side down. Squeezes her eyes shut, decides she can't bear the black behind her lids, opens. Sees the iPhone zhizha she collected months ago sitting on the windowsill across from her—she wonders if there's cellular connection in the afterlife. Could the dead ever call the living?

Her phone vibrates.

"Hello?"

"I'll be there soon." Kevin's voice.

"Wait, what about Angela? I'd love to see you both," Vicky says. Would prefer to see Angela, she does not say.

The call ends without a response.

She stares at the screen, confused. Maybe they broke up, which would explain Kevin's coming alone—Kevin stealing Angela's phone in revenge, going around to each lover informing them of Angela's awfulness. Exes could be vindictive. But rationality whispers this scenario is delusional, a desperate explanation, because if she is the flighty bird, then Kevin and Angela are the branches to land upon. The strong, sturdy solidity who would always be connected to the same trunk. In all her nonmonogamous chaos, she's never encountered such steadiness as found between Kevin and Angela. The guilt rises from her stomach into her throat—maybe Angela is sick of her, hates her, detests her for her ghosting. Vicky's rationality agrees. Vicky wouldn't forgive herself either. Never has. The guilt ascends to her throat, and she coughs, unable to swallow, unable to breathe—

The apartment bell.

Vicky tries to buzz him in but fails. It's broken. She rarely has guests, only Jen, who usually texts her upon arrival, so she has no frame of reference for when it turned faulty. Rushes down the stairs without wasting time to put on a winter coat or shove her feet into shoes. Throws open the apartment door—

Kevin, in a puffer jacket and beanie, his long hair curling out from under.

"Hi," she says, breathless.

Kevin stares at her.

"What's going on." She says this not as a question but as a demand. *Tell me.*

A chorus of weeping—if Vicky could tear her gaze away from Kevin toward the left, she'd see the funeral parlor mobbed by wailers leaving a funeral. Arms around one another's shoulders, exchanging tissues and hugs, drowning in sorrow. But she's trained on Kevin and the visible envelope in his hands on which she reads her name in Angela's scrawl: *Vicky*.

The guilt. Flooding every aspect of her body: her limbs, tongue, teeth, nails. "What's going on," she says again, louder, rising above the laments, every strand of hair on her body rising with goose bumps in tune with the backdrop of grief. Because there is always guilt in grief. What more could have been done. How time could have been better spent. What words could have been said.

Kevin thrusts the envelope at her. She accepts it with a trembling hand.

She clears her throat. "Want to come in?"

Kevin shakes his head. "I'll leave soon."

"Should I open this here?" She waves it like a white flag. A surrender.

"Yes."

She slides open the flap hastily sealed shut with a sliver of Scotch tape, as if someone had been desperate to read its contents only to feel guilty for snooping afterward—Vicky is sure the culprit had been Kevin. The letter, an 8½-by-11-inch sheet of paper creased into thirds, slides out. She unfolds it and finds her paper body lying atop Angela's handwriting. Her zhizha self. The gift returned, unwanted. Her zhizha legs are wrinkled, rippled, as if formerly damp or splashed upon and now dried. Like it had been propped up by a bathtub or sink.

The guilt, shattering.

She slides her paper self into her hoodie pocket.
She reads:

Dear Vicky,

I know you think that nothing happens to us after we die, but I still hope I'll turn into a butterfly. I want to reincarnate into something more beautiful than I was before. You should walk around Central Park in the springtime and say hello to the butterflies because one of them could be me. Do butterflies have long memories? I wonder if I'll remember you because of how much I love you. Will I be afflicted with unsolvable yearning? Maybe when you die, you'll be turned into a butterfly too. We'll find each other. Thunder will clap. We'll fly off into the horizon as eternal butterfly lovers. Or maybe I'll just forget everything that ever happened and emerge blank. It would be too painful to hold on to every memory of every life we've ever lived.

Onwards helped me prepare. You were right. You guys made it easy. I chose the Lucy urn because you said it's your favorite. You should be proud of your work. Thanks for lessening Kevin's funerary burden. I hope he won't grieve too much.

Your zhizha self has kept me company. I thought about burning it before I left so I'd have you in the afterlife, but I don't think that's fair. Because I want you to live. So I'm giving yourself back to you. Take care, okay?

I'm sorry.

       Angela

Vicky drops the letter. Her hands shake.

Kevin stoops to pick it up, crumpling it in his fist.

"How—" she croaks. She stops herself. What matters is not the how but the where. And the where is that Angela is not here, but Onwards.

"You didn't expect it?" Kevin scoffs. "She talked about it all the time. Did you even pay attention?"

She looks down at her feet, ashamed. Can't return his accusatory gaze.

"You never loved her at all," he spits.

She snaps her head up. "How can you say that?" How could he *think* that? Hadn't she shown how much she loved Angela through her actions? Sure, she might have disappeared for several weeks, but she could swear there had been evidence of love: the honest conversations, the zhizha gift, the cumulative time spent together over the many months. Didn't actions matter most? Angela was the one who had taken action: Angela had left. So. Maybe it was Angela who had never loved either of them at all. If she had, why would she leave?

She volleys back: "If you expected it, why didn't *you* help her?"

"I—" He falters. Swallows. His face scrunches. "I tried."

Seeing his forlorn expression, Vicky descends back into guilt. "I'm sorry."

"Sorry for what? You caused this. You and Onwards. Didn't you read the letter? You helped her prepare."

"That's not true."

Kevin shoves the letter at her. She refuses to take it. He crushes the paper into a ball and throws it at her. It bounces off her shoulder and onto the ground. Kevin glares at her, his lip trembling, and she knows he cannot blame himself if he is to survive this grief, and so he blames her. She accepts. It is her fault.

Hers, and Onwards's.

She wonders if she should comfort him in their shared galaxy of pain or give him space to explode. But before she can do anything, make any sort of decision that could repair or destroy their relationship, he speaks: "I never want to see you again."

He stomps away, his boots thumping against the concrete.

Her suffocating heart—

"Kevin—wait!"

He disappears from her sight.

The ground underneath her is tipping over. She can't hold her balance, and she collapses into a crouch over the threshold of her apartment building, her body rocking back and forth. Hands clutching her face, her tears leaking between her fingers onto the pavement as her shoulders convulse. She'd dreamed of this, hadn't she? A strange shadow floating in a bathtub wearing a mutated mask of Angela's features, discarded sleeping pill containers on the floor. If she'd dreamed it, then she'd made it come true. This is her fault. Everything is her fault. Her dreams, her work at Onwards, and her bitter self, all combining forces to kill the one she loved. Loves. Her weeping joins the peripheral funeral chorus, loud enough that the parlor mourners briefly discontinue their crying to wonder if this new girl had been familiar with their deceased and had only just learned the news. Did this girl know of death too?

Residents and tourists walk past, eyes flitting to her sniveling form. They are curious. What terrible news has befallen this spectacle of despair? They avert their eyes while still giving in to the temptation of furtive peeks. Then they glide their gazes away and hurry to their destination in fear that the distress will latch on to them too. In her anguish, Vicky does not notice their stares, but if she had, she wouldn't have minded. She understands. She had gawked too, with Urnie and his lover and his family. Salivated over the spectacle from her screen. Used his tragedy as her protection against death. Her dreams stopped but death did not, not in real life. Death always came. And no one could prepare for its strike. She couldn't, and Urnie couldn't either. It had been foolish to even try. How silly of her, and how stupid of Urnie. Urnie! Is this terrible destabilization—that the world has flipped and she is falling endlessly through clouds—how Urnie had felt at the scene of the crash too? Torment etched into every inch of his body? She thinks of her own current crumpled posture and remembers the prostrate form of Urnie at the scene, his knees pressed painfully into the gravel, as if paying penance for living while his loved ones could not. Had Onwards been simply a coping mechanism to stay busy in order to forget grief? An entire business stemming from a fanatical delusion by somebody who had too much money? Who believed that in conquering death his loved ones would return to him, unharmed? A revelation. Vicky understands him. Vicky understands herself. Autumn dusk has settled into the concrete cracks around her. Vicky can't believe she began the day infuriated at work only to be moved by paintings, thinking Angela alive, now sobbing here on the sidewalk, knowing Angela is—no. She can't think the sentence.

She is freezing. Numb from cold. She searches the pavement for the crumpled ball of Angela's note, that last message, but it has disappeared, kicked away by a pedestrian in a makeshift game of sidewalk soccer. She returns to her crouch.

Her neighbors recognize her as the mopey girl on the top floor. Vicky ignores them; she does not move aside. They step over her to enter the building, shaking their heads. Two brush their hand over her back to offer a human touch of comfort. One hands her a tissue; three ask if she is all right. She does not answer. Does not accept their kindness. How dare they enter her sphere of pristine grief? There is a sort of perfection in heartbreak and loss. An all-consuming validity. If Vicky cannot hold on to Angela, she will hold on to this purity of feeling. Her lungs spasm. Her chest aches. She runs a hand over her cheeks, swabbing the tears. Rubs the bottom of her nose, stinging from the snot. Attempts to clean herself up. Another revelation: She has never cried like this before. She's cried in public, yes. A symptom of being a New Yorker. Riding the F train after Dan had told her she needed to be less absent-minded at work. Walking down 32nd Street after being broken up with over sundubu-jjigae by a girl she really had felt things for, even if, yes, she had been absent then too. Sitting in Central Park's Strawberry Fields, when the saxophonist began to play a haunting tune, stirring something in her that she's never been able to find on any music streaming platform. And now, here in Chinatown, in the doorway next to the funeral parlor, with her heart ruined, wrecked, ravaged.

She collects the pieces of herself. Stands. Takes out her phone from her back pocket. There is only one person who deserves to know.

kevin said angela killed herself. (It is easier to place Angela's actions into the mouth of somebody else than to confront them directly.)

i'm going onwards to see where she went. i don't know if i'll find her but i need to try. will you burn my zhizha? burn the mansions and the alcohol and the cars and the tech and the vacations.

and i'm sure every cigarette you smoke will find me too. they'll remind me of you.

dont forget all that paper stuff we couldn't afford during this stupid life so maybe i can share the riches in the after.

burn the hot pot one too ok? i'll save it for you when you arrive.

i'm sorry. give eric my love.

**Clicks send, moves to put her phone away. Hesitates. Types out three more sentences:**

i hope you know that i love you. so much. thank you.

## onwards

Vicky stands on Onwards's penthouse rooftop. Wind whips her hair into tornadoes.

She's resolved to fly off, skies cracking open with a thunderclap. She'll morph into a butterfly to match Angela. Behind her, the ghosts of the previous time she'd been here—the office party—dance in their ugly costumes. She hates them.

After hours. The building empty, storefront closed, streets devoid. She stares at every pinprick of city illumination she can see from her perch: streetlights, building windows, car headlights. She wishes she could snuff them out. How dare signs of life flicker when she is experiencing death? The pain, the pain, the pain—an aching in her chest. She steps up onto the ledge and looks directly down—vertigo strikes. Her courage loses her—she steps back. Finds firm footing, clutches her forehead, dizzy. She steadies, wraps her arms around her core, and hugs herself tight. She's all she has left—she must jump. She must go—the pain is too much to bear. Would Urnie arrive at the office tomorrow only to faint at her carcass smeared over the sidewalk? Would her tangle of guts and brain and bone remind him of his lover's; would his tears be actor-trained crocodile or legitimate? Would rats emerge from trash bags and gutter grates as soon as she splatters to munch at her corpse so quickly that she'd disappear, her death unnoticed? Or would the NYPD—or whoever cleans up the sidewalks, she has no idea if the city employs a specific post-suicide squad—draw a chalk outline around her gore before her coworkers like Anthony and Lani show up for the workday with their double shot espressos in hand? The task of crafting a public relations spin to ensure the company would weather an employee's suicide, especially a death off the famous office's roof, would likely be delegated to Anthony. Vicky whispers an apology to him into the wind, which then pushes against her—she tips forward, the air caressing her. As if nature itself is promising it will catch and carry her upward into the atmosphere of oblivion—oblivion is seductive. To be nothing after feeling everything would be a welcome comfort.

She steps forward again.

Left foot, then right foot, both on the ledge.

Braces her thighs to leap into emptiness, and then—

"I'm here, I'm here!" comes a scream. "*Stop!* Vicky! STOP!"

Vicky teeters. And the wind that had just been blowing her forward sends a breeze in the opposite direction—she topples backward onto solid ground—is it not time yet? Soon, she tells herself. She should say goodbye to whoever this is who knows her. She does not want to traumatize a witness. She turns around.

Jen.

Sprinting toward her.

Jen, panting, in sweatpants, a puffer, and mismatched shoes—a running sneaker and a combat boot. Jen, hair askew, sweat beading on her forehead despite the temperature. Jen, who clearly sprinted out the door without care upon reading Vicky's texts. Jen, who throws her arms around Vicky in a full-body hug, reminding Vicky of the tackle at the Halloween anniversary party—and Vicky sobs for this protective embrace—and for the host of that party, no longer here. Vicky tumbles onto the ground, shaking.

"What are you doing?" Jen huffs, her breath ragged.

Vicky does not know how to vocalize *I am going to kill myself*. The sentence is too dramatic. Too overbearing, too absurd. She stays quiet. Wiggles out of Jen's grasp.

Jen seizes Vicky's hands with both of hers. Holding on to her. Not letting her go. "No. Vicky. I'm tired of death. I hate it. I don't want to read about it, I don't want to think about it, I don't want to live it—don't make me go through it again," Jen begs. "I can't lose you." She coughs, her lungs spasming. "Please."

Vicky, again, silent, speechless. Turns her head to the ledge—

"Vicky!" Jen screams, her hands gripping tighter. "Look at me!"

Vicky snaps back to Jen, but the pleading on her best friend's face is excruciating—she looks upward to the stars, planets, moon, because nobody could understand her sorrow better than the celestials: companions magicked into eternal constellations; Chang'e rising to the moon in the hopes of staying close to her mortal husband; birds forming bridges out of their own backs to connect separated lovers. Vicky opens her mouth and screams. She screams like the song of the Kaua'i 'ō'ō bird she'd once read about while researching for an Onwards Valentine's Day campaign: the last two 'ō'ō alive, a pairing, until the female died from a hurricane, the male left alone, his bird call recorded by an environmental historian before disappearing into extinction as well. The sound of desperate loss heard in that last sound recording—Vicky hears this loneliness in her own scream too.

"Is it always this painful?" she wails.

"The pain never ends," answers Jen.

"Why not?"

"I don't know."

Vicky hiccups, sobbing. "Why did it have to end like this? I wanted Angela to live forever. For *us* to live forever. All of us, together."

"Then you can't leave me," begs Jen.

Vicky collapses onto her back, pulling Jen along with her.

Jen hugs Vicky, keeping her arm on top of Vicky's stomach as much of a consoling pressure as an anchor to the here and now as she waits for Vicky's tears to settle.

She'll stay for as long as Vicky needs.

"I didn't know I could feel this much," Vicky sniffles. She stares up into the night.

"How could you be dead inside when you've built this much life?"

Vicky lets out a strangle of a laugh.

"This love," Jen says. "I love you, you love me, Angela loved you, you loved her. It's a privilege to love. To love is to build a life."

Jen grabs her hand, squeezes.

Vicky squeezes back.

Vicky shudders.

Her body. Heavy.

The wind above them howls.

"I'm here for you," Jen whispers. "I'll always be here for you."

Vicky releases a watery chuckle, then a full-body laugh. Laughter is all she has left. "Jen."

"Yes?" Jen responds carefully.

"Do you have a cigarette?"

Jen, relieved. "Lucky you. I had just opened the window of my apartment to smoke when I read your text. Here." She reaches into her sweatpants pocket, pulling out her Hello Kitty lighter and slightly crumpled cigarettes. "Come on. Sit up."

Vicky groans.

Jen pulls her up by her wrists.

Vicky moves because it is easier to ascend with a friend.

Jen shakes out two cigarettes and hands one to Vicky, who shoves it in her mouth. She ignites the Hello Kitty lighter, but the flame goes out. Vicky cups her palms to protect the spark from the wind, then guides the flame to Jen.

They release exhalations of smoke.

"Remember when—" Vicky chokes off because she is not ready to look back.

Jen, a comfort, who knows Vicky could have been talking about anything: "I'll never forget."

Shivering, Vicky scooches closer to Jen.

"How'd you get in? Wait. How'd you even know I was here?"

Jen takes a key card out of her other pocket and dangles it in front of Vicky's eyes. "You left your extra card at mine, like, months ago. And I have your location, remember?"

"Ah."

"Want to talk about her?" Jen asks.

Vicky shakes her head.

Jen tucks her forehead against Vicky's neck.

"She gave me back to myself," says Vicky.

"What do you mean?"

Vicky slides her hand into her hoodie pocket and pulls out the zhizha. "Why didn't she burn me? I could've been there with her in the afterlife," she whispers, fingers moving to crumple her paper self into a ball, the legs squeezing flat, but Jen quickly grasps her wrist, stopping her.

"She just wanted you to live." Which is what the note had said, but Vicky still couldn't quite understand why Angela would want that, or how Jen could know that.

"I wouldn't have minded if she took me along," says Vicky.

"She would have minded, though."

"Why?"

"I don't know why. But staying makes more sense than going. I promise."

Vicky stares at her paper self. What would she look like lit by flames? Burned to ash, poured into an Onwards urn? She's seen pictures of human ashes. Variations of gray and brown. Her ashes would be pitch black, representing depths where no light could reach.

"I should never have worked here."

"Huh?"

"Angela's note said Onwards helped her prepare. It's my fault she's gone. I made her think it would be too easy."

Jen looks incredulous. "It's *not* your fault."

"But it is. What if by helping people plan for death, we just made it easier to die? What if it would be better to fight against death, rather than welcome it with open arms?"

Jen is quiet. Then: "I don't know, Vicky. I don't know the answer. I don't know anything."

"I can't work here anymore."

"What do you want to do next?"

"I don't want to do *anything* next."

"Use your imagination."

"Fine." Vicky pauses, thinks. "Well, I have no marketable skills other than copywriting, which is fake anyway. Maybe I'll be an artist. I love art, and I always have ideas I want to explore but end up ignoring. How cool would it be to create zhizha-inspired sculptures? Maybe I should pay attention to what makes me feel alive. But if I become an artist, I can already predict the financial drain and how much I'll hate what I make. And all the good artists have day jobs anyway." Vicky then remembers Kevin. She is wrong. Kevin is a good artist without a day job, and it makes her so jealous that it stops her from being in love with him the way she is—was?—in love with Angela. "Maybe I'll become a mortician. I'm sure my death résumé will bolster my application. Even though I'll flunk out of all the biology and chemistry courses. I've always sucked at science."

"Okay. I support you."

"I just can't work at Onwards. Not anymore. Fuck this place. I'm a bad person for working here for so long."

"No, Vicky, you're not a bad person."

"I am. I'm a bad person, because I should have told Angela that I didn't want her to die. I should have said those words directly, instead of telling her it would be easy. What the fuck was I thinking?"

"Vicky, you're a good person."

"No."

"Fine. Vicky, you're just *a* person who's made some bad choices and some good choices. A person who is trying to survive and figure out how to live. A person who loves people—and to love someone means to hurt someone. Not all the time, and not on purpose. But . . . yeah. Sometimes."

"Why does to love mean to hurt?" Vicky asks, thinking about how she'd been correct in avoiding love if love meant to hurt. Love led to grief and pain. Why would anybody choose to love?

Jen laughs. "That's what everyone who has ever loved someone else wonders. It's just the way it is."

"Have you and Eric hurt each other before?"

"Of course."

"How'd you two come back from it?"

"The same way you and I did."

"What do you mean?"

Jen exhales. "Why do you act like you are incapable of loving? Or of hurting? Don't you remember? You and I, we've fought before. Then we apologized, and then we moved on. Sure, in some relationships, the hurt can be too much and there's no way back. But most of the time, when the connection is worth it, like with me and Eric, and like with you and I, we choose to stay. Relationships are difficult. But . . . love is real. Love should be savored and saved."

A pause. Then: "I took too long to realize I should've done that with Angela."

"But you did, eventually," Jen says.

"Too late."

"It's never too late."

"I don't know what I'm doing," Vicky says.

"None of us do."

"You don't think Urnie knew? He created all this: the company, the suicides, the death—"

Jen, fair and tough: "You enjoyed it, didn't you?"

"Yes. Maybe. But not anymore! How come Urnie gets to live on and Angela can't? Why does this stupid building and its stupid urns still stand while Angela—" Vicky cuts herself off. She grabs a stone and hurls it. It lands with a useless clatter. The physical exertion is not enough to express her pain or her anger. She hates herself for selling death. She hates herself for loving other people, and she hates herself for forcing them to love her back.

The hatred provokes her. Vicky flaps the zhizha of herself in her hands, slapping her paper head against her other palm, her mind churning with ways to quit, though quitting would not be enough. She wants to punish, destroy, self-destruct—

The solution comes to her the way all her best ideas have. Bursting free. Awoken from her subconscious.

Seized by a reckless abandon, Vicky leaps upward, gesturing wildly. Hadn't she known it would come to this? The meaning of the zhizha: not to be rich when dead, but to have the chance to try again after life. To destroy, to start anew. To *burn*. The answer, so brilliant; her idea, always right. She even had everything she needed to see it through, the materials waiting for her patiently inside the building, as if placed there by an efficient producer, the set working smoothly, like clockwork, rushing to its final scene.

"What if we burn? Burn this to the ground?"

Jen, still sitting, stares at her. "What are you talking about? Burn what?"

"Come on." Vicky grabs Jen's hand and tugs her.

Jen stumbles to her feet.

They cross the roof hand in hand.

Vicky jerks open the door leading to the floors below and begins sprinting down the stairs. "We gotta get to the fifth floor," she says as they descend.

Jen, fit, pulls ahead of Vicky as they progress.

"Here," Jen says.

They enter. Though they had been clattering carelessly down the stairs, they tiptoe through the hushed, darkened floor, desks lumpy and misshapen from picture frames and coffee mugs. Vicky doesn't turn on the light.

"Is anyone here?" Jen whispers, swiveling her head to stake out the space.

"There shouldn't be," says Vicky in a normal tone. She'd scanned her key card and walked in without disturbance, no security guards or system flagged, for Urnie left the office unbothered to allow his hardworking employees to enter at any hour whenever their passion for death work struck. She rubs her thumb along the edge of Jen's in an attempt to comfort. "It's past the hour for janitors. And Urnie thinks our lives' greatest purpose is to send off emails at three a.m."

Vicky halts in front of a closed door with a placard reading STORAGE. "In here." She toggles the handle, and it swings open, the room stocked with chrome racks piled with indistinguishable shadows. Vicky flips the switch and floods the room with light, revealing alcohol bottles, hastily taped cardboard boxes, and miniature urn models.

"Figures it's unlocked. Office supply dude is pretty careless, and account people go in and out to ship Onwards-branded packages to media—it'd be too much of a hassle." She's not sure whom she's explaining this to, but she needs to talk now, to fill the world with noise instead of silence. Vicky pulls the hesitant Jen inside, the door clicking shut behind them. "We're looking for a box labeled fireworks. Or annual party supplies. Halloween explosives? Something like that."

*"What?"* Jen wrenches her hand out of Vicky's to cover her mouth in horror. "What are you planning?" She squints at Vicky's face. "You look . . . strange."

Vicky grins, baring her teeth. "Thanks." She stalks around the shelves scanning the boxes as Jen watches her. A lid labeled HALLOWEEN. "Here it is." She throws the lid to the ground carelessly and looks inside. "Yes."

Vicky takes out cylindrical packages decorated with comic book–style sparkles and labeled CAPTAIN THUNDERBOOM, stacking them on an empty space on the shelf. When the fireworks are all removed, she grabs the lid off the ground and places it onto the empty box, pushing it back into its original position. She gestures toward the cylinders, speaking to Jen: "This is the shit they used at the party. I thought I was gonna die when they were set off close to me." She gathers them in her arms, cradling them like a baby.

"Vicky, this is a bad idea," Jen says.

"Please."

"We've never done anything this illegal."

"Not yet."

"It's dangerous."

"When has that ever stopped us?" Vicky asks, staring at Jen in gentle confrontation.

Between them flows the quiet stream of understanding strengthened over the years by supporting decisions that were not the safest, kindest, or easiest, yet felt the most *right*, because they had the other's support.

Jen takes a cylinder, then a second and a third, continuing until she's shouldering half of Vicky's burden.

Jen nods.

They exit the storage room, coming to a stop in the center of the open room.

"Here," Vicky says. She drops her cylinders on the floor, nudging them into a pile with her toe. Jen adds hers. They take a step backward, holding hands, staring at their bunch of kindling.

Vicky experiences déjà vu: She's suddenly returned to the last week of senior year in college with Jen, when they had pledged to burn everything they hated from the previous four years there, from unused plan B packages collected from their medicine cabinets, stocked up in case of nights with people whose names they couldn't remember, to printed mock advertisements selling nonexistent products with lines of copy rewritten ten times.

"Are you sure?"

Vicky has never been so sure of anything else. "Give me the lighter."

"Vicky—"

Vicky thrusts her hand into Jen's pocket before she can react. Filches the Hello Kitty lighter with the swift fingers of someone who swipes museum entry tickets, who used to shoplift lip gloss and candy bars simply to feel in control of something.

Vicky uses her thumb and pointer finger to hold her zhizha self from the neck. Ignites the lighter. Holds the flame to her dangling paper legs. Her feet smoke, then curl in glowing orange, disintegrating—her legs, waist, arms, shoulders—

Then Vicky chucks her paper self onto the fireworks and bends forward to light the Thunderbooms—

"Move back!" yells Jen. "Be careful!"

Sparks in a rainbow of color. That rush of heat. Deafening gunshot bangs, the blinding explosions—

Ideal kindling: the wooden desks specially designed into shapes reminiscent of headstones, carefully sourced from sustainable California lumberyards by ENBY; the stacks of printer paper bundles for designers to compare urn designs; the corkboards where urn release rollout calendars and strategy grids are pinned.

Vicky throws the Hello Kitty lighter into the flames. The sacrifice of the friendship token that had seen the two through long nights over cigarettes and discussions and hugs. The object gone, but the person, still here—

"Vicky! We have to go!" Jen splutters.

Their hands find each other—together they scramble to the exit. Vicky makes for the elevator, but Jen shakes her head, pulling her to the stairs, the safer option in a fire—they spiral down so quickly it feels like the steps beneath them have flattened into a slide. They reach the lobby, Jen attempting to charge through the front door to the outside, but she's interrupted by Vicky's deadweight—despite the whirling alarms and roars of collapse above their heads, Vicky has stopped in her tracks.

Jen turns around, pulling at Vicky's arm desperately with both hands, but Vicky is stubbornly frozen.

Jen gives up tugging and gestures frantically toward the sidewalk. *What?* Jen mouths, smoke inhalation leaving her unable to vocalize.

Vicky shakes her head no, eyes wide and fearful. She can't. She'd rather hurl herself into the flames. To exit would mean to face another day, and another night, where nightmares of Death and his cloak swallow her, and she's sure that she'll see Angela there in her slumber: Angela falling off a building, Angela's lifeless hand drooping down the side of a bathtub, Angela shaking out sleeping pills into her steady palm. Another day, another night, and another, and another, until—Vicky is terrified that she will one day wake up and be fine. Because scar tissue will have coated her tender heart. She will move on, and she will stop dreaming of Angela, and she will forget how much Angela had meant to her. Grief is illuminating yet brief; tomorrow would fade to dull. She would default again to her stasis: Alone. Numb. Just fine. Vicky stares at the panicking Jen and wonders why her best friend is her best friend when Vicky is so insistent on her own cranky solitude. Why did her best friend come today? *Jen deserves better,* she thinks. *She deserves a friend who shows up for her the way she shows up for me.* Vicky knows if she had gotten the same sort of text from Jen, she would not have come—she wouldn't have even opened the text until hours later, too late. Yet here is Jen, trying to save her from burning her life down. Vicky gapes at Jen in wonder and thinks about how beautiful she is, even when Jen has just assisted in committing arson and is now panicking with soot staining her forehead, and Vicky smiles to herself despite the roar of flames, because of course her best friend is beautiful—it is through love that she is made beautiful. *I love you don't die,* Vicky thinks as she watches Jen tug at her arm, mouthing pleas for Vicky to move. *I love you don't die*—this is the clearest thought Vicky has had in weeks, settling down in her heart like a soaring bird returning to its nest. Vicky wishes she had told Angela this before it was too late: *I love you don't die.* But Vicky is wiser now. She will remember to tell the people she loves that she loves them.

She lets Jen pull her through to the dark outside.

They run to the opposite side of the street, the hour still dawn, no cars to dodge. Then they are on the sidewalk, gulping fresh air, lungs shaking in relief. Jen drops Vicky's hand and bends over, clutching her thighs and panting, catching her breath. Vicky turns to look at the office building on fire, so bright that her eyes hurt. She wonders where in the blaze is her paper self. Is her soul ascending in search of Angela? Angela, who could have stayed to see Onwards burn. She hopes Angela is proud of her. Vicky begins to cry. A tear, then more tears, washing down her ashy cheeks. She feels a hand on her shoulder and turns to look—there's Jen next to her. Jen, her best friend. Synchronized, they turn to watch the building engulf in flames: its windows shattering and exploding; the sandstone exterior blackened and crumbling; smoke billowing upward to the celestials. Vicky bids goodbye to the copy she's written, the urns inside, the death room, the hallways through which Urnie had stalked. She apologizes to Lani and Anthony, because they had been kind, worth knowing, good to work with. *So long, Onwards. Fuck you, Urnie. Farewell, farewell, farewell.* Goodbye and good riddance to this death-driven chapter in the novel of her stupid, pathetic life. She's off. She's running away again just like she always ran away from love when she was younger, in the fear of facing eventual grief. But this time is different—this time, she's running away *with someone.* So she's not running *away,* but *toward.* Toward somewhere, and that somewhere, so dear, so warm, is love—Jen. She feels a hand squeeze her shoulder again, and she turns away from the inferno to look at Jen, beautiful Jen, whose face reads terrified, rightfully so, for firetruck and police sirens are growing audibly nearer. Jen opens her mouth, and Vicky leans in to listen, and Jen whispers in fear and in enlightenment, because the two things have always been the same, the terror of a newfound realization and where it will lead: "Vicky, what did we do, what did we do, what did we do?"

*What did we do? What do we do next? And where do we go from here? I don't know, dear friend, but shall we figure it out together? Take my hand. Let us run onward to love; let us refuse death; let us stay alive in love, together.*

*note*

For help or simply someone to talk to, https://www.mind.org.uk/ contains resources that can be accessed 24/7.

Befrienders Worldwide will offer support regardless of where you are in the world.

http://suicide.org/international-suicide-hotlines.html contains a list of international hotlines.

# acknowledgments

Hui Cheng, Ethan Song, and Jesse Song. David Pomerico and DongWon Song. Serena Arthur, Amy Evans, Flora Willis, Jodie Lewis, and the marvelous, hardworking team at Footnote. Emily Xueni Jin, Sara Bresciani, Marie Koullen, Kuzey Baykal, Catherine Ho, and Imani Parks. Pear for the bathtub; Josh and Chiyeung for commiserating; Henry and Deepa for the solidarity, the education, the belief. 天天 for the poetry. The Q train. Green-Wood Cemetery. Brighton Beach. Sunset Park and Prospect Park. Metrograph. The workers of the Metropolitan Museum of Art. My cozy, darling apartment. New York City's Chinatowns. KTV. The HarperCollins Union. Books Through Bars. Art Against Displacement. The artists. The translators. The booksellers. The librarians. The readers. My friends, for our conversations that inspired much of this book, and for understanding friendship like Derrida, who wrote that friendship is more *being-friend*, which makes it a verb and not a noun: showing up, checking in, reaching out, being there, building despite the persistent destruction around us. Community will keep us alive. Thank you. I love you.

## about the author

Jade Song is an artist, writer and filmmaker, based in New York. Their debut novel, *Chlorine*, received wide acclaim on publication in 2023 and was translated into multiple languages. *I Love You Don't Die* is their second novel.